Young Jane Young

Also by GABRIELLE ZEVIN

BOOKS FOR ADULTS

Margarettown

The Hole We're In

The Storied Life of A. J. Fikry

BOOKS FOR YOUNG ADULTS

Elsewhere

Memoirs of a Teenage Amnesiac

All These Things I've Done

Because It Is My Blood

In the Age of Love and Chocolate

Young Jane Young

a novel

Gabrielle Zevin

VIKING

VIKING

an imprint of Penguin Canada, a division of Penguin Random House Canada Limited

Canada • USA • UK • Ireland • Australia • New Zealand • India • South Africa • China

Published in Viking hardcover by Penguin Canada, 2017
Simultaneously published in the United States by Algonquin Books of Chapel Hill,
a division of Workman Publishing, New York

www.penguinrandomhouse.ca

*Publisher's note: This book is a work of fiction. Names, characters, places and incidents
either are the product of the author's imagination or are used fictitiously, and any
resemblance to actual persons living or dead, events, or locales is entirely coincidental.*

LIBRARY AND ARCHIVES CANADA CATALOGUING IN PUBLICATION

Zevin, Gabrielle, author
Young Jane Young / Gabrielle Zevin.

Issued in print and electronic formats.
ISBN 978-0-7352-3438-3 (hardcover).--ISBN 978-0-7352-3439-0 (EPUB)

I. Title.

PS3626.E95Y69 2017   813'.6   C2017-900165-5
                                             C2017-900450-6

Cover adapted from a design by Phil Pascuzzo / pepcostudio.com
Text design by Steve Godwin

Printed and bound in the United States of America

10 9 8 7 6 5 4 3 2 1

Penguin
Random House
Canada

VIKING

I know
Not these my hands
And yet I think there was
A woman like me once had hands
Like these.

"Amaze" by Adelaide Crapsey

CONTENTS

I

Bubbe Meise

RACHEL

ONE

My dear friend Roz Horowitz met her new husband online dating, and Roz is three years older and fifty pounds heavier than I am, and people have said that she is generally not as well preserved, and so I thought I would try it even though I avoid going online too much. Roz's last husband died of colon cancer, and she deserves her happiness. Not that this new husband is anything special—his name is Tony and he used to be in the auto glass business in New Jersey. But Roz fixed him up and took him shopping for shirts at Bloomingdale's, and now they're taking all these classes at the JCC together—Conversational Spanish and Ballroom Dancing and Massage for Lovers and Creative Soap and Candle Making. I don't particularly want a husband. They're a lot of work, but I don't want to spend the rest of my life alone either, and it would be nice to have someone to go to classes with is what I'm saying. I thought online dating was for younger people, but Roz says it's not. "Even if it is," she says, "Rachel, you're younger now than you'll ever be."

So I ask Roz if she has any advice and she says don't put a picture that makes you look younger than you are. Everyone on the Internet lies, but ironically, the worst thing to do on the Internet is lie. And I say, "Roz, my love, how exactly is that different from life?"

The first man I meet is named Harold, and as a joke, I ask him if he always had that name because it seems like an old man name to me. But Harold doesn't get the joke, and he gets huffy and says, "Haven't you ever heard of *Harold and the Purple Crayon*? Harold is a child, Rachel." Anyway, this date goes nowhere.

The second man I meet is Andrew, and he has dirty fingernails so I can't notice if he is nice or not. I can't even eat my brown sugar and butter crêpes because, *oy gevalt*, I'm so distracted by these fingernails. I mean, what was he doing before he came on this date? Competitive gardening? Burying the last woman he dated? He says, "Rachel Shapiro, you eat like a bird!" I think about packing up the crêpes, but what's the point? Crêpes don't keep. Reheat them, and they end up eggy and rubbery, and even if you force them down, it's a tragedy because you're thinking of the crêpes they might have been and all that wasted potential.

Andrew calls me a few weeks later to ask me if I want to go on another date, and I very quickly say, No thank you. And he asks why. And I don't want to tell him the thing about the dirty fingernails because it seems petty and maybe it is. My ex-husband was meticulous about his fingernails, and he still turned out to be a piece of garbage. While I'm thinking of what to say, he says, "Well, I guess I have my answer. Don't bother making up some lie."

And I say, "Honestly, I think we lack chemistry, and at our ages"— I'm sixty-four—"it doesn't make sense to waste time."

And he says, "So you know, your picture makes you look ten years younger than you are." A parting blow.

I know this is the insult of the insulted, but I show Roz the picture anyway, just in case. I had thought of it as recent, but upon closer consideration, I determine it's from the end of the second Bush administration. Roz says that I do look younger in it, but in a good way, not so much that it's ridiculous. She says if I pick the right restaurant, with the right lighting, I'll look exactly the same age as the photo. And I say that's starting to sound like Blanche DuBois putting scarves on the lamps. Roz takes a new picture of me with her phone on my balcony, and that's that.

The third man I meet is Louis, and he has very nice glasses with titanium arms. I like him immediately even though the first thing he says is, "Wow, you're prettier than your picture," which leaves me wondering if I've swung too much in the other direction with this whole picture foolishness. He's a professor of Jewish-American literature at the University of Miami, and he tells me he ran marathons until his hip started bothering him and now he runs half marathons. He asks me if I work out, and I tell him yes, I teach Pilates for Seniors, as a matter of fact—maybe I could help with his flexors? He says, I bet you could, or something like that. Then, to establish we aren't bimbos, we schmooze about books. I say I love Philip Roth, even though that's probably a cliché for a woman of my background and my age. And he says, no, Philip Roth is wonderful. He once gave a public lecture about Philip Roth's books and Philip Roth came to it and sat in the first row! Philip Roth sat through the whole thing, nodded occasionally, crossed and uncrossed and recrossed his long legs, and when it was over, he left without saying a word.

"Did he like it?" I ask. "Was he offended?"

Louis says he'll never know and it'll always be one of the great mysteries of his life.

I say, "Philip Roth has long legs?"

He says, "Not as long as mine, Rach."

It's a nice thing to flirt.

And then he asks me if I have any children. And I say, I have a daughter, Aviva. And he says, Aviva, that means springtime or innocence in Hebrew, what a beautiful name. And I say, I know, that's why my ex-husband and I chose it. And he says, I haven't known many Avivas, it's not a very common name, just that girl who got into trouble with Congressman Levin. Do you remember that whole *mishegoss*?

"Um," I say.

He says, "It was a blight on South Florida, a blight on Jews, a blight on politicians if that's even possible, a blight on civilization in general."

He says, "Can you honestly not remember it? It was on the news every day here in 2001, until September eleventh happened and everyone forgot about her."

He says, "I wish I could remember her last name. You really don't remember her? Well, Rach, she was like Monica Lewinsky. The girl knew he was married and she seduced him. I guess she was drawn to the power or the limelight. Or maybe she was insecure. She was slutty and a bit zaftig—one of those such-a-pretty-face types—so it probably raised her self-esteem to attract a man like Levin. I can't feel much sympathy for people like that. What the heck was her last name?"

He says, "It's a real shame. Levin's been a solid congressman. He might have been the first Jewish president if not for that *farkakte* girl."

He says, "You know who I feel sorry for? Her parents."

He says, "I wonder whatever happened to that girl. I mean, who would ever hire her? Who would marry her?"

He says, "Grossman! Aviva Grossman! That's it!"

And I say, "*That's it.*"

I excuse myself to go to the ladies' room, and when I come back, I tell the waiter to pack up the rest of my paella, which is very good and way too much for one person. Some restaurants skimp on the saffron, but not La Gamba. You can't microwave paella but it will reheat on the stovetop very nicely. I say let's go halfsies on the check, and Louis says he was planning to pay. But I insist. I only let a man pay for me if I'm planning to see him again. Roz says this is either feminism or the opposite of feminism, but I think it's plain manners.

We walk to the parking lot, and he says, "Did something happen back there? Did I say something wrong? I thought it was going very well until suddenly it wasn't."

I say, "I just don't like you," and I get in my car.

TWO

I live in a three-bedroom condo on the beach. I can hear the
ocean and everything's the way I like it, which is the best
thing about living alone. Even when you're married to a doctor who's gone most of the time, he'll still feel like he should weigh
in on the décor. And his opinions are, *I think I'd prefer a bed that
was more masculine* and *Definitely blackout curtains, you know my
schedule* and *Sure it's pretty, but won't it get dirty?* But now my couch
is white, my curtains are white, my duvet is white, my countertops
are white, my clothes are white, everything is white, and no, it doesn't
get dirty, I'm very careful. I bought near the bottom of the market—I
have always been lucky in real estate, if nothing else—and the condo
is worth three times what I paid for it. I could sell it and make a killing, but honestly, where would I go? You tell me where I would go!

Back when I was married and back when Aviva was young,
we lived across town in a Tuscan-style minimansion in Forestgreen

Country Club, which is a gated community. Now that I no longer live there, I can admit that the gates always troubled me—we lived in Boca Raton; who were we keeping out? People were always getting robbed in Forestgreen anyway. The gates seemed to attract thieves. Put up gates, people will think there's something worth protecting. But Forestgreen's where I met Roz, who has been my best friend through some times, let me tell you. And that's where we met the Levins. The Levins moved in when Aviva was a freshman in high school, fourteen.

When we first knew him, Aaron Levin was a lowly state senator. His wife, Embeth, was the one who made the money—she worked as in-house counsel for a conglomerate of South Florida hospitals. Roz's nickname for Aaron Levin was "Jewish Superman" or "Jewperman." And honest to God, that's what he looked like. He was six feet two inches tall in New Balances, with black curly hair and blue-green eyes and a big, kind, dopey smile. The man could wear a dress shirt. He'd gone to Annapolis and served in the navy, and he had the shoulders to show for it. He was a few years younger than Roz and me, but he was not so young that Roz didn't like to joke that one of us should try to sleep with him.

The wife, Embeth, always looked unhappy. She was thin from the waist up but frumpy on the bottom—thick calves and hips, puffy knees. How the woman must have suffered to keep her brown curly hair in that straight blond bob. Roz used to say, "In this humidity, *oy vey iz mir*, maintaining a hairstyle like that is nothing short of madness."

For the record, I tried to make friends with Embeth, but she wasn't interested. (It wasn't just me, because Roz also tried.) Mike and I had them over for dinner twice. The first time, I made beef brisket, which takes all day. Even with the AC blasting, I was *shvitzing* on my Donna Karan open-shouldered dress. The second time, I made maple-glazed salmon. No big deal. Marinate for fifteen minutes, thirty in the oven, and done. Embeth never reciprocated. I can take a hint. Then when Aviva was a junior in high school, Aaron Levin ran for Congress, and they moved to Miami, and I thought I'd never see or hear from them again. You have a lot of neighbors in a lifetime and only a few of them turn out to be Roz Horowitzes.

But it's not Roz I've been brooding about all day, it's the Levins, and I'm still thinking about them when the phone rings. It's the history teacher from the public school, wanting to know if I'm Esther Shapiro's daughter. She has been trying to reach Mom to see if she will be able to be a speaker for Survivor Day at the high school, and Mom's not been answering her texts or her phone. I explain to her that Mom had a fairly devastating stroke about six months ago. So, no, Esther Shapiro will not be able to attend Survivor Day. They will have to find other survivors this year.

The history teacher starts to cry—annoying, indulgent—and says it is harder and harder to find enough survivors, even here in Boca Raton, which is, roughly, 92 percent Jewish, the most Jewish place on earth aside from Israel itself. Twenty years ago, when she first started doing Survivor Day, it was easy, she says, but now, who's left? Maybe you survive cancer, maybe you survive the Holocaust, but life'll get you every time.

That afternoon, I visit Mom at the nursing home, which smells like a combination of a school cafeteria and death. Mom's hand is limp and her face has collapsed on the left side. I mean, why mince words? She looks strokey.

I tell her that the indulgent schoolteacher was asking about her, and Mom tries to say something but it comes out as vowels and no consonants and maybe I'm a bad daughter, but I don't understand. I tell her that I almost had a very good date until the man, out of the blue, insulted Aviva. And Mom makes a face that is inscrutable. And I say, I miss Aviva. I only say this because I know Mom can't say anything back.

As I'm leaving the nursing home, Mom's younger sister, Mimmy, arrives. Mimmy is the happiest person I've ever known, but she isn't always trustworthy. Maybe this is unfair. Maybe it isn't that Mimmy isn't trustworthy but that I don't trust happy people or happiness in general. Mimmy wraps her big, flappy wings around me. (When we were kids, my brother and I called arms like these Hadassah arms.) Mimmy says that Mom has been asking about Aviva.

"How precisely was she doing that, Mimmy?" I ask. Mom can't say anything.

"She said her name. She said UH-VEE-VUH," Mimmy insists.

"Three whole syllables? I highly doubt that. Besides which, everything Mom says sounds like 'Aviva.'"

Mimmy says she doesn't want to argue with me, because we need to start making plans for Mom's eighty-fifth birthday party. Mimmy isn't sure if we should have the party here, at the home that is not her home, or if Mom will be well enough to travel. Obviously, Mimmy thinks it would be better to have the party somewhere else, somewhere more scenic—the Boca Raton Museum of Art or that nice brunch place in Mizner Park or my apartment. "Your apartment is gorgeous," Mimmy says.

I say, "Aunt Mimmy, do you think Mom would even want a party?"

Mimmy says, "There is no one on earth who loves parties more than your mother."

I wonder if Mimmy and I are speaking of the same woman. Once, I asked my mother if she and Daddy had been happy. "He was a good provider. He was good to you and your brother. Happy?" my mother said. "What's that?" This is to say, I am reminded for the millionth time that it is a very different thing to be a woman's sister than it is to be her daughter.

I say, "Mimmy, is it really the right time for a party?"

Mimmy looks at me as if I am the most pitiable person she has ever met. "Rachel Shapiro," she says, "it's always the right time for a party."

THREE

Sometime before my marriage ended, Mike and I drove down to the University of Miami to have dinner with Aviva, who said she had an announcement for us. At long last and a few semesters behind schedule, she had decided on a major: Spanish literature and political science.

Mike said that sounded impressive, but he was always such a softie where Aviva was concerned. I was the one who had to ask her what she was planning to do with a degree like that, which sounded like a whole lotta nada. I had visions of my daughter living in her childhood room forever.

Aviva said, "I'm going into politics." The Spanish literature, she explained, was because she noticed that everyone who won elections in our part of the country spoke Spanish fluently. The political science, she felt, was obvious.

"Politics is a dirty business," Mike said.

"I know, Daddy," Aviva said, kissing him on the cheek. Then she asked Mike if he was still in contact with Congressman Levin. Though it had been a while since we had lived next door to the Levins, Mike had performed heart surgery on the congressman's mother about a year earlier. Aviva hoped this connection would help her to land an entry level job or an internship.

Mike said he would give the congressman a call the next day, which he did. Where Aviva was concerned, Mike was more than reliable. She was daddy's little girl. I find the term *Jewish-American princess* offensive, but if the tiara fits. At any rate, Mike talked to Levin and Levin gave Mike the name of someone in his office, and Aviva went to work for the congressman.

In those days, I was vice principal at the Boca Raton Jewish Academy, which serves students from kindergarten to twelfth grade. I had held this position for the last ten years, and one of the reasons I had not driven down to Miami to see Aviva much that fall was because my boss, Principal Fischer, had been caught *shtupping* a senior girl. The girl was eighteen years old, but still . . . A grown man and an educator should know how to keep his schlong in his pants. Eli Fischer was foolishly determined to keep his job and wanted me to advocate on his behalf with our board. "You *know* me," Fischer said. "*Please*, Rachel."

I did know him, which is why I told the board that Fischer should be fired immediately. While they searched for a replacement, I became the principal of BRJA, the first woman ever to hold that post, for what such distinctions are worth.

When Fischer returned to pack up his desk, I brought him a black-and-white cookie. It was a peace offering but also an excuse to see how the packing was going. I wanted him out of what was to become my office. He opened the white wax paper bag, and he flung the black-and-white cookie at my head, like a Frisbee. "Judas!" he yelled. I dodged just in time. The cookie was from King's—six inches in diameter with an almost petit-four-like consistency. What a stupid man.

By the time I saw Aviva at Thanksgiving, she had lost some weight, but she was otherwise rosy and happy, so all I could think was that the employment was doing her good. Maybe Aviva has found her calling, I thought. Maybe politics is her calling? I entertained a fantasy of myself at her inauguration for some office, dabbing my eyes with a red, white, and blue silk Hermès handkerchief. Aviva was always a girl with smarts and energy, but it often went in many directions, like sun rays or a bag of marbles dropped on the floor—maybe this is just youth, though? I asked her, "So you like working with the congressman?"

Aviva laughed. "I don't work with him directly, not really."

"What do you do, then?"

"It's boring," she said.

"Not to me! Your first real job!"

"I don't get paid," she said. "So it's not a real job."

"Still, this is exciting stuff," I said. "Tell me, my daughter. What do you do?"

"I get the bagels," she said.

"Okay, what else?"

"They send me to Kinko's."

"But what are you *learning*?" I said.

"How to photocopy double-sided," she said. "How to make coffee."

"Aviva, come on, give me one good story to take back to Roz."

"I didn't take this job so you'd have stories for Roz Horowitz."

"Something about the congressman."

"Mom," she said impatiently. "There's nothing to tell. The congressman's in D.C. I mainly work with the campaign staff. Everything's raising money and everyone hates raising money, but they believe in what they're doing and they believe in the congressman, and I guess that makes it all right."

"So you like it?"

She took a deep breath. "Mommy," she said, "I'm in love."

For a second, I thought we were still talking about the job, that she was saying she was in love with politics. I realized that we weren't.

"It's early," she said. "But I think I love him. I do."

"Who is he?" I asked.

She shook her head. "He's handsome. He's Jewish. I don't want to say too much."

"Did you meet him at school?"

"I don't want to say too much."

"Okay," I said. "Well, tell me one thing. Does he love you, too?"

Aviva flushed prettily, like when she was a baby and had a fever. "Maybe."

She wasn't saying something. It is probably obvious what she wasn't saying, but it didn't occur to me. She was only twenty years old, just a kid, a good girl. I didn't believe that my Aviva could get herself mixed up in something dirty like that. I had faith in her.

"How old is he?" I asked. The worst I thought was that he could be older.

"Older," she said.

"How much older?"

"Not as old as Daddy."

"Well, that's something," I said.

"Mom, he's married," Aviva said.

Oh God, I thought.

"But he's unhappy," she said.

"My love, I can't caution you strongly enough—please don't get yourself mixed up in someone else's marriage."

"I know," she said. "I know."

"Do you? In this life and the next one, all you have is your good name."

Aviva began to cry. "That's why I had to tell you. I'm so ashamed."

"You must end this, Aviva. This can't go on."

"I know," she said.

"Stop saying 'I know'! 'I know' doesn't mean anything. Say 'I'll do it,' and then go do it. Nothing has happened yet. No one knows except me."

"Okay, Mom. I'll do it. Promise you won't tell Daddy."

ON THE FOURTH or fifth night of Chanukah, I drove down to Miami to make certain Aviva had sacked the married man. I was anxious so I went overboard with offerings for Aviva's dorm. I brought an electric menorah, and a netted bag of gold chocolate coins, and new face towels from Bloomingdale's (I paid seven dollars per towel for in-store monogramming), and two black-and-white cookies from King's because these were her favorite when she was little.

"So?" I said.

"Mom," she said, "the marriage is over, but he can't break up with the wife at the moment. The timing isn't right."

"Oh, Aviva," I said. "That's what every married man says. He will never break up with the wife. Never."

"No," Aviva said, "it's true. He has a very good reason he can't break up the marriage right now."

"Yeah," I said, "what?"

"I can't tell you," she said.

"Why? I want to hear this *very good reason*."

"Mom," she said.

"How can I advise you if I don't know the details?"

"If I tell you the reason, you'll know who it is," Aviva said.

"Maybe not," I said.

"You will," she said.

"So tell me. What difference does it make if I know who it is? I'm not going to tell anyone. I'm a vault when it comes to you."

"The reason is"—she paused—"the reason is because he is in the middle of a reelection campaign."

"Oh God," I said. "Please end this. Aviva, you must end this. Think of his wife—"

"She's awful," Aviva said. "You always said that yourself."

"Then think of his sons. Think of his constituents, of the people who have voted for him. Think of his career. Think of your own! Think of your reputation! And if that's not enough, think of Daddy and of me and of Grandma!"

"Stop being a drama queen. No one will ever find out. We'll keep it a secret until he can get divorced," Aviva said.

"Please, Aviva. Listen to me. You have to end this. Or if you can't end this, put it on ice until he gets the divorce. If it's really love, it will keep until next year."

Aviva nodded in a considering way, and I thought I might be getting through to her. She kissed me on the cheek. "Don't worry. I'll be careful." This must be what it's like when your child joins a cult.

I could not sleep that night. I called in sick to work, something I never do because I am never sick, and though I was forty-eight years old at the time, I went to see my own mother for advice.

"Mom," I said. "Aviva's in trouble." I described the situation for my mother.

"Aviva is smart," Mom finally said, "but she is young and she does not know what she does not know. Go to Levin's wife. You know the woman and have a context from which you can request a meeting. The wife will talk sense into the congressman."

"But isn't that a betrayal of Aviva's confidence?"

"Aviva will be hurt in the short term, but it will be a temporary hurt and it is for her own good."

"Do I tell Aviva that I'm going to do this?" I asked.

"It's up to you, but I wouldn't. She will not see reason. She will not see things from your point of view, and whether or not it is a betrayal, she will surely see it as one. If you don't tell her, in all likelihood she will never find out it was you."

Just before I married Mike, my mother and I went shopping for bridal shoes. And I remember thinking, Why bother? Do I really need to wear white shoes? But then I saw a diamanté-covered pump with a three-inch stiletto heel. "Mom," I said, "look at these beauties."

"Meh," she said.

"What?" I said. "They're gorgeous."

"They're pretty," she said. "But your dress is to the floor. No one will see your shoes. You may as well be comfortable."

"I'll know they're there," I said.

She made her signature moue.

"I'm a seven and a half," I told the salesman.

I tried them on and determined them to be bearably painful.

"Your legs look amazing," the salesman said.

"No one's going to see her legs," Mom said. "Can you even walk?"

I walked.

"Those tiny baby steps. You look hobbled," she said.

"I feel like Cinderella," I said. "I'm going to get them."

"These are investment shoes," the salesman said.

My mother snorted audibly.

"You'll have these shoes your whole life," the salesman said.

"They'll sit in your closet your whole life," Mom said. "You'll never wear them again."

"You have shoes like these, you find places to wear them," the salesman said.

"You don't have to pay for them," I said to my mother. I put my credit card on the counter.

In the car, my mother said, "Rachel—"

"Stop with the shoes already. It's done. They're paid for," I said.

"No, it's not that. I don't know why I was so sour about the shoes. If you love them, you should have them. What I wanted to say was"— she paused, but barely—"you could just as soon not marry him."

"What?"

"You know, I guess I mean, you could marry him or you couldn't." She said this casually, as if she were saying she could have either sandwiches or soup for dinner, it didn't matter to her.

"Are you saying you don't like him?" I asked.

"No, I like him fine," she said. "But while I'm thinking about it, I wanted to point out to you that it's as easy to call off a wedding as to go through with one."

"What?"

"My point is, it's tempting," she said. "It is certainly tempting to continue on with something because it has already begun. Think of Hitler, Rachel."

There was no one Mom despised more than Hitler. He was rarely invoked and when she did invoke him, it was for situations she considered most grave. "I don't know where you're going with this, Mother."

"Maybe at some point, that piece of shit had doubts about the Final Solution. Probably not, he was not a man known for introspection, but you never know. But maybe at one million Jews or two million Jews, in his secret, diseased heart, he was like, 'Enough. This isn't solving anything. If anything, it's creating more problems! I don't know why I ever thought this was a good idea.' But he'd gotten the ball rolling, so . . .'"

"Are you seriously comparing Mike to Hitler?"

"No, in this metaphor, you're Hitler, and your wedding is the Final Solution, and I'm the good German who doesn't want to sit idly by."

"MOTHER!"

"Don't be so literal. It's a story. People use stories to make a point."

"Not you! You don't do that. Not with Hitler!"

"Calm down, Rachel."

"Why are you saying this? Do you know something about Mike?" This was the woman who said she didn't know what happiness was, after all. I couldn't imagine where this was coming from.

"I know nothing," she said.

"You seem like you know something."

"I *know* nothing," she said. She removed a tin of French lemon drops from her purse. My mother was never without candy. "Would you like one?"

"No."

With a shrug, she returned the tin to her purse. "I know nothing," she repeated. "But maybe I *feel* that you do not always have his complete attention."

My hands were shaking. "What *else* is he paying attention to?"

"I don't know," she said. "But you are a free woman, mine daughter, and you have options. You bought the shoes, but maybe you wear them to the opera instead. They'd be great at the opera. This is the last I'll say about it." She smiled at me and patted my thigh. "The shoes are very pretty."

I did wear those shoes to my wedding, and I ended up twisting my ankle on the way out of the synagogue. I limped through the entire reception. I couldn't dance at all.

My mother's advice had always been sound.

FOUR

I left a rambling message on Embeth Levin's answering machine. "Embeth, it's your old neighbor, Rachel Grossman"—I was still Rachel Grossman then—"Rachel Grossman from Forestgreen Country Club, from Princeton Drive, from Boca Raton, from Florida, from planet Earth, ha ha! Anyway, I was thinking of you, and the kids"—oh God, that was one way to put it—"and when the kids were young, and I was wondering if we might have lunch, just to catch up and talk about old times."

A week passed, and she hadn't called me back. But why would she? She'd eaten my brisket, she'd eaten my salmon, but we hadn't been friends. I decided to call her at her work. Her assistant put me on hold. The hold music was the Three Tenors Christmas album, and I remember sitting through at least two versions of "Ave Maria" in the time it took the assistant to return. "Embeth's in a meeting," the assistant said.

"Is she really in a meeting?" I asked.

"Of course," he said.

I started to wonder if the best thing to do wouldn't be to send her an anonymous note about the affair. But how could I be certain that she alone saw it and that it wouldn't be intercepted by the assistant or someone even more indiscreet?

I was considering driving down to her office, which was forty minutes away in Palm Beach, when Embeth called me back.

"Rachel, hello," Embeth said. "I was surprised to get your call. How are you? How's Dr. Mike? Alisha?"

Normally, such an error would have insulted me (*We'd been neighbors! They'd been invited to Aviva's bat mitzvah!*), but at that moment, I felt relief that she didn't remember Aviva's name. It meant she couldn't know about the affair. "Aviva's good," I said. "She's interning in the congressman's office."

"I didn't know that," Embeth said. "That's wonderful."

"Yes," I said.

I knew there would be no better moment.

But I couldn't ruin a woman's marriage over the phone.

"How about lunch?" I said.

"Oh, Rachel," she said. "I wish I could! But I'm incredibly busy with work and with the congressman's reelection campaign."

"It could be short," I said. "Drinks even."

"The soonest I could think of doing it would be this summer," Embeth said.

I needed to invent a reason for us to see each other, something she couldn't put off. I remembered what Aviva had said about the campaign and money. *Money*, I thought.

"Well, I wasn't only calling to catch up. I thought we might discuss the possibility of a fund-raiser," I said. "I don't know if you've heard, but I've recently become the principal of BRJA, and I'm always on the lookout for opportunities for our students to meet with Jewish leaders. So, I thought, wouldn't it be marvelous if the school hosted an evening ticketed lecture with the congressman? Our students get to meet with the congressman, and we could invite the parents, too, and we could make it a real thing. It would be win-win for us and for the congressman. The Boca Raton Jewish Academy presents a Night of Jewish Leaders. Is that something you and I could discuss?"

She laughed. "The only time the zookeepers let me out is for campaign business." Her voice was bashful. "How about lunch next Thursday?" she said.

In honor of the occasion, I bought a new suit at Loehmann's. St. John. Black, with gold buttons and white trim. It was deeply discounted— the fabric was heavy for South Florida—and my size-ish.

The dressing room at Loehmann's was communal, which meant the other shoppers weighed in on what you tried on.

"You look great in that," an older woman (younger than I am now) in her bra, underwear, and a chunky turquoise necklace said to me. "So svelte."

"It's not really my style," I said. "I like your necklace."

"I got it visiting my son in Taos, New Mexico," she said.

"I've heard it's nice there."

"It's a desert," she said. "If you like the desert, it's fine."

I swung my arms. It felt like I was wearing armor.

"The suit looks made for you," the older woman said.

I looked at myself in the mirror. The woman in the suit looked frumpy and severe, like a prison matron. She didn't look like me, which was exactly the look I was going for.

When I arrived at the restaurant, Embeth was there as was Congressman Levin's director of fund-raising, I don't remember the exact title. His name was Jorge, and he seemed like a very nice man, but I wanted to stab him with my fork. How irritating that she had brought someone! I had to pretend to talk about a fund-raiser that I had no intention of throwing. An excruciating forty-five minutes into lunch, Embeth said she had to leave Jorge and me to continue plan-ning the fund-raiser without her. "This was lovely, Rachel. Thanks for getting me out of the office."

"So soon?" I said.

"We should do it again," she said, in a tone that meant that we shouldn't.

I watched her leave, and as she rounded the maître d's station, I stood and said, "Jorge."

"Yes," he said.

"Excuse me. I have to go to the ladies' room!" I knew I was being oddly specific, but I didn't want him to suspect my real purpose.

"Well, you don't need my permission," he said lightly.

I walked at a measured pace toward the bathroom, but as soon as I was past the maître d' and out of Jorge's eye line, I sprinted toward the parking lot. She was still walking to her car. Thank God, I thought. I ran and I called her name like a madwoman: "Embeth! Embeth!"

The pavement was so hot it had almost turned back into tar, and my heel sank into it. I tripped and I skinned my knee.

Through my panty hose, I could see glistening flecks of pavement, embedded in my flesh like jewels.

"Rachel," she said. "Oh my God, are you all right?"

I immediately stood up. "It's nothing. It's . . . the pavement is sticky," I said. "What a klutz I am."

"Are you sure you're okay? I think you're bleeding," she said.

"Am I?" I laughed, as if my own blood was a great joke.

She smiled at me. "Well, this was fun. So great that we could do this. We should . . . Yes, you're definitely bleeding. Maybe I have a Band-Aid?" She began to dig through her handbag, a shiny leather pentagon with brass corners, the size of a small suitcase. In a pinch, the bag could double as a weapon.

"You carry Band-Aids?" She didn't strike me as a Band-Aid carrier.

"I have sons," she said. "I'm basically a registered nurse." She continued searching through her bag.

"It's fine," I say. "It's probably best to let it breathe anyway. That way, it can dry out."

"No," she said, "that's an old wives' tale. You keep a wound moist for the first five days and it heals faster and leaves fewer scars. Found it!" She handed me a Band-Aid with dinosaurs on it. "You really should wash it out first."

"I will," I said.

"Maybe I have some Neosporin?" She began to dig through her bag again.

"It's like a magician's top hat, that bag," I said.

"Ha," she said.

"Enough!" I said. "You've done more than enough."

"Well," she said, "we should do this again."

And I said, "Yes, we should."

And she said, "Was there something you wanted?"

I knew it was now or never, but I was having trouble saying the words. There was no polite way to deliver such news and so I just said it. "Your husband is having an affair with my daughter, I'm sorry."

"Oh," she said. The music of that syllable reminded me of the flat line of a heart monitor: shrill but final, dead sounding. She smoothed down her own St. John suit, which was navy blue and almost identical to the one I was wearing, and she ran her fingers through her straightened, scarecrow hair, which was growing frizzier every moment we stood in that infernal parking lot. "Why not go to him?"

"Because . . ." Because my mother told me to go to you? Why *hadn't* I gone to him? "Because I thought I should handle this woman to woman," I said.

"Because you don't think he'll end it without a push from me."

"Yes."

"Because you don't want your daughter to know that you're the one who betrayed her," Embeth filled in. "Because you want her to *love* you, to think of you as her best friend."

"Yes."

"Because she's a slut—"

"Come on," I said. "She's just a mixed-up kid."

"Because she's a slut," she said, "and you're a coward."

"Yes."

"Because you want it to end and you thought I would know what to do."

"Yes."

"Because you look at my husband and you look at me and you suspect I've been through this before. Is that right?"

"I really am sorry."

"Sure you are. I'll take care of it," Embeth said. "And I'll let Jorge know there isn't going to be a fund-raiser. A Night of Jewish Goddamn Leaders! Next time you want to ruin someone's marriage, do it over the effing phone."

I felt guilty, but lighter. I had turned my problem into someone else's. I went back inside the restaurant and had a vodka tonic with Jorge. I asked him what it was like to work for the Levins.

"They're wonderful people," he said. "Beautiful people. The best. We all think they're a rocket ship. You see it, don't you?"

FIVE

After Louis the asshole, I decide I'm done with online dating for a while and it's fine to be a third wheel with Roz and Tony the glass guy. The glass guy says he likes having two women, and honestly, *he's* the third wheel because Roz and I have a friendship that predates their relationship.

Roz and Tony decide to subscribe to the Broadway series at the Kravis Center, and Roz wants me to subscribe with them. Three seats together? I say. That'll make me an institutional third wheel. And she says, Why not? Tony says he'll sit in the middle.

So once a month, on theater nights, Tony and Roz pick me up, and we have early bird somewhere, and then we go to the theater. Tony starts calling me "Legs" after the first show, *A Chorus Line*. He says I've got dancer legs. I tell him I've got Pilates legs. Roz says she has turkey legs and a turkey neck, too. We have a good laugh over this.

And that's how it is with the three of us. Maybe it's not particularly deep, but it's pleasant and it passes the hours.

The third show in the series is *Camelot*, and Roz gets a cough, so she can't go. Roz says she doesn't want to be coughing through the whole show. I tell her this is South Florida and a musical in South Florida is more coughs than notes anyway. Be that as it may, Roz says, she'd rather not be in the South Florida Senior Citizens' Cough Chorus.

Tony and I end up going alone, and at dinner, what we talk about is Roz. He says how lucky he was to find her, how she fixed his whole life. And I say there isn't a better person in the world than Roz Horowitz. And he says he feels grateful to have made friends with Roz's friends.

During the show, during Guinevere's number "The Lusty Month of May," his elbow makes its way across our shared armrest, and I nudge it back to his side. The elbow returns during Guinevere's act 2 number, "I Loved You Once in Silence." This time, I push it into his seat. He smiles at me. "Sorry," he whispers. "Guess I'm too big for the theater."

On the walk back to his car, he says, "Did anyone ever tell you, you're a ringer for Yvonne De Carlo?"

"You mean Mrs. Munster?" I say. "Is she still alive?"

He says she was in a lot of things before that. "Wasn't she Gomorrah in *The Ten Commandments*?"

"Gomorrah's not a character," I say. "It's a city."

"I'm pretty sure she was Gomorrah," he says. "I've seen that movie a thousand times."

"It's a city," I say. "It's a disgusting, violent city where people are terrible to strangers and have all kinds of crazy sex."

"What kinds of crazy sex?" he says.

I'm not going to get into that with him. "Fine," I say. "Have it your way."

"Why can't you be nice to me, Rachel?" he says. "I like it when you're nice to me."

When he drops me off at my apartment, the glass guy makes a big show of walking me to my door. "This is unnecessary," I say. "I know how to get to my door."

"You deserve full-service treatment," he says.

"I'm fine," I say.

"I promised Roz I'd see you home," he says.

We walk to my front door, and when we get there I say, "Good night, Tony. Give my love to Roz."

He puts his hand on my wrist and he pulls me toward him. His red, corpulent lips leech on to my own. "Aren't you going to invite me in?"

"No," I say, pulling my lips and my wrist away. "You've got the wrong idea. Roz is my best friend."

"Come on," he says. "You've been flirting with me for months. Don't deny it."

"I strenuously deny it!"

"I think I know when a woman is flirting with me. I'm not usually wrong about these things."

"You're dead wrong this time, Tony." I dig out my keys from my purse, but my hands are shaking—anger, not fear—and I have trouble opening my door.

"What was all that talk about 'teaching Pilates'?" he says.

"It's my job," I say. "And I do think strengthening your core would help with your sciatica."

"Let's start on my core tonight," he says.

"I think you need to leave," I say.

"Okay, relax," Tony says. He starts massaging my shoulders with his thick, lumpy hands. It feels good, but I do not want his hands there. "Don't be so tense. Roz and I have an understanding about these things."

"You do not. She is not that kind of person."

"There's a lot you don't know about Roz," the glass guy says.

"There is *nothing* I don't know about Roz. Even if you do have an 'arrangement,' which I highly doubt, I do not want you!"

I get the key in the lock, and he tries to follow me inside. I push him away, and I kick his foot off the threshold. I close my door and I put on the dead bolt.

I hear him breathing, and then he says, "I hope we're not going to be little children about this, Rachel." He means that he doesn't want me to tell Roz and he means that he wants Broadway nights to go on as usual.

Finally, the glass guy leaves, and I want to call Roz and tell her about it, but I don't. Nothing happened, not really. The key to happiness in life is knowing when to keep your mouth shut.

BEING SIXTY-FOUR YEARS old is like being in high school again.

IT'S NOT SO much the betrayal I want to report—the betrayal is depressing and makes me sad for my friend. It's that I want to tell her the story.

I'M STARING AT the phone, willing myself not to call Roz, when the phone rings.

"Roz?" I say.

It's Louis the asshole. "I thought about it for the longest time," he says. "I know what I did. I know what I said, and I'm sorry. I shouldn't have said that thing about your picture."

"What thing about my picture?" I say.

"I don't want to repeat it," he says.

"You're going to have to repeat it," I say. I have no idea what he's talking about.

"That thing where I said you were so much better looking than your picture. It was stupid of me," he says. "I mean, how are you supposed to respond to that? Maybe you think I'm insulting your judgment? Maybe you think I'm saying your picture is ugly? And your picture isn't ugly, Rachel. Your picture is dynamite."

I tell him that wasn't it.

"Then what was it?" he wants to know. "It was something, I know it was something."

I say to him, "Is it possible that I just don't like you?"

"Impossible," he says.

"Goodnight, Louis," I say.

"Wait," he says. "Whatever I did, whatever I said, can you try to forgive me?"

"Goodnight, Louis," I say.

I thought literature professors were supposed to be more astute.

The way I see it, I am glad he said what he said about Aviva. It is better to know what someone is like up front.

SIX

I waited for Aviva to call me, wailing that the wife had found out and the congressman had broken up with her.

When she did not call, I thought, Perhaps she is working through this on her own, perhaps this is what maturity looks like. I knew the stereotype of an overbearing Jewish mother—as aforementioned, I am a Philip Roth fan—and I probably met some of those criteria. But honestly, I wasn't one and I'm still not one. I had a job that fulfilled me. I had friends. My daughter was my love, but she was not my life.

So I decided to leave her be. I sent her lavender-scented hand lotion from Crabtree & Evelyn, but that was all. Lavender was her favorite.

I did not hear from Aviva, not even a thank-you. But that next week, I did hear from Jorge. "Well, Rachel," he said, "summer's coming quick. We probably need to get moving if we want to do this before the end of the school year."

"Didn't Embeth speak to you?" I said.

"Uh-oh," he said. "Are you having cold feet?"

"No, nothing like that," I said. "It's . . . Well, maybe it's *my* misunderstanding, but I thought Embeth had decided the fund-raiser wasn't a good idea."

"Nope, I spoke to her this morning," Jorge said. "She was still completely on board. She said she was pumped for it."

"'Pumped'?" I said. "Embeth said she was pumped?"

"I don't know if those were her exact words. One second, Rachel— yes, I'll be off soon," Jorge called to someone in the other room. "It's madness here today," he apologized.

"Something exciting happening?"

"It's always madness. So, Rachel, if you're still good to go, we're still good to go."

I don't know why I didn't say no. In my defense, I was confused. I think it's like when you're on a cell phone call with someone and the reception goes bad and you continue to pretend as if you can hear for a bit, hoping that the cell phone reception will work itself out before the person catches on that you haven't been hearing her for five minutes. Why don't you immediately say, I can't hear you? Why does it feel shameful?

"I'm good to go," I said, "but I will need to talk to my board." Of course, I had no intention of going to the board. There was no way they would let me host a *political* fund-raiser at the school. Politics was a landmine at BRJA. God forbid Levin bring up, for instance, the Rabin assassination!

"Yes, of course. How's the second Thursday in May? That's May eleventh."

"May eleventh," I repeated. I made an imaginary mark in my calendar. I'd call Jorge back in a couple of days to tell him that the board was unwilling to approve a political fund-raiser, and that would be the end of that.

The thing that left me disquieted was Embeth's behavior and what it meant about Aviva's silence.

I phoned Aviva and I asked her how she was and how it was going and did she get the lotion.

"It's a little thin," she said. "The lotion. I think they changed the formulation since the last time you bought it."

"No," I said. "Last time, I bought the hand cream and that's thicker. This time I got the body lotion."

"We haven't broken up," she said. "I know that's what you really want to know."

I did want to know that, but I also wanted to know if Embeth had spoken to the congressman. "Aviva, what will you do if his wife finds out?"

"Why would she find out?" Aviva said. "Who's going to tell her?"

"There are a lot of eyes on the congressman," I said. "He's a public person."

"I'm careful," Aviva said. "We're both careful."

"I want you to have the kind of man where you don't have to be careful," I said.

"Mom, he's not like other men. He's worth it. He's—"

"He's too old for you, Aviva. He's married. He has children. I didn't think I raised you to have such terrible judgment."

"How many times are we going to do this?" Aviva said.

"I don't understand his interest in you," I said.

"Nice, Mom. Is it so hard to believe that a man like him could be interested in a girl like me?"

"That's not what I meant. I mean, he's a grown man, Aviva. He's *my* age. What do you two have in common?"

"This is why I don't call you anymore."

"But what if she *does* find out? Will you end it then? Will he?"

"I don't know," she said. "Good-bye, Mom."

"Aviva, I—" I heard her hang up the phone.

MAYBE A WEEK later, Rabbi Barney, the head of the school's board, came into my office without knocking.

"What's this about us doing a fund-raiser for Congressman Levin? A man named Jorge Rodriguez says he spoke to you."

Jorge had left word for me three times in the past week, and I had ignored him. This was a mistake on my part. A man in Jorge's job was used to being blown off and used to doing whatever it took to get someone to pay attention to him. Of course he would have gone over my head.

I laughed to give myself time. "Oh, it's nothing. You know how pushy those political people can be, always looking for money. I took a courtesy meeting with Embeth Levin—she used to be my neighbor in Forestgreen. I couldn't get out of it—Aviva's working for the congressman now, I don't remember if I told you."

"That's not what Jorge Rodriguez said. Jorge said that you pitched them on the idea of a Night of Jewish Leaders, and now it's on the congressman's public schedule."

"No," I said. "I specifically did not agree to anything. I was having a discussion with them out of courtesy."

"Politicians." Rabbi Barney sighed. "Well, the local press has picked up on the event. I don't see how we can *not* do it now."

Why the hell not? "Why not?" I said.

"If we cancel the event, it will look as if we *were* supporting Levin and now we *aren't* supporting Levin. We don't want to appear to be supporting Levin, but we don't want to appear to *not* be supporting Levin either. It's an extremely awkward position, Rachel. I don't blame you for what happened, but you must be careful about who you agree to meet with. You're the principal of BRJA now."

It was clear that he did blame me. On some level, I was offended. If it had happened as I had described it, then it wasn't my fault. Of course, it had not happened this way—and so it *was* my fault—but he didn't know that.

Rabbi Barney instructed me to plan the event but to try to keep it as low-key as possible. "Let's all try to keep our jobs, Rachel," he said.

As soon as Rabbi Barney left, I called Jorge.

"I was starting to get hurt feelings. I thought you were ignoring me on purpose," he said.

AVIVA PHONED ME that evening. "What are you trying to do to me?" she yelled.

"Did I raise you to be this self-centered?" I said. "Not everything has to do with you. Knowing what I know about the congressman, you think I want this fund-raiser at my school? I have nothing to do with this."

"Then why did you call the congressman's office?"

"No, Aviva." I expected God to strike me dead, I had never lied so much in my life. "I called them months ago, before you even went to work for Levin. Someone at the school had an idea for a Night of Jewish Leaders. I called the Levins because the school asked me to, because I knew them, because your father had operated on his mother, because Levin is the most prominent Jewish leader I know. It is a coincidence, my love, nothing more. Maybe Embeth had the idea to turn it into a fund-raising event? But it did not come from me."

"Then end it," she said. "You're the principal. You can end this. Nothing happens at that school without your say-so."

"It's not that simple," I said. "His staff put it on the schedule. And some guy named Jorge?"

"Yes, Jorge Rodriguez. He's in charge of fund-raising."

"Okay, so you know him. This Jorge fellow went over my head to Rabbi Barney. And now the whole thing's become political, I guess. My hands are tied."

I could hear Aviva breathing, but she had not hung up.

"Fine, Mother," Aviva said. "I believe you. I need you to promise me you won't say anything about"—she lowered her voice—"my relationship to anyone. Promise me you won't talk to the congressman or to his wife."

"Aviva, God forbid, of course not. I won't mention your relationship, but I'll have to talk to them. It isn't practical for me not to talk to them. They used to be our neighbors."

Aviva began to sob.

"Aviva, what is it?"

"I'm sorry," she said, the bully from her voice gone. "I'm tired," she said. "I miss you," she said. "And I'm twenty and I feel so old," she said. "Mommy," she said, "I think I should break it off. I know you're right. I just don't know how to do it."

My heart bloomed like a hothouse rose. All the lying had been worth it if this was going to be the result. Even if I got fired for this *narishkeit* fund-raiser, it would have been worth it if I had managed to save my daughter and her good name. "Are you saying you want my advice?" I said cautiously, not wanting to scare her off.

"Yes," she said. "Please."

"Talk to him without bitterness. Tell him that you loved the time you have spent together, but that neither of you is in the right place in your life for this relationship to continue."

"Yes," she said.

"Tell him that you understand that his life is complicated. Tell him that you are too young to settle down with one person. Tell him that the end of a school year is a good time to reassess. It is, Aviva."

Aviva began to sob again.

"What is it, my love?"

"I'll never meet anyone as good as him again."

I bit the tip of my tongue so hard, I could taste the blood in my mouth. The things I did not say!

If I ever write my memoir, that should be the title. *Rachel Shapiro: The Things I Did Not Say!*

SEVEN

I t had been six years since I had seen Aaron Levin in the flesh, and what I noticed about him was that he had a small bald spot in the middle of his black curls.

Aviva was there, of course. How could she not attend Boca Raton Jewish Academy Presents a Night of Jewish Leaders? It was a hot ticket, and she worked for the congressman and she was my daughter. She was wearing the St. John suit I had bought for my meeting with Embeth—I hadn't even known she had taken it from my closet. It was too tight across her bosom, but she still looked like a little girl in it. I did not know if she had broken up with him, or he with her.

The congressman greeted me warmly. "Rachel Grossman, you look wonderful. Thank you for setting this up. It's going to be a grand night." And other politician schlock.

"Happy to do it," I said. This was how civilized people behaved.

Nothing in his behavior suggested that he was screwing my daughter. Though what he was supposed to do, I do not know. What behavior of his would have pleased me? I led him and one of his aides into the dressing room behind the auditorium. The students were going to give speeches about what being a Jewish leader meant to them, and then the congressman would come out to give his own speech and present a small cash prize to the graduating senior who showed the most leadership potential. I had invented the prize about a week ago to make everything seem legit.

The congressman's aide had excused himself to take a phone call, and for a moment, the congressman and I were alone. He looked me right in the eyes. His eyes were clear, kind, and honest, and he said, "Aviva is doing a wonderful job."

I looked around. "Excuse me," I said.

"Aviva is doing a wonderful job," he repeated.

I considered the possibilities.

1. He didn't know that I knew about the affair.
2. He did know that I knew about the affair, and he was making a repulsive sexual innuendo.
3. He did know that I knew about the affair, and Aviva was genuinely doing a wonderful job.

There may have been other options, but this is what occurred to me at the time. All three of the options made me want to slap him, though I did not slap him. If Aviva had already broken up with him, what good would my slapping him have done?

"Yes," I said. I could tell he was put off by my terse reply. He was one of those people who needed people to like him.

"How's Dr. Mike?" he asked.

"Very well," I said.

"I was hoping to see him tonight," the congressman said.

"Well, his medical practice keeps him busy," I said. And I'm not certain why I said this next thing, but I did. "Also, his social life."

"His social life?" the congressman asked with a laugh. "What kind of social life does Mike Grossman have?"

"He cheats on me," I said. "He has a woman I know about, but there may be others, too. It's been humiliating for me. I don't know if Aviva knows about it. I've tried to keep it from her. I want her to be able to love and respect her father. But I have a feeling that children sense things even when you don't tell them. Still I worry, Aaron, what it will do to her morals, having a father like that."

"I'm sorry," the congressman said.

"It is what it is," I said and then I left to organize my students.

THE CONGRESSMAN'S SPEECH was about being one of very few Jewish kids at Annapolis and how it was not a bad thing to find you were the "only one" from time to time. Being the "only one" was good practice for imagining what it was like to be a minority or even a poor person, the congressman said. Government's greatest danger was myopia and egocentrism. Good leaders and good citizens had to consider the needs of those who were not like us, too.

It was a fine speech from a putz.

I ushered everyone into the lobby of the auditorium for a reception with the congressman. Somehow, I had misplaced the congressman. I went backstage and I was about to knock on the door of the dressing room when I felt a hand on my shoulder. Jorge shook his head. His smile was the feigned amusement of a peasant made to listen to a king's off-color joke.

"Don't worry, Rachel. I'll get him," Jorge whispered. "I'll bring him to you in a moment."

The congressman opened the door. Aviva's lipstick was smudged, and her chin was pink and raw. The room smelled musky, salty. Oh, why be polite? It smelled of sex.

"Aviva," I said, "here." I reached into my pocket and handed her a tissue.

"Congressman," I said, "you're needed in the lobby."

The congressman told Jorge and Aviva to go on ahead.

"Rachel," the congressman said in a low voice, "that wasn't what it looked like."

When someone tells you 'it's not what it looks like,' it's almost always *exactly* what it looks like. "You're a disgrace," I said.

The congressman nodded. "I am," he said, but this admission did not please me.

"She is twenty years old," I said. "If you have any interest in doing the right thing . . . If you were any kind of a man, you would end this right now."

"Yes . . . ," he said. "It's funny," he said. "Around us . . . Lockers, baseball bats, a judge's bench—what show are the kids doing this year?"

"*Damn Yankees*," I said. I wondered if he had even heard me.

"*Damn Yankees*," he said. "What's that one about?"

"Well, there's this baseball player . . ."

By that time, we had arrived at the reception. The congressman put on a smile, and so did I.

AROUND ONE IN the morning, Aviva let herself into our house, but I knew she was coming because the guard at the gatehouse had called me. God bless those Forestgreen gates.

Her eyes were swollen, like cherries. She pointed at me like a prosecutor in a legal movie. "I know you said something, Mother!"

"What's happened?" I asked.

"Don't play innocent," she said. "I know this is your fault."

"I'm not *playing* anything. I don't know what's happened," I said.

"He ended it," she said. Her lip trembled and then she began to sob. "It's over."

Oh God, the relief felt like oxygen. The relief felt like getting off a plane, after a long winter and a turbulent flight, and finding yourself outside the airport in a tropical clime. The relief was so profound, I felt undone. I wanted to smile, to laugh, to scream, to weep, to fall to my knees and thank God. I went up to her, and I tried to take her hand. "I'm so sorry," I said.

"Don't touch me!" she said, pulling her hand away.

"I am sorry for you," I said. "But I am relieved for you as well."

"You don't care if I'm happy!" she said.

"Of course I do."

"I don't understand it. Did you say something? You must have said something. Tell me, what did you say?"

"I said nothing," I told her. "The congressman and I barely spoke."

"What about after you gave me the tissue? Did you say something then? Your face looked so judgmental."

"No," I said.

"What exactly did you talk about?"

"Aviva, I don't even remember. It was chitchat, nothing more. We talked about Daddy! We talked about *Damn Yankees*."

"*Damn Yankees*? You mean the SHOW?"

"It's the senior musical."

"It's my fault," she said. "I shouldn't have . . ." She did not say what she shouldn't have done.

Aviva flopped on the dark leather couch, which Mike had chosen. I mistook her body language for retreat. There was a whitish stain on her suit jacket—*my* suit jacket. This is motherhood, I thought. Your daughter stains your jacket, and you get to clean it up. "Take off the jacket, Aviva," I said. "I should get it dry cleaned."

She removed the jacket, and I hung it in the hall closet.

"Maybe it's a blessing, my love," I said. "Weren't you thinking of ending it anyway?"

"Yes," she said. "But I never would have."

"Let me make you something to eat," I said. "You must be starving."

Aviva stood up. My offer of food re-enraged her. "You say I'm fat and then you're always trying to stuff me like a pig!" she yelled.

"Aviva," I said.

"No, you're very clever. You never say I'm 'fat'—you just talk about my weight obsessively. You ask me if I'm eating right, if I'm drinking water. You say some dress looks a little tight."

"That isn't true."

"You say I shouldn't cut my hair too short because it makes my face look round," Aviva said.

"Aviva, where are you getting this?" I said. "You're a beautiful girl. I love you, just as you are."

"DON'T LIE!"

"What? Your hair does look better longer. I'm your mother. I want you to look your best. Is that a crime?" I said.

"Just because you think about your body all the time, just because you never eat more than three bites of dessert, just because you work out like a crazy person doesn't mean I have to feel or behave the way you do!" she said.

"Of course you don't have to feel the way I do," I said.

"Which bothers you more? That I could attract a man like Aaron Levin, or that you couldn't?"

"AVIVA!" I said. "Enough. That is a ridiculous and ungenerous thing to say."

"And I know you said something! I know you said something or did something! Admit it, Mom! Stop lying! Please stop lying! I need to know what happened, or I'll go crazy!"

"Why does it have to be anything I said? Maybe being at the school reminded him of how young you are and how inappropriate this relationship is? Isn't that possible, Aviva?"

"I hate you," she said. "I am *never* speaking to you again." She left the house and she shut the door.

• • •

NEVER LASTED UNTIL August.

At the end of the summer, Mike and I rented a house in a little town outside of Portland, Maine. I called Aviva and said, "Haven't we not been speaking long enough? I'm sorry for anything I've done and anything you think I've done. Come to Maine with me and Daddy. I miss you terribly. And Daddy misses you, too. We'll eat lobster rolls and whoopie pies every day."

"Lobster, Mom? What's come over you?" Aviva said.

"Don't tell Grandma, but I refuse to believe in a God who doesn't want me to eat lobster," I said.

She laughed. "Okay," she said. "Okay, I'll come."

We had been there about four days when she said, "It feels like last year was a dream," she said. "It feels like I had a fever, and the fever has finally broken."

"I'm glad," I said.

"Still," she said, "sometimes I miss the fever."

"But you don't see him anymore?"

"No," she said. "Of course not." She corrected herself. "I mean, I don't see him socially. I see him at work."

I was impressed with her that she had somehow managed to keep working for the congressman. "Is that hard?" I asked. "Seeing him, but not being with him?"

"I almost never see him," she said. "I'm not that important now that I'm not that important."

EIGHT

A few days after *Camelot*, Roz calls me and asks if she might use my ticket for *The Mystery of Edwin Drood*. Her sister is coming to town, and wouldn't it be nice for the three of them to go together? I say yes, because who wants to see a musical version of *The Mystery of Edwin Drood*? Whenever you subscribe to a regional theater season, there're always a few duds. She says she'll pay me for the ticket, and I say your money's no good here, Roz Horowitz. It's a mitzvah to *not* have to go to *Edwin Drood*.

Roz laughs and then she says, "Oh, Rachel, how could you?"

I know what she is going to say before she says it. I know that Mr. Elbow in My Seat has told her that I tried to kiss him and not the other way around. He's made a preemptive strike. I should have called her, but in my defense, who wants to get in the middle of someone's marriage? Even knowing what he's done, I'm still not sure how to proceed. She's not the first woman in the world to end up married to a cheating louse. It can happen to anyone. Do I really want my friend to have to divorce? At her age? Do I wish her a future that involves profile pictures and swiping and squeezing into Spanx to go on dates with *alte cockers*? No, I do not.

"Roz," I say, "Roz, my dear one, I think it was a misunderstanding."

"He says you tried to give him"—she lowers to an outraged whisper—"a hand job, Rachel."

"A hand job? Roz, that is fantasy." I tell her what happened. Why in the world did he make up the hand job? What is wrong with him?

"I know you're lonely, Rachel," Roz says. "But you've been my best friend since 1992, and I know what you're like. You're lonely and you're vain and you meddle. I believe him."

I say, "I would never betray you for him. For the *farkakte* glass guy? I would never. After all that we've been through together."

Roz says, "Rachel, stop."

So I stop.

I'm sixty-four years old. I know when to stop.

NINE

When she went back to the University of Miami in the fall, Aviva decided to move off campus to a tiny studio apartment in Coconut Grove. We had a good time decorating that little place together. We did a whole "shabby chic" thing. We bought wood furniture from Goodwill and sanded it and painted it cream, and we bought faded floral sheets, and a beige quilt from an antique store, and we had a turquoise bowl filled with seashells, and gardenia and lavender scented soy candles, and we painted the walls white, and we hung sheer voile curtains. And we lucked into a genuine Wegner Wishbone chair in birch. This was before the midcentury craze, so I think we got it for about thirty-five dollars. The last thing I bought was a white orchid.

"Mom," she said, "I'll kill it."

"Just don't overwater it," I said.

"I'm not good with plants," she said.

"You're twenty-one," I said. "You don't know what you're good with yet."

It was so beautiful and perfect and blank, this little place, I remember wishing I could move in with her, and I felt almost jealous of Aviva. Everything in her apartment could be exactly the way she wanted it.

It was a happy time in our relationship and a happy time in my life in general. The board had decided not to seek out a new principal, and I was made permanent principal of BRJA. They had a cocktail party for me. They served smoked salmon on toast points. Unfortunately, the salmon had turned, and though I did not eat the salmon, everyone who did got sick. I did not take this as a sign.

Roz took me out to lunch for my forty-ninth birthday. She said that I looked great and asked me what I'd been doing.

I said, "I'm happy."

"I'll have to try that," she said.

I don't know why—maybe I'd had too much wine—but I started to cry.

"Rachel," Roz said, "oh my God, what is it? Has something happened?"

"The opposite," I said. "Something that I thought was going to happen didn't happen, and I feel so relieved and grateful."

"You don't have to tell me," Roz said. She poured me another glass of wine. "Was it your health? Mike's health? Did you find a lump?"

"No, nothing like that."

"Aviva?" Roz said.

"Yes, something to do with Aviva."

"Do you want to tell me? You don't have to tell me," she said.

"Roz," I said. "She was having an affair with a married man, and now it's over. It's over, thank God."

"Oh God, Rach, that's nothing. She's young. It's the special privilege of youth to make mistakes."

I lowered my eyes. "It wasn't just the affair. It was who it was with."

"Who was it, Rachel?" she said. "You don't have to say."

I whispered the name in her ear.

"Good for Aviva!"

"Roz!" I said. "You're wicked. He's married, and he's our age, and he was her boss!"

"Well, he's not hard to look at," Roz said. "And we did used to joke about him being our 'spring fling.' Do you remember?"

As if I could have forgotten.

"Do you think Aviva could have heard us?" Roz said.

"I don't know," I said.

"That wife of his." Roz was pleasantly soused. "I change my mind, good for *him*. Aviva's a catch. They would have had be-yoo-tee-full babies, those two."

"Well, it's over now," I said. "No babies, thank God."

TEN

I want to begin by saying, the accident was neither Aviva's nor the congressman's fault.

An eightysomething woman, driving with a suspended license and in the beginning stages of dementia, wasn't looking when she took a left turn, and she slammed into the side of the congressman's Lexus sedan. The old woman was killed, which meant there was an investigation. The investigation found that the old woman was at fault, and also that my daughter, who was in the passenger seat at the time, was having an affair with the congressman. This was the beginning of South Florida's Aviva Grossman obsession. Avivagate.

But I get ahead of myself.

Before Avivagate, before the story had a name, there was a period of time when we waited for the story. We waited to see if the story would even become a story, or more precisely, if Aviva would be a character in the story. For a brief but shining moment, she was the "unknown female intern" who was traveling in the car with the congressman. We didn't know if her name would be released, and I believe the congressman tried to keep Aviva out of it. He may be an immoral man, but he is not a cruel one. Unfortunately, interest in the story grew beyond the congressman's power to protect my daughter. The public would not be sated until it knew who had been in the car with the congressman that night.

Aviva couldn't bear to tell her father. She waited until the day before the police's release of her name and the congressman's press conference addressing that release. I offered to tell Mike for Aviva, but to her credit, she said she wanted to tell him herself.

We took Mike to the sleepy restaurant at what used to be the Bridge Hotel but is now a Hilton. Roz and I like to joke that everything in the world eventually becomes a Hilton. The restaurant was a favorite of our family's, mainly for the view of the Intercoastal and the boats passing by, but the food was nothing special. Pool food. Club sandwiches. Steak fries.

Aviva ordered a Cobb salad, which she did not touch. And then, to prolong the meal, she ordered a coffee, which she did not drink. We talked about things: my job, Aviva's classes, Mike's job. We did not talk about Congressman Levin, though the story—sans Aviva's name—was already in the air. That kind of gossip didn't interest Mike, though. So we talked about nothing, and time flew. I knew Mike was planning to go back to the office. I considered prompting Aviva, but I decided against it. It was not my secret to tell.

As Mike was going over the bill, he told a story about a woman whose heart he'd operated on a few years back. "Sixty-one years old. Quadruple bypass," he said. "No complications, but the recovery was long. Anyway, about a year after the surgery, she was playing with her granddaughter, and out of the clear blue sky, she made a perfect replica of the family's dachshund out of Play-Doh."

"Play-Doh!" Aviva said too enthusiastically.

"Yes! Can you imagine? And the granddaughter says, 'Make another, Dodie.' So Dodie does one of the granddaughter and the house and Dodie's childhood home in Yonkers, which she hasn't seen for years, and by this point, the whole family is gathered around to witness this miracle. And Dodie's son says, 'Maybe we should get you to a sculpture studio, Mom.' Before the heart attack, she'd never been in the least artistic. She had no sense of perspective, could barely draw stick figures. And now she's making these photorealistic three-dimensional busts out of marble, clay, whatever medium she can get her hands on. She did the whole family, all of her friends, a few celebrities. She's so good, the story gets picked up by the local news. They're calling her the Grandma Moses of sculpture. And now Dodie's taking commissions, and she's getting paid thousands of dollars to do sculptures for towns, for public spaces, for celebrations."

"You should get a percentage," I said. "She owes it all to you."

"I wouldn't go that far, but she is making a bust of me right now," Mike said. "Gratis."

"You can put it in the lobby of your office," I said. *The Head of a Great Man.*"

"What do you think caused it?" Aviva asked.

"You unblock the heart, and the increased blood flow will improve brain function. And maybe the improved brain function creates new neural pathways, resulting in the discovery of heretofore undiscovered talents. Who knows?" Mike said.

"The heart is mysterious," I said.

"That's garbage, Rachel," Mike said. "The heart is fully explicable. The brain is mysterious, I'll give you that."

"The heart is explicable to you," I said. "The rest of us are in the dark."

Mike signed the receipt.

"Daddy," Aviva said.

"Yes?" Mike looked up.

She kissed him on the cheek. "I love you," she said.

"I love you, too," Mike said.

"I'm so sorry." Aviva began to cry.

"Aviva, what is it?" Mike sat back down at the table. "What can it be?"

"I screwed up," she said.

"Whatever it is, we'll fix it," he said.

"This can't be fixed," she said.

"Everything can be fixed," he said.

AVIVA DROVE BACK to Miami, and Mike, who had canceled the rest of his day, and I drove back to our house to argue pointlessly.

"I suppose you knew about this," he said.

I sighed. "I had suspicions," I said. "I did suspect."

"If you suspected," Mike said, "why in God's name didn't you do something?"

"I tried," I said.

"You didn't try hard enough!"

"She's a grown woman, Mike. I can't lock her in her room."

"I thought the one thing I could say for you was that you were a good mother," Mike said.

He had always been lousy in an argument, and this is one of the many reasons I do not miss being married to him.

"How could you let her do something so immoral?" Mike said.

"It's not as if you set a great example," I said quietly.

"What? What did you say?"

"I said, there's no point in us trading insults. We have to figure out what we're going to do."

"What can we do?" Mike said. "Other than get her a lawyer and wait for this to pass?"

"We have to support our daughter," I said.

"Obviously," Mike said. He put his head in his hands. "How could she do this to us?"

"I don't think she was thinking of us," I said.

"Would you have done something like this at that age?"

"No," I said. "But I wouldn't have done something like what the congressman did at his age either. I wouldn't have slept with an employee, young enough to be my daughter. Would *you*?"

He didn't reply. He was flipping through his address book. "I've operated on about a million lawyers. There's got to be a good one in here somewhere."

AVIVA AND THE congressman both claimed that the affair had been over for some time. I know what she told me, but I cannot say if this is true or not. It may have been, as he said, that he had been giving the intern a ride home. (I will tell you that they were not going in the direction of her apartment in Coconut Grove or our house in Forestgreen at the time of the crash.) It was certainly bad timing that she was in the car when that old woman turned left.

Occasionally, a news story captures the imagination of a region, and so it was with the congressman and my daughter. I could tell you the details of how the story played out, but even if you didn't live in South Florida, there is nothing you haven't heard or can't imagine. It played out exactly as these stories always play out.

The congressman and Embeth went on a news show. They claimed that the affair had occurred during a time of trouble in their marriage. The time of trouble had passed, they said. They held hands. He had manly tears in his eyes, but he did not cry. She said she had forgiven him. She said that they had a real marriage, not a storybook one. Something like that. I remember she wore an ill-fitting purple tweed jacket. What must she have been thinking?

Because it was an election year, the congressman's staff took great pains to distance itself from Aviva. They characterized her as the Lolita intern, a Lewinsky wannabe, and a variety of other synonyms for "slutty."

It did not help Aviva's cause that she had kept a blog, detailing her months working for the congressman. The year was 2000, and I did not even know what a blog was when I found out that Aviva had been keeping one. "Blog?" I said to Aviva. The word felt foreign on my tongue. "What's that?"

"It's short for weblog, Mom," Aviva said.

"Weblog," I repeated. "What's a weblog?"

"It's like a diary," Aviva said. "It's a diary that you keep on the Internet."

"Why would anyone do that?" I asked. "Why would *you* do that?"

"It was anonymous. I never used names. Until everything happened, I had about three readers. I was trying to make sense of my experiences by writing about them," she said.

"Then buy a diary, Aviva!"

"I like typing," she said. "And I hate my handwriting."

"Then make a folder on your laptop and save a Word file called Avivasdiary.doc in it."

"I know, Mom. I know."

Aviva's blog was called "Just Another Congressional Intern's Blog." As she said, she didn't use his name or her own, but people still figured out it was her. Decoding Aviva's blog became an unofficial South Florida pastime for a while. She tried to have it taken down, but it wouldn't be taken down. This blog was like a zombie. It would not be killed. She'd have it removed and it would show up somewhere else. You can probably still find it somewhere on the Internet if you look hard enough. I will tell you that I read it—most of it; some of it with one eye closed—but it was really quite boring except for the sexy parts. And the sexy parts gave me no pleasure. I felt the same way when Roz's and my book club read the *Story of O*.

Aviva was forced to take a leave from U of Miami because the press were disturbing the other students in her classes.

She moved back home, and she waited out the storm as best she could.

One other thing I could say about this period is God bless the Forestgreen gates. The press could not wait on our lawn but instead had to wait outside those gates for us to leave. Roz brought us food. Her offerings included matzo ball soup, sweet and savory kugels, tongue sandwiches on rye, loaves of challah, bagels, lox, herring, and hamantaschen, as if we had a sick friend or a death in the family.

A quick story about hamantaschen, while I'm thinking about it. A week before the end of the school year, Rabbi Barney summoned me to his office. He held out a fig hamantaschen. "Rachel, have a hamantaschen," he said.

"No thank you," I said. In general, I do not care for hamantaschen as I find them low on fruit filling and often dry in the cookie part.

"Please, Rachel, take the hamantaschen. My mother bakes them twice a year. It's a big production for her. She has a special recipe. Also, she has lung cancer. This might be the final batch of Harriet Greenbaum's famous hamantaschen."

I thanked him for the generous offer, but I told him it would be wasted on me. I told him my feelings about hamantaschen. But he kept insisting so I took it, and I bit into it, and honestly, it was delicious. High fruit to cookie ratio, and not dry in the least. She must have used a stick of butter. It was so delicious and sweet, I almost wanted to moan.

"Rachel," he said, "we'd like you to resign."

I was in the middle of chewing the hamantaschen. I needed a beverage but none had been offered. It took me almost twenty seconds to swallow the hamantaschen. "Why?" I asked. Of course I knew why, but by God, he was going to say it.

"The scandal with Aviva. It's no good for us."

"But, Rabbi," I said, "I am not the one in a scandal. It's my daughter, and she is an adult, a human being separate from myself. I cannot control what she does."

"I'm sorry, Rachel. I agree with you. It's not Aviva's affair, it's the fund-raiser that's the problem. The board felt that you compromised yourself by advocating for the fund-raiser with the congressman last year. It has the appearance of impropriety."

"I didn't know about the affair!" I said. "And I had nothing to do with the fund-raiser. You must remember. I didn't want anything to do with it."

"I do remember and I believe you, Rachel. I believe you. It's how it looks."

"I've given twelve years of my life to this school," I said.

"I know," said the rabbi. "It's a rotten business. We want to make it as copacetic an exit as possible. You could say you're resigning to spend more time with family. Everyone would understand that, the year you've had."

"I won't say that!" I said. "I will not lie!" I had half a haman-taschen left, and I was considering throwing it at the rabbi. Last year, that Fischer idiot threw a black-and-white cookie at me, and I started to wonder if every principal exited this school with a ceremonial baked good fling.

"Is something funny?" the rabbi asked.

"Everything's funny," I said.

"Well, sleep on it."

"I don't need to sleep on it."

"Sleep on it, Rachel. No one wants to fire you. No one wants another scandal. If you resign, you can still find work somewhere else."

I SLEPT ON it. I resigned.

AFTER I PACKED up my desk, I drove across town to a dumpy pink apartment building on Camino Real. I rang the bell for M. Choi. The woman's voice asked who it was, and I said it was a delivery, and the woman said she wasn't expecting a delivery, and I said it's flowers, and the woman said who are the flowers from? And I said they're from Dr. Grossman. The woman buzzed me in.

I climbed the stairs, and M. Choi had the door open. She was still wearing her nurse's uniform, not a sexy costume one—blue scrubs with a neon geometric pattern.

My husband's mistress said, "Hello, Rachel. I guess Mike didn't send me flowers."

I said, "Mike's not a flower guy."

"No," she said.

I said, "I got fired today."

She said, "I'm sorry."

I said, "It's been a rotten year."

She said, "I'm sorry for everything. For Aviva. And for everything."

"I don't want an apology," I said. "I don't even know why I'm here."

"Do you want a cup of tea?" she said.

"No," I said.

"I'm making one for myself. The water's already on. It won't be a moment. Have a seat," she said. She went into the kitchen, and I poked around her living room. She had pictures of her family, pictures of a cat and then a different cat. She had one picture of Mike, but it was a group photo with her and the other people who worked in Mike's practice. Mike wasn't even standing next to her. I was still looking at the photo when she returned with the tea. I set the frame back on the mantel, though I know she saw me looking at it.

"Do you take sugar?" she asked. "Milk?"

"No," I said. "Plain."

"I like a touch of sweetness," she said.

"I like my sugar in dessert," I said, "but I try to avoid it everywhere else."

"You're so trim," she said.

"I work for it," I said. "Inside me, there is an angry fat woman."

"How do you fit her in there?" the mistress asked me.

"You're funny," I said. "I hadn't expected you to be funny."

"Why?" she said.

"Because I'm funny," I said. "If he wanted funny, he could have stayed home."

"I don't think I was always funny," she said. "I was too in awe of him to be funny."

"In awe of Mike? That is funny," I said.

"When it started, I was only twenty-five, and he seemed so powerful and accomplished. I was amazed that he could take an interest in me."

"How old are you now?" I said.

"Forty in March," she said. "Take out the bag. The tea gets bitter if it oversteeps."

I did as I was told. "Fifteen years," I said.

"A tea bag left to steep for fifteen years will definitely make bitter tea," she said.

"I meant, that's how long you've been with Mike."

"I knew what you meant. I feel terrible half the time and the other half of the time, I wonder where my life has gone," she said.

"I know," I said. "But you're still young."

"I am," she said. "Relatively. Or at least I'm in the middle." She took a long look at me. "You are, too."

"Don't be condescending," I said.

"I'm not meaning to be. My point is, it may not seem like it but Aviva is lucky this came out now and not fifteen years from now. She still has choices."

I sneezed.

"Bless you," she said. "Are you getting a cold?"

"I'm never sick," I said. "Never."

I sneezed again.

"But I'm so tired," I said.

She said she had some chicken matzo ball soup in the fridge. "I made it myself," she said. "Lie down on my couch."

I wasn't sure if I wanted my husband's mistress to give me chicken soup, but I felt so run-down all at once. Her apartment was small but comfortable and clean. I wondered how long she had lived there. I imagined her getting ready to go on dates with my husband. Putting on lipstick for him. Tarting herself up. I imagined her young, waiting for Aviva to grow up so that Mike would divorce me. I felt sad for all of us.

She brought the soup in a pretty blue imitation delft bowl.

I ate the soup, and I immediately began to feel better. My sinuses cleared and my throat felt less raw.

"See," she said, "it's not just an old wives' tale about chicken soup."

"I hate that phrase," I said. "Old wives' tale."

"I'm sorry," she said.

"No, it's not you. But it's so hateful and sexist and ageist when you think about it. 'Old wives' tale' means something that's untrue or not scientifically proven? 'Old wives' tale' is basically a way of saying ignore everything that dumb old woman says."

"I hadn't thought of it that way," she said.

"I hadn't thought of it that way either. Not until I became an old wife myself."

THREE MONTHS LATER, terrorists crashed two planes into the World Trade Center, and just like that, Avivagate was over. People stopped talking about the scandal. The news cycle moved on.

That winter, Aviva finished college. She received her diploma in a windowless office at the university.

That spring, she applied for jobs. She wanted to continue working in government or politics, but in South Florida, everyone had heard of her and not in a way that was helpful. Anyone who hadn't heard of her googled her, and that was that. She switched her focus to finding work in PR or marketing, thinking that these employers would be less—I suppose the word is *moralistic*—than public sector employers. They were not. I will admit, I have more sympathy for her situation now than I did then. At the time, what I wanted was for her to move out, move on, get her life together.

By the end of the summer, she'd given up. I'd always find her floating in our pool, letting her skin bake to a deep brown.

"Aviva," I said. "Are you even wearing SPF?"

"No, Mom. It's fine."

"Aviva, you'll damage your skin."

"I don't care," she said.

"You should care!" I said. "You only get one skin."

"I don't care," she said.

She was working her way through the Harry Potter books. I think there were four out at the time, but I don't remember. I know that adults read Harry Potter, but I took it as a bad sign. They looked so childish to me, with the drawing of the cartoon boy wizard on the front.

"Aviva," I said, "you like to read so much. Maybe you should apply to grad school?"

"Oh yeah?" she said. "Who's going to write me recommendation letters? What school isn't going to web search me?"

"Well, you could apply to law school. Plenty of people from dubious backgrounds go to law school. I saw a show where a convicted murderer did law school by correspondence so that he could try to get himself acquitted."

"I'm not a murderer," she said. "I'm a slut, and you can't be acquitted of that."

"You can't stay in this pool forever."

"I'm not going to stay in this pool forever. I'm going to float on top of it, and I'm going to finish reading *Harry Potter and the Chamber of Secrets* for the fourth time, and then I'm going to take a shower, and then I'm going to read *Harry Potter and the Prisoner of Azkaban* for the fourth time."

"Aviva," I said.

"How's *your* job search coming, Mom?" Aviva said.

It is awful what I did.

It is awful.

I had never raised a hand to that girl. I walked into the pool, my belted summer-weight cashmere cardigan getting wet and billowing around me. I pulled the floating mat out from under her. Harry Potter fell in the pool and so did Aviva.

"Mom!" she screamed.

"GET OUT OF THE GODDAMN POOL!" I yelled.

Harry Potter sank to the bottom of the pool. She scrambled to get back on the floating mat, and I pulled it out from under her again.

"Mom! Stop being such a bitch!"

I slapped her across the face.

Aviva's expression was hard, but then her nose turned red and she wept.

"I'm sorry," I said, and I was sorry. I tried to put my arms around her. She was resistant at first, but then she let me.

"Sometimes I feel crazy, Mommy," she said. "He did love me, didn't he?"

"Yes," I said, "I think he probably did."

In retrospect, I would say she was depressed.

I WENT TO my mother and I asked for advice.

"You've been too much of a friend to her and not enough of a mother," Mom said.

"Okay," I said. "How do I stop doing that?"

"You have to tell her to move out," she said.

"I can't do that," I said. "She is shunned. She has no money, no job. What will she live on?"

"She is able-bodied and smart. She will figure something out, I assure you."

I couldn't do that to Aviva.

"And stop worrying about Aviva," Mom said. "Try worrying about your own life. There are things to figure out there, I assure you, my daughter."

But a few months later, Aviva did move away.

She did not consult me; she did not leave a forwarding address. I have a cell phone number. She calls me once or twice a year. I believe I have a grandchild. Yes, I would call this a sadness in my life.

How can I blame her for leaving? There was nothing for her in South Florida. These people feel as Louis the bad date felt. They know a few punch lines. They don't think they are talking about a human being. They don't think they are talking about someone's daughter.

Mike and I divorced a few months after Aviva left. I would not say we had stayed together for Aviva, but in the absence of Aviva, I felt no particular connection to him. We were Aviva's parents. I will tell you, it was no tragedy to return to my maiden name.

I run into Mike every now and again. He is remarried. Not, I might add, to the mistress. That poor woman waited and waited, only to have him marry someone else. I almost feel more outraged for her than I do for myself. The new wife—what can I say about her? She is younger than me but older than my daughter, thank God.

Should I tell you about Levin? He's still in Congress. I think he's managed to keep his schlong out of other people's daughters. What a mensch.

ELEVEN

A month before Mom's eighty-fifth birthday, the nursing home calls me. Mom is being transferred to the hospital. She has pneumonia, and she may not live through the night.

I dial Aviva's cell phone number. She never picks up, but I dial it anyway. The robot voice recites her number.

"It's Mom," I say. "If you want to see Grandma before she dies, you may want to get on a plane to South Florida. Give me a call."

I sit in the lobby and wait for her to call me back. I fall asleep and when I wake up, Mimmy is sitting next to me.

"Good news!" she says. "We can have the birthday party at the Boca Raton Museum of Art. The people who were using the garden for the wedding canceled!"

I say, "Mimmy, are you kidding me? Mom is on life support. Mom will probably die."

"She'll pull through," Mimmy says. "She always does."

"No, Mimmy," I say. "She may not pull through. She is eighty-four years old. One of these days, she is definitely not going to pull through."

"You're a hard one, Rachel Shapiro," Mimmy says.

"If you mean I'm a realist, then yes, I guess I am a 'hard one,'" I say.

"Anticipating the worst doesn't provide insurance from the worst happening," Mimmy says.

The crazy thing is, Mimmy turns out to be right. Mom does pull through, and we have the party at the Boca Raton Museum of Art. Mom seems delighted as a five-year-old that we are having an eighty-fifth birthday party for her.

"Museum," she says.

"Art," she says.

"Wonderful," she says.

"Rachel," she says.

"Aviva," she says.

I think that is what she says.

I've put Mom in the van back to the rehab and I'm on the way to my car when someone calls my name. It's Louis the bad date. He's visiting the museum with his grown son and daughter-in-law.

"Rachel Shapiro," he says. "I have been so hoping I'd run into you. I want you to know: I would never have said it, if I'd thought *that* Aviva was *your* Aviva."

"You finally figured it out," I say.

"I didn't," he says. "I'm a dunce. I was at the synagogue for the Torah unrolling ceremony, and Roz Horowitz was there, and it came up that she was your good friend, so I asked if she knew what had happened, and she told me."

"Roz and I aren't good friends anymore," I say.

"Meh, I doubt that," he says. "Friendships ebb and flow."

"Roz was at the synagogue?"

"She's not doing so great," he says. "Her husband died."

"The glass guy died!" I say.

"A heart attack," he says.

"Poor Roz," I say. "I'll have to give her a call."

He says, "When I like someone, I get nervous and I talk too much. I was showing off for you, trying to be funny and smart, and I'm sorry, it backfired. I know I come off as gregarious, but I'm a bit shy actually."

I don't care.

"Obviously," he says, "I don't know your daughter. I know what the story on TV was, but I don't know her. And it's bad luck, plain and simple, that we hit upon that subject."

"It's not bad luck," I say. "You asked me about my children."

He can't argue with that.

And then I say, "What if Aviva weren't my daughter? Should you talk about anyone's daughter that way? Levin was an adult man and an elected public official, and my daughter was a dumb kid in love, and he ended up fine, and she's a punch line. So, fifteen years later, why should she have to be some *alte cocker*'s dating banter?"

"I am sorry," he says. "I know I stuck my foot in it. I wish I could go back in time and rewind the tape of our date."

"There aren't tapes anymore, Louis. Just zeros and ones, and they never disappear."

"You're smart and you've got moxie," Louis says. "I like a woman with moxie. At our age, can we afford not to try again? Don't we owe it to ourselves to give this another shot?"

"I have been alone a long time," I say. "I am fine with continuing to be alone."

"Even so," he says. "I think we can be better than fine."

"I'm fine with fine."

"You're a tough one," he says.

I tell him my aunt said the same thing.

"I like tough," he says. "Please," he says. "Let's try this again."

Just because I am sixty-four and a woman, people think I should be happy to be with anyone. But I would rather be alone than be with a bastard like the glass guy, may he rest in peace, or a blowhard who insulted my daughter.

A FUNNY THING happens. Mom loses an earring at the museum. Mom didn't even know she lost it, but a few weeks after the party, a docent at the museum calls and says, I think I have your mother's earring. She describes the earring—emeralds, opals, jade, and diamonds, cut to look like grapes and leaves. I ask her how did she ever figure out it was Mom's? The docent says, "Did you know your mom used to speak at the high school for Survivor Day? She used to talk about her father the jeweler, and I remembered that his name was Bernheim, and the earring backing says Bernheim."

"What a strange thing for you to remember!" I say.

"I used to love when your mom would come in to speak. It really left an impression," she says.

I drive to the museum after Pilates class, and I can't find the docent anywhere, so I wander around the museum for a spell. I come across a class of older elementary schoolers, maybe fifth graders, and an older man—by which I mean *my age*—is teaching them how to make block prints. He's teaching them to carve simple designs into wood, and to dip the wood in ink-filled trays, and to go over the papers with rollers. It's very messy and I do not generally care for messy things. The man doesn't wear gloves, which seems like lunacy, and his hands are covered in ink. He has green eyes, a rust-colored beard, and no hair on his head. He is exquisitely patient. The man looks up at me and says, "Can I help you?"

"No," I say, "I'm meeting someone, but I couldn't find her. I like watching you work."

He shrugs. "Stay if you like."

So I sit in the back and honestly it's very peaceful, watching the man make the ink prints with the children. The ink has a pleasant medicinal smell. I enjoy the rhythmic swish of the blocks in the trays. But the thing I like most is the low hum of the children concentrating on a task. It was one my favorite things when I used to be an educator.

When the kids leave, the man says, "Do you want to try?"

I say, "I'm wearing white. I shouldn't."

He says, "Some other time."

He washes his hands in the sink, but they still don't come clean. And that's when I remember who he is. He is Andrew with the dirty fingernails. He's an artist! Had he said he was an artist? I couldn't even tell you, I was so distracted by those nails. But now I know the dirt is ink, the whole thing feels different.

"Andrew," I say.

"Rachel," he says.

"I didn't recognize you."

"I recognized you immediately."

"You thought of my picture and added ten years," I joke.

"That wasn't kind of me," he says.

"Ah, it's fine. I'm thick-skinned," I say. "By the way, it's not that I'm vain. It's, well, it's embarrassing to admit, but I honestly forgot how old the picture was. You know, 2004 doesn't seem that long ago in certain ways."

"Really, I was awful. I'd gone on quite a few dates that went nowhere and I'm afraid I took it out on you," he says. "I know what you mean, though. Once your children are grown, you lose track of time a bit. Do you have any children? I don't think you said."

"One," I say. "A daughter. Aviva."

"Aviva," he says. "That's a beautiful name," he says. "Tell me something about Aviva."

II

Wherever You Go, There You Are

JANE

ONE

In the middle of a particularly brutal political season, I began to have dreams about Aviva Grossman, Florida's answer to Monica Lewinsky. Unless you lived in Florida at the turn of the century, you probably won't remember her. The story briefly made national headlines because Aviva Grossman had foolishly kept an anonymous blog, where she detailed some of the "highlights" of the affair. She never mentioned him by name—but everyone knew! It was speculated that Aviva wouldn't have kept a blog if she hadn't *wanted* everyone to know, but I don't think so. I think she was young and dumb, and I also think people didn't truly understand the Internet back then, if indeed they can be said to understand it now. So, okay, Aviva Grossman. As a twenty-year-old intern, Aviva had an affair with Aaron Levin, a congressman from Miami. He was not her "immediate supervisor," to quote the squishy statement he made during the press conference. "At no time was I the woman's immediate supervisor," Congressman Levin said, "and so, while I am deeply sorry for the pain I caused my loved ones, particularly my wife and sons, I assure you that no laws were broken." The woman! He could not even bring himself to say Aviva Grossman's name. The details of the affair, which were as tawdry and clichéd and human as you would expect, were on every local news channel and newspaper for months. One station even had a recurring segment called Avivawatch, as if she were a hurricane or an orca that had mysteriously beached itself. Fifteen years later, Levin's still in Congress; Aviva Grossman, whose résumé included a dual degree in political science and Spanish literature from the University of Miami, a tenaciously googleable blog, and of course that infamous stint as an intern, couldn't get a job. They didn't put a scarlet letter on her chest, but they didn't need to. That's what the Internet is for.

In my dream, though, Aviva Grossman had managed to get past all of that. In my dream, she was in her forties and she had smart, short hair, and she was wearing a neutral pantsuit and a turquoise statement necklace, and she was running for national political office, though my dream wasn't clear which one. It felt like Congress to me, but maybe that's too poetically just. But it's *my dream*, so let's call it Congress. In any case, she was at a press conference when a journalist asked her about the affair. At first, Aviva gave a politician's response—"It was a long time ago and I'm sorry for any pain I caused"—and she sounded not unlike Congressman Levin. The journalist persisted. "Well," Aviva said, "being the age I am now and being in the position I am now, I can tell you with absolute certainty, I would *never* sleep with one of my campaign interns. But looking back and thinking about my part in it, my conduct, the only thing I can say . . . the only thing I can say about it is, I was very romantic and I was very young."

TWO

My name is Jane Young. I am thirty-three years old, and I am an event planner, though my business mainly consists of weddings. I was raised in South Florida, but I now reside in Allison Springs, Maine, which is about twenty-five minutes from Portland and which is a popular summer spot for destination weddings. It is less popular in the fall and still less popular in the winter, but I manage. What else can I tell you? I like my work, but no, I did not see myself doing this when I was a kid. The thing I went to college to do, I didn't end up doing for a variety of reasons, and I found I had a knack for the combination of discipline, communication, psychology, politics, stagecraft, and creativity that planning a wedding requires. Oh, I have a precocious eight-year-old daughter, Ruby, whose father is not in the picture. Ruby is truly clever, though she has probably been around brides more than is healthy. Last week, Ruby told me, "I never want to be a bride. They're all miserable."

"Come on," I said. "Some of them seem happy."

"No," she said with certainty. "Some of them seem *less* unhappy."

"Unhappy brides are each unhappy in their own way," I said.

"Sure, I guess," Ruby said. Her brow furrowed. "What's that supposed to mean?"

I explained that I was riffing on that old Tolstoy saw, and Ruby rolled her eyes. "Be serious," she said.

"So you'll never marry?" I said. "That's not much of an advertisement for my business."

"I didn't say that," Ruby said. "I don't know if I'll ever marry. *I'm eight.* But I do know I don't ever want to be a bride." Ruby is at a perfect age. She is old enough to talk to and not yet a teen or a tween. She is nerdy and slightly round, but it is delicious. I want to eat her. I want to bite her solid arms. By the way, I never mention her weight because I don't want her to end up with a complex. I was overweight when I was her age, and my mother discussed it exhaustively. And yes, as a result, I would say I am the proud owner of several complexes. But who isn't? When you think about it, isn't a person just a structure built in reaction to the landscape and the weather?

THREE

My storefront is located between a stationers and a chocolatier, in the main part of town. It was November, and things were slow. After catching up with some of my spring and summer couples, I spent the morning shopping online for things I didn't need. How many black shift dresses could one woman have? A lot, if you're me. Seventeen, at last count. A wedding planner dresses for a wedding as if it is a funeral. I was thinking of what Ruby had said about every bride being miserable when Franny and Wes walked through my door. They didn't have an appointment, but this time of year, they didn't need one.

Franny was Frances Lincoln. She was twenty-six years old, unformed. She was pretty enough but somehow like dough that had not been allowed to rise. She was a kindergarten teacher—of course she was! no one had ever looked more like a kindergarten teacher than she—but she said she was on leave. Wes was Wesley West—based on his name, I suspected his parents would be awful and I looked forward to meeting these monsters. Wes was a Realtor, and he informed me that his office was around the corner from mine though I had never noticed him before. He also told me that he had political aspirations. "I just thought you should know," he said in a conspiratorial tone that suggested I should not plan the wedding for the future whatever of Allison Springs and be caught unaware. He was twenty-seven, and his handshake was too firm—what are you trying to prove, bro? As far as my clientele went, these two were not exceptional in any way. Weddings had a sneaky way of turning people into old-fashioned stereotypes of husband and wife.

"We were thinking about hiring someone from the city," Wes said. "The city" referred to Portland, and this was meant as a dig.

"I'm from a city," I said with a smile.

"But I thought, why not try someone local? I mean, I pass your office every day. Nice place. I like how clean everything looks, how white everything is. Also, I'm hoping to run for city council, so I like getting to know the local businesses. My constituency, you know. Must be pretty slow for you this time of year."

I asked them if they had set a date.

He looked at her, and she looked at him. "We'd like to get married a year from now, next December," she said. "Is that enough time?"

I nodded. "Plenty."

"She thinks winter weddings are romantic," he said. "But what I like about it is the value. We'll have our pick of venues, and for half the price of summer, am I right?"

"Not half, but definitely less," I said.

"Winter weddings *are* romantic, don't you think?" she said.

"I do," I said. The bride and the bridesmaids would freeze and, if it snowed, half the out-of-town guests might not show up. I suppose there was a romance to that. Winter pictures always turned out great, though, and I'm not sure that people don't remember the pictures more than the actual event anyway. In any case, these were grown-ups, and I was not going to talk my way out of winter business.

FOUR

Some weeks later—perhaps after they'd visited one or more of those big city wedding planners—they arranged to come in for the second time so that they could give me their signed contract and a deposit for my services. Only Franny showed, which was not unusual, although she was embarrassed by his absence. "Is it weird?" she asked. "Does it seem like a bad sign? I mean, he should be here, right?"

"It isn't at all weird," I said as she handed me the check. "I often end up working more with one member of the couple than the other. People can't be everywhere at once."

She nodded. "He's showing a house," she said. "And he can't always control when that happens."

"Perfectly understandable," I said. "How did he propose? I don't think I asked." I put her contract into my filing cabinet.

"Oh, it was romantic," she said. *Romantic* was a big word with her. "Well, I think it was romantic. As I'm about to say it, it might seem weird to you." *Weird* was another of her words.

He had proposed at her mother's funeral. Not *at* it, but just after it. I had a sense that it had happened in the parking lot of the cemetery, but I wasn't clear. She was crying and grieving, mucus everywhere, and he had gotten down on one knee, and he had said something like, "Now this can't ever be the saddest day of your life." *Gross.* Again, I suppose he had meant well, but this was truly the worst thing I'd heard about him yet. For God's sake, some days are *meant* to be the saddest days of your life. Also, should she have been making major life decisions when her mother had just died? I didn't know these people, but it was almost as if he had preyed on her when she was at her most vulnerable. I was starting to hate Wes West. A little bit, I was starting to hate him. I often ended up hating the groom, but not usually so fast.

"Oh, it *is* weird," she said. "It is weird, isn't it?"

It *wasn't* weird, but it was awful. It was awful, but it was ordinary. I didn't know her, and it was not my business. To make the moment about something other than what I had been thinking and what my face may have betrayed, I did something that was unlike me. I reached across my desk and I grabbed her hand. "I'm so sorry about your mother," I said.

Her lip quivered, and her large blue eyes teared. "Oh gosh," she said. "Oh gosh."

I handed her a tissue.

"I'm a big baby," she said.

"No, you're grieving," I said. "You must feel so unmoored."

"Yes, that is exactly what I feel. Unmoored. Is your mother alive?" she asked.

"She is, but we don't see each other much," I said.

"How awful," she said.

"I have a daughter," I said. "So I can imagine something of—"

"And your mother doesn't want to see her? Her own granddaughter? I can't believe that!"

"Maybe she does. It's complicated," I said.

"Nothing's that complicated." Franny smiled at me. "I've overstepped," she said. "I'm sorry. You have a very comforting way about you, so I forgot we aren't friends."

She was sweet. "Did you do your homework?" I had asked them to assemble an inspiration board for their fantasy wedding.

She took out her tablet from her purse. They had pinned a bride in cowboy boots *and* a groom wearing an ascot and tails; a buffet of pies *and* a seven-tier wedding cake; a silver bucket of gerbera daisies *and* a three-foot-tall arrangement with white lilies and roses; gingham tablecloths *and* white linen tablecloths; barbeque chicken *and* filet mignon. It was the wedding of City Mouse and Country Mouse.

"We didn't get very far. Some of these are his ideas and some of these are mine."

"I can tell," I said.

"He wants it to be elegant, but I want it to be more rustic," she said. "Can you do anything with this, or are we hopeless?"

"You're hopeless," I said.

Franny laughed and flushed. "We kind of had a fight about it. Only a little fight. He says my taste is basic," she said, "but I want our guests to feel relaxed and comfortable. I don't want it to feel all—" She searched for a word before settling on "corporate."

"Elegant and rustic. Let me think. Chandeliers and white tablecloths in a barn. Or, considering it's going to be December, mason jars with red-and-white gingham ribbons and baby's breath and pine boughs and burlap tablecloths in a crisp hotel ballroom setting. Twinkly white Christmas lights strung across the dance floor and place cards written on tiny chalkboards. Tulle canopies and white linen napkins. BBQ and pies. A crackling fire. Yes, I see it." And I literally had seen it. Everyone wanted elegant and rustic lately.

"It sounds so beautiful," she said.

The bells on my door jingled, and Ruby came in, dumping her backpack on the floor. "This is my assistant," I told Franny.

Ruby shook Franny's hand.

"I'm Franny," Franny said. "You look pretty young to be an assistant."

"Kind of you to say, but I'm fifty-three years old," Ruby said.

"She's very well preserved. Franny wants a wedding that's elegant and rustic," I told Ruby.

"You should have an ice cream truck," Ruby said. "Mom did a shabby chic one with an ice cream truck. Everyone loves an ice cream truck."

"You're not supposed to call me Mom at the office," I said. "You're supposed to call me Boss."

"Everyone went out to the parking lot," Ruby continued, "and they could pick any ice cream they wanted for free. It was pretty much the best thing."

"It *was* great, but Franny's wedding is in December," I told Ruby.

"True," Franny said. "But it sounds so fun. Couldn't we do it in December? It's not like everyone stops eating ice cream just because it's December. And it's almost more fun to have an ice cream truck in December. Like, shouldn't we *embrace* the cold?"

That night, I got a call from Wes letting me know that he didn't "get" the ice cream truck thing. "I think it looks like foolishness," he said. "These people I'm inviting, some of them may have to vote for me someday and some of them might even have to donate to my campaign, and I don't want them thinking that I'm the guy who had an ice cream truck at a winter wedding."

"Fine," I said. "No ice cream truck."

"I don't mean to be a buzzkill, but it seems . . . feckless."

"Feckless," I said. "That seems strong."

"Feckless," he said. "Not considered and the product of a disorderly brain. I love Franny, but she can get ideas."

Yes, I thought, she has a brain and those do peskily tend to make ideas. "You obviously have strong feelings about this," I said. "Honestly, it was only at the brainstorming stage, Wes. We hadn't rented the truck or anything."

"Well, the thing is," Wes said, "would you mind telling Franny that you aren't able to get an ice cream truck in winter? Because she has her heart set on it now. She thinks it's whimsical, I don't know."

"Wouldn't it be easier for you to tell her you don't like it yourself? I mean, she liked it, yes, but I don't think it was that big a deal to her. She likes a lot of things. She's a very positive person."

"Yeah," he said. "Yeah, I think you should do it. If I do it, I'm the guy who is taking the fun out of the wedding. If you do it, it's just a fact: the wedding planner can't get an ice cream truck in December."

"But I probably *can* get an ice cream truck," I said.

"Well, sure, but Franny doesn't know that," Wes said.

"Actually, I'm not comfortable lying to your fiancée," I said. "I try never to lie to my couples. And it seems silly to me for either of us to lie over something as inconsequential as an ice cream truck."

"Since it's silly, why does it matter? And it's not really lying. You're executing the wishes of the person who is paying for your services," Wes said. "I believe in you, Jane."

I thought about telling this weenie that he could take his business elsewhere, but I did not. I didn't mention it before but my bookish and lovely Ruby had been having trouble with bullies at her elementary school. I had done all of the things you are supposed to do when your child is being bullied. I had met with school administrators. I had called other parents. I had monitored her online activity. I had enrolled Ruby in a variety of purportedly self-esteem-boosting activities—gymnastics! Girl Scouts! I had talked to Ruby extensively about strategies for dealing with unpleasant people. Nothing had worked. I was thinking of transferring her to private school, but that cost money. Money meant you didn't have the luxury of liking every-one you worked with.

"Jane," he said, "do we have an agreement?"

"Fine," I said, thinking that I would never vote for this man and, if he ever ran for anything, I would actively campaign against him. This marriage was doomed.

I did not lie to Franny. I told her that I had thought about it, and the logistics of the ice cream truck would be too difficult in winter. And really, they would have been. The checking and rechecking of coats alone. It would have been a nightmare.

FIVE

hat's fine," Franny said. "It was just a whim. I had another thought I wanted to run by you. I know we had mostly settled on mason jars and cabbage roses, and I could not love that more. But I was wondering if you knew anything about orchids."

"Orchids?" I said.

"Well," she said. "I see you have one over there on your windowsill. And the thing I like about it is, it never dies. It has looked exactly the same every time I've come in here. And, I don't know, there's something comforting and homey to that."

I had never heard someone refer to an orchid as homey. "They die sometimes," I said. "But as long as you keep watering them, eventually they come back."

"Oh, I love that," she said. "I don't know if it fits with the elegant rustic theme—"

"Everything fits with that," I said.

"But I was wondering if we could use potted orchids as centerpieces and then people could take them home with them. It would be so elegant, but also . . . what's the word?"

"Rustic?" I filled in.

"I was thinking 'green.' That's something that's important to both Wes and me. Well, at least it's important to me. I don't know, maybe it seems more special than roses."

I took Franny to Schiele's. Eliot Schiele was the florist I went to when the wedding couple wanted something unusual. He was the most serious florist I had ever met. I don't mean to tar him with the word *artisanal* because that has a particular connotation, but it would not be wrong to refer to Schiele's flowers as artisanal. He was a perfectionist, a tad obsessive, and also pricey.

Schiele said, "Winter wedding? The only difficult thing will be getting them from the truck to the space. Orchids do not love the cold."

"But people will be able to take them home?" Franny said.

"Yes, as long as you tell your guests not to dawdle in the parking lot. Also, I could print up booklets with care and handling instructions. You know, how often and how much to water, when to start fertilizing, where to cut the spike, how to repot, how to select potting medium, how much sunlight. Franny, did you know that orchids like it when you touch their leaves?"

"Neat," she said.

"I never touch my orchid's leaves," I said.

"Then I bet your orchid is feeling pretty blue, Jane," Schiele said.

"What kinds of orchids are there?" Franny asked. "Jane has a white one that I love."

"Jane has your typical, beginner, grocery store phalaenopsis. No offense, Jane. And we could definitely do that, no problem. But there are thousands of orchids. You shouldn't settle down with the first orchid that catches your eye."

"Hey, Schiele," I said. "That's my orchid you're talking about. I've had it since college."

"It's a great orchid, Jane. It's a solid starter orchid. But this is a wedding. This is the beginning of young lives! We can do better." He got out his big binder of orchids.

She chose the brassavola, which looked like clusters of delicate calla lilies.

"Ah," said Schiele, "the Lady of the Night."

"It's actually called that?" I asked. "Or is that your weird pet name for it?"

"It releases a perfume in the evening," he said. "Don't worry, Franny. It smells great."

Schiele said he would run estimates for how much it would cost.

A few days later, he sent his estimate to my office, along with another orchid, a purple one with leaves that looked like bamboo shoots, and a note: "My name is Miniature Dendrobium. I want to be friends with your grocery story phalaenopsis, even though he is incredibly pedestrian. He is very lonely and longs for companionship."

I called him on the phone. "My phalaenopsis is a girl."

"I don't think so," he said. "And actually, I think you're being quite sexist. Not every flower is a girl."

"I didn't say that. I only said mine was a girl. Do flowers have sexes?"

"Didn't you take biology in high school?" Schiele said.

"I didn't pay attention."

"Pity. Some plants have all flowers of one sex. Some have flowers of both sexes. You have to consider each flower and each plant individually. And in point of absolute fact, most orchid blooms, including yours, are hermaphrodites, and many flowers are bisexual."

"But I stand by my original point," I said. "My phalaenopsis, whatever her sexual presentation or preference, is a girl. For you to insist otherwise is to confuse gender and sex."

"Maybe we could have coffee sometime to settle this matter? I'll examine your orchid for you."

"I'm not sure I'm comfortable with that."

"The orchid won't feel a thing."

"No, I meant the coffee. I don't drink coffee," I said.

"Tea then," he said.

"Schiele," I said. "Just to be clear, this isn't a date."

"No," he said. "Of course not. But it's good for us wedding business folks to stick together, don't you think? Anyway, I'd like us to be friends. I know you use Maine Event Blooms more often than me, and I'd like to be your number-one flower guy."

"It's not personal. Maine Event Blooms is cheaper," I said.

"And they do have that pun," he said. "Who can compete with that?"

"So I hope this won't be presumptuous," Schiele said at the restaurant, "but having worked with a fair number of wedding planners, you don't exactly strike me as the wedding planner type."

I asked him what he meant.

"The kind of woman who has been planning her wedding since she was a little girl, and then when she actually had her wedding couldn't get enough of weddings, so she decided to go into the business," he said.

"I feel like you're being quite sexist, or quite something," I said.

"Sorry," he said. "I mean, you seem very solid," he said. "As a person, not like your body, though that seems admirably solid as well. I'm sticking my foot in it."

"You are," I said.

"To be clear, I think you're gorgeous. You remind me of a *Cleopatra*-era Elizabeth Taylor. And by 'solid,' I meant intellectual and thoughtful—not what I associate with people in your line of work."

"And you'd been doing so well," I said.

"Crap. What I'm trying to say is what led you to wedding planning? What did you study in school? Did you go to school? What did you want to do when you were young? Who are you, basically? Who is Jane Young?"

"You could google it," I said.

"What fun would that be?" he said. "Also, I tried. You've got a very common name. There are about a thousand Jane Youngs."

"You ask a lot of questions," I said.

"I used to be a teacher and I believe in the Socratic method."

"I feel like I'm on a job interview," I said. "Why did you stop teaching?"

"I don't know. I wanted to have more time to spend with my plants."

"Of course," I said.

"Plants respond more readily to care and attention than people do. As a teacher, I felt like I was boring the kids. Why do questions make you anxious?" he said.

"They don't," I said.

"They seem like they do," he said.

"I'm an open book," I said. "Go ahead. Ask me anything."

"What did you study in college?" he said.

"Political science and Spanish literature," I said.

He looked at me and he gave a small nod. "Now that makes sense."

"I'm glad you approve. To be clear, even if it's not what I thought I'd do, I like planning weddings," I said. "I like the ceremony. And people invite you into their lives on what they believe to be the most important day. It's a privilege." This was my spiel.

"You know everyone's secrets," he said.

"I know a few," I said.

"You might be the most powerful person in town."

"That's Mrs. Morgan," I said.

"What did you think you'd do?" Schiele asked.

"I thought I'd go into public service, government, politics," I said. "I briefly did."

"You didn't have the stomach for it?"

"I loved it," I said. "But then I had Ruby, and I needed to reinvent myself. What did you study?"

"Botany," he said. "You probably guessed that. Why Spanish literature?"

"Because where I grew up, it was useful to be fluent in Spanish if you wanted to work in politics," I said. "I had high school Spanish already, so I thought I could get more out of studying literature. But honestly, I made the decision pretty impulsively, in about two minutes. It was my junior year. The clock was ticking, and I had to choose something."

"Tell me something from Spanish literature," Schiele said.

"I'll give you a line from my favorite novel. '*Los seres humanos no nacen para siempre el día en que sus madres los alumbran, sino que la vida los obliga a parirse a sí mismos una y otra vez.*'"

"I like that," he said. "What does it mean?"

The door chimed, and Mrs. Morgan walked into the restaurant like she owned the place, which, in point of fact, she did. Mrs. Morgan had just turned seventy. She was outspoken in the way of the very rich. In addition to the restaurant, she owned half the town and the newspaper. Mrs. Morgan and I were in the middle of planning a benefit to restore the statue of Captain Allison in Market Square.

"Jane," she said, stopping at our table, "I was planning to call you, but as long as I have you here, any word on the yacht club? And Mr. Schiele, how is your lovely wife, Mia?"

Mrs. Morgan sat down at the table. She signaled the waiter and ordered a glass of red.

"Very well," Schiele said.

"Do you know Schiele's wife?" Mrs. Morgan asked me.

"I don't," I said.

"She's a ballet dancer," Mrs. Morgan said.

"She's retired now," Schiele said.

"Well, still. What a thing to have a talent like that," Mrs. Morgan said. "Excuse me, Mr. Schiele. How rude of me. Were you two about done? I have a few things to discuss with Jane about our little benefit."

Schiele stood. "It's fine," he said. "Jane, I'll give you a call."

THAT NIGHT, SCHIELE did indeed call me. "We got cut off there," he said.

"Sorry about that," I said. "Mrs. Morgan doesn't understand that the universe won't always bend to her will. Was there something else you needed?"

"The thing is, I like you," he said.

"And I, you," I said. "You're the most exacting florist I know."

"Come on, Jane. What I'm saying is I can't stop thinking about you," he said. "You must have noticed."

"Well, you're going to have to stop thinking of me," I said. "I don't date much, and I definitely don't date married men."

"I feel like you think I'm a scumbag," he said. "You should know that the marriage has been over for some time. It's been bad for some time."

"It's good that you know that. It takes real courage to recognize when you're unhappy," I said. "I'm glad you called, though. Franny wants to know if we can get a discount on the pots if we order them separately from the orchids."

"I'll price it out," he said. "Can I give you a call back in a couple of days?"

"Why don't you e-mail me?" I said. "Good-bye, Schiele."

I really had liked him. Something I have learned, though, is that even a bad marriage isn't to be trifled with.

My grandmother was married for fifty-two years, until my grand-father died. She used to say that a bad marriage was one that hadn't had enough time to get good again. And not to put too fine a point on it, but since Schiele was a florist, I will tell you that there have been times when I thought my "pedestrian" orchid would never bloom again, when it looked dead as dead can be. I think of a time when Ruby and I went to San Francisco on vacation, and I left it on the radiator, and every last leaf fell off. I watered it for a year, and first a root, and then a leaf, and maybe two years later, voila! Flowers again. And that's what I know about marriages and orchids. They're both harder to kill than you think. And that's why I love my grocery store orchid and I don't do married men.

SIX

Franny and I were touring yet another hotel ballroom when she said, "They're starting to blend together. I think I like this one better than the last one, but I'm not sure."

"It's more a feeling. What does it make you feel?" I was saying words, but I was barely paying attention. I was thinking of Ruby. I had gotten a call from Ruby's school. She had locked herself in a girl's bathroom stall and was refusing to come out. As soon as we were done here and I had dropped Franny off at her house, I was going down to the school to see who I needed to kill.

Franny's gaze moved from the slightly dingy floral carpet to the mirrored walls. "I don't know," she said. "Nothing? Sad? What should it make me feel?"

"Well, you have to imagine it filled up," I said. "Imagine it with the orchids and the Christmas lights and the tulle. Imagine your friends and family and . . ." What was the instinct in kids that when they encountered another kid who was different or weaker, they pounced on it? Was it some vestigial survival instinct from a time when resources were scarce?

"What?" she said.

"No, that was all," I said.

Franny nodded. "I think I'd like to maybe see some other options, if that's all right."

"Honestly, we can keep looking, but unless you want to go in another direction entirely, like not a hotel ballroom at all, you've pretty much seen what this area has to offer in terms of ballrooms. They're empty rooms, Franny." I snuck a glance at the clock on my phone. I wanted to get to Ruby's school before lunch started.

"Which one would you choose?"

"The first one we saw. The Lodge at Allison Springs." I resisted saying, *That's why I showed it to you first.* "If it's still available."

"You're right," she said. "Maybe this is silly but I thought when I walked into the reception room, I would feel like, 'This is where the most romantic night of your life happens, Franny,' and I didn't feel that. The room gave me no feels. All that dark wood."

"You wanted rustic," I said.

"But it felt sort of, I don't know, masculine."

"It won't once there are orchids and—"

She interrupted me. "Tulle, I know. Maybe we could drive down there right now so I could have one more look at it? I think I could commit to it today if I could just see it one more time."

I took a deep breath. "I can't," I said. "Trust me. I want nothing more than to put this to bed, but I've got to get to Ruby's school. She locked herself in the bathroom and she won't come out. And if I don't get her out before lunch starts, all the kids at her school will know about it, and maybe a small thing becomes a big thing, you know how kids are." I laughed. "I'm sorry to burden you."

"It's no burden," she said. "We can look at ballrooms some other day."

"WHY DO YOU think she locked herself in the bathroom?" Franny asked when we were in the car.

"Probably to escape the bullshit kids at her bullshit school."

"That's awful," Franny said.

I hated Ruby's school, which seemed to be populated by a particularly high percentage of assholes. I *loathed* the vice principal, who referred to himself as the "bullying czar." *Czar*, can you imagine? He had the mean good looks of a porn actor. You knew the only reason he had been named the "bullying czar" was because he probably had done a lot of bullying himself. This man had the rhetoric of antibullying down (inclusiveness, safe environment, no tolerance), but on some level, I could tell that he actually thought everything was Ruby's fault. *It would be easier for everyone if Ruby could kindly stop being so darned bullyable.*

"I was bullied, too," Franny said. "But when I went to high school, it stopped."

"What happened?" I asked.

"Oh, well"—she laughed—"I got hot. I don't want to sound conceited."

"Lucky you," I said.

"I mean, I was glad it happened, don't get me wrong. I was glad not to have to throw up every morning before school. But I knew it was wrong and also, it was not to my credit. I knew those people were still the same terrible people and that I was still the same person they had hated," Franny said. "Were you bullied?"

I slammed on my brakes. I had almost run a stop sign. I waved at the jogger who'd been crossing and mouthed the word "sorry." The woman gave me the finger. "I was," I said.

"It's hard to believe. You seem so strong," Franny said. "You seem like a wall, not in a bad way."

"The good kind of wall. Everyone loves a wall."

"Untouchable," she said. "Unflappable."

I laughed. "Once upon a time, I was easily touched and easily flapped."

"What happened?" she said.

"I grew up," I said.

I KNOCKED ON the bathroom door. "Ruby, it's Mom."

The door unlatched. I asked her what had happened, and the situation was so stupid I couldn't believe it. In her gym class, a male classmate of Ruby's had "hilariously" taken to running his hand up and down the girls' legs to determine who had shaved and who had not. Ruby had not shaved her legs. Indeed, she had not shaved her legs ever. She said she was the only one, which I found hard to believe. They were eight years old and it was the middle of the winter in Maine. I had not personally shaved my legs for three weeks. Since when were eight-year-olds shaving their legs?

"Why didn't you tell me I was supposed to shave my legs?" she asked.

I sat down on the bathroom floor. "Once you start shaving, you can't stop," I said. "As long as you don't shave, your hair is silky and downy, but once you start, it gets all spiky and itchy. I thought it would be good to put it off as long as possible. And honestly, what is so bad about leg hair? It grows there. Who cares?"

She looked at me as if she were very old and I were very young. "Mom," she said in a serious voice, "if I am going to get through this year, you need to keep me informed about the right things to do. I don't want to call any attention to myself."

"You're breaking my heart," I said.

"I don't want to do that. But as a strategy . . ." She looked at me to see if I was following.

"Strategy," I repeated.

"This is how it has to be. I'm a good person, I think. I'm smart. But these girls—they pounce on any little thing about me. There's no negotiating with them."

"I understand," I said.

On the drive home, we stopped at the drugstore to shop for razors.

SEVEN

I called Franny on the phone to apologize if I had come off brusquely.

"Oh, no. It's not a problem. I don't know why I was being so irritating about the ballroom," she said.

"Franny, you're not irritating. And even if you were, you're a bride, which means you're allowed to be irritating."

"You'll be glad to know I drove down to the lodge this afternoon, and I walked around. The sun was going down, and you can see the lake through the windows, and by December, it will be frozen over so the view will be even more beautiful! And everything smelled like cedar, and I imagined the lace and the orchids and Wes in his plaid bow tie, if we can convince him to wear plaid, and I thought to myself, 'Franny, you dope, of course Jane is right.' I'm so grateful for you, Jane," Franny said.

"That's a nice thing to hear," I said. I felt like all I'd done was screw up that day.

"Actually, I'm glad you called, because I had a thought. Have you ever heard of Steineman's?"

"Of course," I said. It was a large bridal dress shop in Manhattan. It was overpriced and a bit hokey. A wedding amusement park for tourists. You could get the equivalent dresses at any local store with a decent bridal department.

"I know it's probably corny, but I have always wanted to go there," Franny said, "and I was wondering if you could come with me. You could take Ruby. You should, obviously. She's your assistant. I'll pay for everything. I have some money from my mom's estate."

This was not normally something I would agree to, but the fact was, Ruby and I were both in need of a change of scenery. "It's a nice offer," I said to Franny, "but wouldn't it make more sense to take your best friend?"

"I don't have one," she said, with an apologetic laugh. "Not one I'd want to take. I think I have trouble making close female friendships."

"Probably because you were bullied," I said.

"Probably so." She laughed again.

"Or your bridesmaids?" She had four. "You could take them."

"Three of them are Wes's sisters, and the last one is Wes's best friend, who is not my favorite person. I could take my aunt, but she'd cry the whole time. And I'd rather have a professional opinion."

BUT SHE BARELY needed one. When it came to wedding dresses, Franny was admirably decisive. She chose the first dress she put on, which left the three of us the rest of the day to sightsee. I had the sense that she had chosen the dress before she even got to the store.

We decided to walk from the dress emporium to the Metropolitan Museum of Art. It was a long walk, but the day was balmy, especially compared to the weather in Maine. Ruby linked arms with Franny and me, but we kept having to switch to single file so that people could move past us.

Ruby said, "Did you know that ninety percent of men or people—I don't remember which—don't move out of the way when you are walking toward them on the street?"

"Where'd you learn that?" Franny said.

"My friend, Mrs. Morgan," Ruby said. "Anyway, I always move out of the way for people, and I notice that you and Mom do it, too. But I was wondering, what would happen if I didn't? What if I kept walking right toward them, would they eventually move?"

"I'm going to try it," Franny said. "I'm not gonna move!" She stood very tall, and in less than a minute, a man in a business suit was walking toward her. He was about a foot away from her face when Franny darted out of the way.

"You swerved!" Ruby said. She was doubled over laughing.

"I did," she said. "Darn it! I really thought I could do it."

Franny frowned, and Ruby said, "Don't be sad, Franny. Maybe we need some percentage of the people to move out of the way, otherwise the world would be in— What's the word, Mom?"

"Anarchy," I said.

"Anarchy," Ruby repeated. "Maybe the people who move out of the way aren't weak? Maybe they just don't care?"

When we arrived at the Met, we went straight to the Temple of Dendur, which has always been one of my favorite city places. Franny was throwing a penny in the fountain when a handsomely patina-ed couple in their seventies stopped me. "We're on vacation from Florida," the woman said.

I could have guessed. These people were as Florida as Disney World and pink lawn flamingoes.

"We're visiting our son and daughter-in-law. Why they want to live in the cold, I will never know. Their apartment is the size of a matchbook," the man said.

"We were saying—I hope you won't be offended, but you look so much like that girl," the woman said. "The one who got into that terrible trouble with the congressman. What was her name?"

"Aviva Grossman," I said. "I know exactly who you mean! I grew up in South Florida, and I used to get that all the time. But in Maine, where I live, no one knows who that is, and it's such a long time ago now."

We laughed about how funny it was to resemble an obscure figure from an ancient scandal.

"The more I look at you, the less you look like her," the woman said.

"I mean, you're much more attractive than her," the man said. "Slimmer."

"That Levin," she said, wrinkling her nose. "He behaved very badly with that girl."

"But he's been a good congressman," the husband said. "You must admit that."

"I will admit nothing about that man," the wife said. "The girl did not behave well, but the man, what he did was—" She shook her head. "No good."

"The girl knew he was married so she got what was coming to her," the husband said.

"You *would* think that," said the wife.

"That woman he was married to, though," the husband said. "She was a piece of work. You could make ice on her ass."

"I wonder whatever happened to the girl," she said.

"Handbags," said the husband with authority.

"Handbags?" the wife asked.

"She went into handbags," he said. "Or hand-knit scarves."

"I think that was Monica Lewinsky," I said, and then I excused myself. "Safe travels," I said.

I went over to where Ruby and Franny were sitting. "Who's Aviva Grossman?" Ruby asked.

EIGHT

When we got back to the hotel, Wes was waiting in the lobby. "Surprise," he said, and he kissed Franny on the cheek.

"Oh gosh," Franny said. "What are you doing here?"

"Wes," I said. "Nice to see you. This is my daughter, Ruby."

"Ruby," Wes said. "Great name."

"Thanks," Ruby said. "I've had it all my life."

"Seriously," Franny said. "Why are you here?"

"I figured you'd be done shopping by now, and I thought I'd take you to dinner." He kissed her again.

"You flew all this way to take me to dinner?" she said.

"Sure," he said. "Why should you get all the fun?"

"This was supposed to be a girls' weekend," Franny said.

"I'm sure Jane doesn't mind," Wes said. "You don't seem happy," he said in a low voice.

"I am," she said. "I'm surprised."

"Well," I said. "Ruby and I can amuse ourselves. Good to see you, Wes." I shook his hand, and Ruby and I left.

We rode the elevator up to our room. "Awkward," Ruby said when we reached our floor.

"I know," I said.

"She could do better," Ruby said. "She looks like a mean girl, but she's so pretty and nice."

FRANNY HAD THE hotel room next to ours, and that night, we could hear them arguing through the wall. Mainly we could hear him. He seemed to be positioned closer to the wall or a connecting duct, and he had one of those voices that carried.

"Thanks for making me feel like shit when I was doing something nice," he said. "Thanks very much for that. I needed that, FRANCES."

She said something, but we could not make it out.

"You're CRAZY!" he yelled. "You know that? I mean, you *literally* are."

. . .

"You know what Audra said? Audra said I was crazy to marry you, considering your history. I have things I want to do with my life, and they do not involve having a crazy girl in it."

. . .

"No, no, I do not accept that. I told her you were just a teenager, but Audra said—"

"I DON'T CARE WHAT AUDRA SAID!" Franny was finally yelling loudly enough for her voice to penetrate.

"You wanna know what else Audra said? Audra said it seemed weird that you were taking the wedding planner to New York City when you have four bridesmaids who would be happy to go dress shopping with you."

"I LIKE THE WEDDING PLANNER!"

"You barely know her. And are you saying you don't like my sisters?" he asked.

"I DON'T EVEN KNOW THEM!" And then she said something we couldn't understand.

A second later, the door slammed. One of them had left.

"Jeez," Ruby whispered.

We had both heard worse. People were often the worst versions of themselves in the months leading up to a wedding. Occasionally, though, the worst version of someone was the actual version of someone, but it was difficult to know if one was in that situation until after the fact. "Average," I said.

"Unhappy brides are each unhappy in their own way," Ruby said. "What did he mean by 'Franny's history,' Mom?"

"That's none of our business," I said.

"We could ask her," Ruby said. "I bet she'd tell us."

"We could," I said. "And she might, but it still wouldn't be any of our business. The only past you have a right to know about is your own."

"And the people you have to study for history class. You're being so boring," Ruby said. "I'm going to google it." Ruby picked up her phone. "Frances—what's her last name?"

"Lincoln," I said.

"It's too common," Ruby said. "Is Franny from Allison Springs, or somewhere else?"

"Hey, Nancy Drew! Seriously, it's none of our business," I said. "Somewhere else, I think."

"We could go on her Facebook," Ruby suggested. "See who she knows."

"You sound like a stalker or a mobster."

"Fine," Ruby said. She plugged in her phone. "I bet she had an eating disorder and she was in a mental hospital."

"That's not nice," I said.

"I'm just, like, imagining what it might be," Ruby said. "She's very skinny."

"Really?" I said. "I hadn't noticed." Of course I had noticed. At the dress store, the shopgirl had needed multiple clamps to get the sample size to stay up. Franny's shoulder blades were as sharp as knives. When I kissed or hugged her, I felt as if I might break her. But Franny could have been naturally that way, who knew? It is foolish to speculate what is happening inside another human's shell. In any case, I wanted my daughter to think that her mother didn't notice the size of other women's bodies because I wanted my daughter not to notice the size of other women's bodies. I believed a mother must act like the woman she wanted her daughter to become.

"You seriously didn't notice?" Ruby said.

"I seriously did not," I said. "I'm not that interested in other women's bodies."

"You are seriously blind." Ruby sighed. "Who's Nancy Drew?"

NINE

He's not that bad," Franny said to me on the plane ride back. I was in the middle seat, and Franny and Ruby were on either side of me. Ruby had on her headphones and she was doing her schoolwork. "He can be very kind," Franny said, "and he cares so much about the community. Like, the animal shelter in town was going to have to close, and he went to every person he'd ever sold a house to or for, and he raised enough money for the shelter to stay open. That's what attracts me to him. He's civic-minded and he's very industrious."

"He's fine," I said. "Weddings are stressful."

"Hmm," she said. "But you still don't like him."

"I like him fine," I said. "I'm not the one marrying him."

"Okay," she said. "Would you marry him?"

"No, because he isn't my type," I said.

"I meant, would you marry him if you were me?"

The truth was, I wouldn't, but she wasn't my daughter or even my friend. I liked her, but she was my client. "I could guess, but I don't know what it means to be you," I said. "So I can't answer that." I paused. "Do you love him?"

"I love you," Franny said.

"No," I said, "I don't think so."

"It's too bright in here. I feel like I'm getting sunburnt. Can you get sunburn through glass?" Franny lowered the shade. "I mean, I love you like a friend. I love how honest you are about things," Franny said.

TEN

The night before Franny's wedding, I had another dream about Aviva Grossman. Aviva was still young, maybe twenty, and I was her wedding planner. "If I blow out my hair," she said, "I'll feel like a liar."

"You should do what makes you feel the most comfortable," I said.

"Aaron doesn't like my hair curly," she said.

"Whatever you decide, it'll be right," I said.

"That's what people say when they aren't listening or they don't want to take any responsibility. Can you help me zip this?" she said. She turned around, and there was a great plane of skin between the two sides of her dress's zipper.

"What is it?" she said. "It's not too tight, is it?"

"Hold on." I wrenched the two sides of the dress, using all my strength, and I somehow forced the zipper up.

"Can you sit?" I asked. "Can you breathe?"

"Who needs to breathe?" She sat very slowly. I heard the creak of the dress's internal boning and I braced myself for the shredding that was surely to come. "Breathing is for real girls." She smiled up at me. "I never thought *you* would become a wedding planner."

I woke up in a sweat. I checked the weather report on my phone: 66 percent chance of flurries.

It did not snow. The weather was cold and clear. The roads were not icy. No flights were delayed. All who said they would attend, attended. But the whole day, despite the meteorological blessing of this union, I was filled with the memory of the prior night's dream, and I felt restless.

Wes's sisters were congenial enough, but they were incredibly close, and they had the kind of intimacy that excluded other people. Audra, the despised best friend of Wes, came on strong, but it was obvious to me—and probably everyone else—that she was in love with him. Today was a tragedy for her, so I cut her some slack and tried to be as kind to her as I could. I knew what it was to be in love with someone who did not love you back.

Schiele checked in with me after he had set up the floral center-pieces. "All orchids present and accounted for, ma'am. Would you like to see them before I leave?"

I followed Schiele into the ballroom. The orchids looked odd to my eye—the blooms were lonely and eerie, almost extraterrestrial, and the pots and the roots seemed awkward and out of place. But that was a good thing. No one wanted a wedding that looked like everyone else's, and the orchids suited Franny, what I knew of her.

"What do you think?" Schiele said proudly.

"You do good work," I said.

"I wish every bride would ask for orchids. It's a lot more fun for me," Schiele said. "This might be my favorite wedding I've ever done." Schiele took out his phone and began snapping pictures. "Would you send me some of the professional photos when you have them? Do you think Franny would mind?"

"I think she'd be delighted," I said.

"Franny's a special woman."

"Yes," I said.

"What? You don't agree."

"I said yes."

"But there was something in your tone," he said.

I didn't think there had been anything in my tone, but I looked around the room to see if we were alone. "This isn't about Franny specifically," I said. "More a thought I have had over the years. These details—the flowers, the dress, the room—all of them seem very important. It's my job to make people believe that the details are important. But ultimately, no matter what they choose, it's still flowers, a dress, and a room."

"But what flowers!" Schiele said. "What a room!"

"Sometimes I feel like the wedding is a Trojan horse. The dream I peddle to distract from the reality of a marriage. They choose these things to distinguish themselves from everyone else. They choose these things to make themselves feel less ordinary. But is there anything more ordinary than choosing to get married?"

"You're a terrible person," Schiele said.

"Possibly."

"My God, you're in a dark mood," Schiele said.

"I think orchids make me melancholy," I said.

"I'M NOT SURE about my hair," Franny said just before the ceremony. "It seems convoluted, and the man did it so tight, I feel like I'm going to have a stroke." The updo consisted of two thick braids coiled into a crown around her head. She had wanted the relaxed look of a girl attending an outdoor musical festival, but instead, the braids looked like hairy snakes that were swallowing Franny headfirst.

"Take it down," I said.

"That's okay?"

"It's elegant and rustic," I said. "That's the beauty of your theme. You can do what you want."

She took down her hair. "What would I do without you?"

"You would have hired a different me," I said. "Maybe one from Portland."

"I had hoped you hadn't heard that. Wes was awful that first time we met you," she said. "He wants people to like him . . . He thought he was impressing you."

"He made an impression," I said.

She laughed, and then she put her hand over her mouth. "Oh gosh," she said. "I'm marrying him so you probably think I'm awful, too." She paused. "You probably think, 'How can she *love* a man like that?' I wonder it sometimes, too."

"I like you," I said. I zipped up Franny's garment bag, and I packed up her shoes and clothes into her duffel.

"Oh you don't have to do that!" she said.

"I'm happy to," I said. "It's my job."

"Okay, Jane. Thank you. You're probably tired of me saying this, but I honestly don't know what I would do without you. My mother . . ." Franny's eyes began to tear, but I didn't want her to cry because the makeup artist had already left. I handed her a tissue.

"Dab at it," I said. "Don't rub. Take a deep breath."

She dabbed. She breathed.

"I read a story about a woman in California," I said. "She pretended to be a bridesmaid so she could rob the rooms where the wedding parties left their things while they were at the ceremony. I think she robbed maybe fifty weddings."

"But eventually she got caught," Franny said.

"Eventually, but it took a long time. It's the perfect crime when you think about it. Everyone's so distracted at a wedding."

"Everyone except you," she said.

"And half the guests don't know one another."

"You're trying to distract me right now," Franny said.

"I don't think you're even one iota awful, and you should know that people get married for every kind of reason, and love is only one of them and—this might sound cynical—but having done a couple of hundred weddings, I'm not even sure love is the best reason to marry someone anyway."

"Oh Jane, it's the *only* one."

"Okay," I said.

"But if I'm wrong about Wes, it seems so permanent," she said.

"But it isn't," I said. "If it turns out you made a mistake, you won't be stoned to death. They won't embroider a scarlet 'D' on your chest. You live in the twenty-first century. You will call a lawyer, and you'll leave with what you came in with—give or take—and you'll change back your name, and you'll go to some other town, and you'll start over again."

"You make it sound easy. What if I've had children?"

"That would be more difficult, yes."

"I sometimes wonder how I let it get so far," she said.

"Listen, if you truly think you're making a mistake, I can go out there and I can tell everyone to go home."

ELEVEN

Wes came by to give me the money I was owed after they'd returned from their honeymoon. "Franny said she would do it, but I said that was silly. Jane's office is about five hundred feet from mine."

I took the check and I put it in my desk. "Is it only five hundred feet?" I asked. The nature of my work leads me to concede most minor points, but something about Wes made me feel contrary. The honeymoon had left him tanned and cockier than ever, and he seemed to expect gratitude for paying what was owed.

"Maybe half a mile," he said.

"Still, that's more than five hundred feet," I said.

"Have it your way, Jane," he said magnanimously. "Franny bought this for Ruby." He set a plastic snow dome on my desk. It was empty except for water and plastic parts: a nose, a top hat, a carrot, three pieces of coal. "It's a Florida snowman," he said.

"That's very sweet," I said.

"Thanks for everything," Wes said. "The wedding was beautiful, and I know your friendship has meant a lot to Franny."

"It's been fun," I said.

He turned to leave. Then he turned back. "Why don't you like me?"

"I like you," I said.

"I don't think you do. Audra overheard you talking to Franny. She said you almost convinced her not to marry me," Wes said.

"I think Audra's in love with you. I think she heard half of a conversation, and she's trying to make trouble," I said. "Because that's not what happened."

Wes nodded. "Is it because I remind you of *him*?"

"I don't know what you're talking about," I said.

"You can play dumb, but I ran a background check on you before we hired you. Just wanted to make sure you weren't a criminal. You aren't—technically. But I know who you are. I know your real name."

Ruby came through the door. "Hi, Mr. West," she said.

"Hey, Ruby girl. Nice to see you." He smiled at her and shook her hand.

"I was showing Wes out," I said.

"Say hi to Franny!" Ruby said.

"Will do," he said, and I walked him to the door. When he reached the threshold, he lowered his voice. "You don't have to worry, Jane. I won't tell anyone. Not even my wife. It's no one's business, and the past is past."

The past is never past. Only idiots think that. I stepped outside and I closed the door behind me. "I don't know what you think you know, but you don't know anything."

"Come on," he said. "There're pictures—"

I interrupted him. "Even if it were true, what does it gain you really?"

"I'm not threatening you, *Jane*. I imagine, though," he said, "it wouldn't be great for a wedding business if people knew you had once been the star player in a sex scandal."

"That's interesting," I said. "That's interesting that you see things this way. Maybe you're too young to remember—I wasn't even born yet myself—but in 1962, Robert McNamara, John F. Kennedy's secretary of defense, gave a speech where he laid out the concept of mutually assured destruction. Are you familiar with it?"

"Sure," said Wes. "It's the idea that you're fine as long as you have more bombs than the other guy."

"That's oversimplifying," I said. "But it's good that you know it, being that you want to go into politics."

"What are you getting at?" he asked.

"You *think* you know something about me. I definitely know something about you," I said. "I know about Franny," I said. "Her past."

"She wouldn't have told you that." He looked at me, and then he looked away.

"If you run for office, this is a small town, and maybe it wouldn't look so great for the future whatever of Allison Springs to have a wife who . . ."

"Shut up," he said.

"But if you tell people about who you *think* I am, what would it do to me? Maybe people would care? Maybe they wouldn't? I'm a private citizen and I don't need anyone to vote for me for anything, you know? I can always move and plan weddings somewhere else." I shrugged.

"You're a bitch," he said.

"Probably. Here's what I think you saw. And the reason I think you saw this is because it is the truth. Aviva Grossman was my roommate at the University of Miami. We were close once, but I haven't seen or heard from her in years. I'll tell you, Wes, I do dream of her sometimes. It's a little embarrassing. What's even more embarrassing, though, is that you would have made such an error, but I can't blame you. Who knows what kind of shoddy background check you get for forty-nine dollars online? Your failure to thoroughly research this matter is understandable. You're a busy man, and I want to assure you I won't hold it against you. People make mistakes. I don't see it as some kind of moral failing."

"Thanks," he said.

"See, I do like you." I offered him my hand. "Shake my hand," I instructed him, and he obeyed. "Good doing business with you. I hope you'll keep in touch."

I watched that weasel walk away. Though he did not run, he walked briskly, eager to put some distance between us. I thought, Wes West, you are not one iota like Aaron Levin.

However, this might be unfair. It's hard to know what I would think of Levin if I encountered him today. Maybe he *would* seem like Wes West—they were both arrogant and ambitious. In Levin, these qualities were leavened with intelligence and an intense, almost painful empathy for his fellow human beings. Still, it must be said . . . Maybe, despite everything, I think kindly of Levin because I knew him when I was easily impressed, because I knew him when I was young.

TWELVE

In May, just before Ruby's tenth birthday, I happened to see Wes West leaving his office. He was heading toward Market Square, and I, in the opposite direction, Schiele's Flowers—I was meeting a wedding couple there, Edward Reed and Eduardo Ontiveros, who went by Reed and Eddie. Reed was a landscape architect—the flowers at his wedding were going to be a serious business; he wanted what he referred to as "architectonic topiaries," and Schiele would be up to it. Eddie was a teacher at Franny's school, and Reed and Eddie had both attended the Lincoln-Wests' winter wedding, and they had liked my work. I think I had also won their favor by not being overly amused that they had variations on the same first name. "People are so annoying about this. Yes, we have the same name," Eddie said when we were discussing the announcements. "We are men with the same name. This happens. It is not so amazing or hilarious." The wedding was set for August. The theme was WASP fiesta.

By the way, Maine had legalized same-sex marriage the prior December, and early signs were that same-sex weddings were going to more than double my business. I was even thinking of hiring a few full-time employees.

So, Wes West was on his cell phone, and he was gesturing and projecting as if he were in a play and no one else in the world existed but him. Or, we did exist, but we were meant to be the audience for his call, for his impressive real estate acumen, or some such. He was walking right toward me, and I was walking right toward him. And I could tell that he hadn't seen me, but if he had, he wasn't going to move over. He hadn't yielded for the dog walker with the tangle of leashes. He hadn't yielded for the woman with the baby carriage and the toddler. He hadn't yielded for the older man coming out of the post office. He hadn't yielded for the two teenage lovers who had arms linked. Why would he yield for me?

I was feeling jaunty that afternoon so I decided to test Ruby's hypothesis. What happens if a person comes toward you and you just don't move? The day was warm, the streets were mercifully ice-free, and so I kept walking and swinging my arms. I walked right toward him until we were about to crash into each other.

Our noses were perhaps six inches apart, but I kept coming.

He moved.

III

Thirteen, or a Few Interesting Facts About Maine

RUBY

To: "Fatima" shes_all_fatima@yahoo.com.id
From: "Ruby"
Young_Ruby_M@allisonspringsms.edu
Date: September 8
Re: Your American Pen Pal, Friends Around the World Pen Pal Program

Dear Fatima,

Allow me to introduce myself! My name is Ruby Miranda Young. I am thirteen years old and I am in the eighth grade at Allison Springs Middle School, which is in the great state of Maine, "the Pine Tree State." Do you eat lobster in Indonesia? A fun factoid about Maine is that most of the lobster in the United States comes from, you guessed it, Maine! I like lobster, but I do not *love* it. My mom says I do not love lobster because it has become "blasé" to me. "Blasé" means that you act bored because something is too familiar. My mom also says if you use a new word in a sentence three times you will remember it:

1. The word "blasé" is not "blasé" to me.
2. Having a pen pal from Indonesia is not "blasé."
3. It is "blasé" to eat lunch in the cafeteria alone, and I have only been in eighth grade one week, and it is already "blasé."
4. BONUS ROUND: My mom finds lobster to be the opposite of "blasé."

There are many ways to cook lobster. I like lobster chowder or lobster roll. (A "lobster roll" is a "sandwich.") My teacher for social studies and world cultures is Ms. Reacher, and she is the one who signed up our class for the "Friends Around the World Pen Pal Program."

She calls it FAW-PUH-PUH. Something I do not like is when people say acronyms, like FAW-PUH-PUH. It is one of my "pet peeves." "Pet peeves" are "especially annoying things." My other "pet peeves" include the cafeteria and "fake" Instagram accounts and people who do not RSVP. My "pet peeviest" thing would be a person who did not RSVP and then said, "Sorry I didn't remember to RIZVIP." If I had a dog or a cat, I would call him Peeves, and then I would say, "This is my pet, Peeves." I cannot have a dog or a cat because I am allergic to dogs and cats and possibly other furry animals. I have not, for example, met a lion or a camel. My other allergies include strawberries and goat cheese and pine nuts. I am not allergic to peanuts, which is excellent, because organic peanut butter is my favorite food. I could eat peanut butter every day and it would never become blasé. Do they use "acronyms" in Indonesia? Something interesting is that up until last school year Ms. Reacher was a "man." Do you have "transgendered" people in Indonesia? I don't know much about Indonesia, which I guess is why it's good that you are going to be my pen pal!

I googled your first name, and did you know that "Fatima" means "captivating" or "shining one" in Arabic? That's very interesting. My name "Ruby" means "precious jewel," which is pretty close to "shining one," which makes us nearly MEANING TWINS! (I just invented that.) How did you get the name "Fatima"? Duh, your parents gave it to you . . . Imagine that I am smacking my forehead. I guess I mean, what made them choose it? Also, do you have a middle name?

I googled pictures of Indonesia. Do you go to the beach a lot? Something to know about me is I google everything. My mom says I should be the Olympic champion in googling.

The instructions say that we should keep our e-mails to "around 250 words," and I have written more than 500! Please write back soon.

Your pen pal,
Ruby

P.S. I know it's weird and probably seems like an invasion of privacy, but I had to have Ms. Reacher read this e-mail before I sent it to you. It *is* an "assignment." I hope you won't take that personally because I *would* want a pen pal even if it weren't assigned. Anyway, Ms. Reacher said my letter was good but that I should probably not have spent so much time on lobster, seeing as I don't have a "particular passion" for lobster. She says the part about lobster felt like "padding," which is when you add extra words to make a certain "word count." I wasn't "padding." I thought the point of this was to learn about each other's cultures, and lobster really is a big thing in Maine. But I'm sorry if the part about the lobster was super blasé.

P.P.S. Also, Ms. Reacher says I should explain that she was always a woman inside and that she only "presented" as a man before. "Presented" means "looked like" or "appeared to be." (I think that's what it means.)

To: "Fatima" shes_all_fatima@yahoo.com.id
From: "Ruby"
Young_Ruby_M@allisonspringsms.edu
Date: September 15
Re: Re: Re: Your American Pen Pal, Friends Around the World Pen Pal
Program

Dear Fatima,

Your e-mail was Very, Very, Very, Very, Extremely Interesting and Not Even One Word Blasé and your English is Very Good even though you said it wasn't. I'm super EXCITED that you joined FAW-PUH-PUH to work on your vocabulary because vocabulary is my "raison d'être." "Raison d'être" means "reason that you are alive." My other raison d'être is oxygen, ha ha. What is your raison d'être?

I didn't know that Muslims don't eat lobster and you can only eat seafood with scales! Also, it is interesting that you are Muslim, as I don't know any Muslims personally, and it is interesting that you are Muslim because none of the other kids in my class have a Muslim pen pal. By the way, I'm sorry if it was awkward that I went on and on about lobster when you can't even eat it. FACE PALM!

I googled so many things while I was reading your letter. Do you wear a "hijab"? And if you do wear a "hijab," what do you do when your head gets hot and you are away from your house? The average temperature in Indonesia is 82.4°F or 28.0°C, but you probably know that already.

Ms. Reacher says that our e-mails should "strike a balance between telling about you and asking about them." She says that "pen pals" are "students and teachers at the same time."

An interesting thing about me is that my mom is an event planner. She doesn't like it when people call her a "wedding planner" though mainly what she plans is weddings. When I'm not in school, I work as her assistant. She says I am "trustworthy" and "strong for my age." I have many responsibilities:

1. Make sure everyone is where they are supposed to be when it's time for the bride and groom to say their vows. Brides and grooms get lost more often than you would think. I also keep track of the location of the "rings" and the "wedding party."
2. Sign my mom's "signature" for deliveries.
3. Answer the phones in the office. I make my voice looooow, and no one ever knows I'm thirteen.
4. Pick up small items, like boutonnieres, from the florist, which is three doors down from my mom's office. "Boutonnieres" are "the flowers that men wear so they don't feel left out."
5. Online and other kinds of "research" for my mom. One time my mom needed to find out if we could get an ice cream truck for

a December wedding, even though that did not end up happening. By the way, you can get an ice-cream truck, in December, in Maine, if you ever need one. (I don't know why you would, seeing as you live in Indonesia!)

6. Putting "place cards" on tables. It is very important to be accurate when I am in charge of this. People get very angry if they are seated in the "wrong" place. Sometimes, they get angry when they are seated in the "right" place, too.

7. Et cetera. ("Et cetera" means "and other things.")

My mom pays me, and so far, I have saved $3,998.93. I also have been given a "business" American Express card. The American Express card says RUBY MIRANDA YOUNG, and underneath that it says, EVENTS BY JANE, which is the name of my mom's company. I am only supposed to use the card "for business." I like to stroke the top of the card with my thumb and pretend that I know how to read Braille. Fun factoid about ME: I am the only thirteen-year-old I know with a business American Express card.

Another interesting thing is that my mom is "running" for mayor of Allison Springs.

Your Meaning Twin,
Ruby

P.S. Ms. Reacher says she is not going to read any more of our correspondence. She will only check to make sure we are doing it. I hope that will ease your mind.

To: "Fatima" shes_all_fatima@yahoo.com.id
From: "Ruby"
Young_Ruby_M@allisonspringsms.edu
Date: September 22
Re: Re: Re: Re: Re: Your American Pen Pal, Friends Around the World Pen
Pal Program

Dear Fatima,
Hello!
It is interesting that you and your sister are interested in politics! It is tragic that there are "quotas" on how many women can run for parliament in Indonesia. (I did not know anything about politics in Indonesia so I googled it.) How old are you, by the way? Are you in high school? I do not have many friends who are my exact age. People my age tend to be pretty blasé.
Here are the answers to your questions.

1. Yes, there are female mayors in the U.S., but Allison Springs has never had one before so if my mom wins she will be the "first female mayor," which is awesome. My mom's "friend" Mrs. Morgan says that this is because Allison Springs is "shamefully patriarchal." "Patriarchal" means that "men control everything." Also, my mom says that she is running for "mayor and not first female mayor."

2. No, I don't think it's usual for event planners to become mayors in the United States or in Maine, but I do not have "exact" numbers. I will have to get back to you.

3. The way my mom became a candidate for mayor is that everyone in Allison Springs thinks that my mom is their best friend, though I am her actual best friend. My mom says the reason people think she is their best friend is because weddings and events give people

"the illusion of intimacy." The "illusion of intimacy" means people "lower their inhibitions." "Lower their inhibitions" means
"people talk and drink and hug too much."

4. One of the people who think they are my mom's best friend is
Mrs. Morgan. My mom says that Mrs. Morgan is not her best
friend but she is definitely her "best client" and "my college
fund." Mrs. Morgan is a "socialite." A "socialite" is a "rich, old
lady who drinks wine and throws parties for charity and gets
in other people's business." Mrs. Morgan also owns the *Allison
Springs Cryer*, which is our newspaper. My mom says it is getting
to be more like a "newsletter." I like Mrs. Morgan A LOT. She
has a colorful vocabulary and a colorful wardrobe.

5. Mrs. Morgan was throwing a benefit "party" for male cancer
of the breast, which is what Mrs. Morgan's husband died of last
year. After the party, Mrs. Morgan "lowered her inhibitions" and
we had to drive her to her mansion in our SUV. My mom took off
Mrs. Morgan's shoes and put her to bed. My mom says that Mrs.
Morgan is a "chatty drunk." A "chatty drunk" is "a socialite
who does not just pass out like a normal person."

SCENE BETWEEN MY MOM & MRS. MORGAN

MRS. MORGAN: You are far and away the best event planner I
have ever hired, but I'm a crutch for you. I have half a mind to stop
hiring you, so that you would go do something better. You should
write a book, have a show like Martha Stewart. Jane, don't lie, did
you want to be an event planner when you were young?

MOM: I like my work. I like the variety. I like working with people
like you. It's a privilege that so many people let me into their lives on
their most important days.

MRS. MORGAN: You're a good girl, Jane Young. Sorry. We're not
supposed to call each other girls anymore, but I mean no offense. A
good woman. A fine woman! The daughter I should have had!

Mom: Thanks.

Mrs. Morgan: Just tell me one thing you wanted to do before you were an event planner. You never say anything about yourself, but you let me blab all my secrets. Tell me what you studied in school.

Mom: Spanish literature and political science.

Mrs. Morgan: Political science. Politics? Did you want to go into politics?

Mom: Yes. But I found that event planning used many of the skills I would have used in politics: the stagecraft, the organization, the ability to bend people to your will. But I've told you all this before.

Mrs. Morgan: I'm going to help you out, Jane Young! And . . . SCENE!

6. A couple of months later, the mayor said he was quitting. His wife has cancer of the anus, which is not a laughing matter, and he needs to take care of her, so he can't be mayor anymore. Mrs. Morgan told my mom if she wanted to run for mayor, she would "back" her campaign. "Back" means "give someone money." Mrs. Morgan also said she was going to have a "benefit for cancer of the anus."

7. My mom asked me if it would be "all right" if she ran for mayor and I said, "All right? It would be SUPER AMAZING!"

8. Then, my mom said that when people run for political office, sometimes "nasty and untrue things" are said and I should be prepared for "nasty and untrue things" to be said about her. She said I should (A) ignore it and (B) not let it hurt my feelings. I said, "If I do part A, there's no need to worry about part B!" She said, "Ruby, I am serious." I said, "Mom, I am tough." I am tough. I don't know if I have mentioned it, but I am "not well liked" at my school. "Not well liked" means that "no one wants to sit with me at lunch."

9. That's how my Mom decided to run for mayor. So far I have not

heard any "nasty and untrue things" about her, but there's still six weeks left until ELECTION DAY!

10. The man my mom is running against is Wes West, and she planned his wedding. I don't have much to say about him.

11. One thing I could say about him is that he was the one who decided not to have the ice cream truck at the wedding. Who doesn't want an ice cream truck?

Your Meaning Twin,
Ruby

To: "Fatima" shes_all_fatima@yahoo.com.id
From: "Ruby"
Young_Ruby_M@allisonspringsms.edu
Date: September 29
Re: Re: Re: Re: Re: Re: Re: Your American Pen Pal, Friends Around the World Pen Pal Program

Dear Fatima,

Hooray, my mom says it would DEFINITELY be possible for us to Skype with your class at the Indonesian Women's Business and Leadership Academy! She says her schedule is "tight" leading up to the election, but as long as we keep it to an hour, it should be fine. It will be UH-MAY-ZING for us to finally see each other! Could you send me a picture so I know which one you are? "UH-MAY-ZING" is "my favorite way to write amazing."

It is interesting that "single mothers" have difficulties getting elected in Indonesia! I told Mrs. Morgan that and she said that was "slut-shaming." I asked Mrs. Morgan what "slut-shaming" was, and she said it is "when a woman is too free and it p*sses people off." The "single mother" thing doesn't seem to be affecting my mom's candidacy too much, but maybe that is because (1) everyone knows my mom, and (2) my father is dead. It isn't a tragic thing for me. I don't remember him, and my mom doesn't like to talk about the past because I think it makes her sad. I don't know much about him. I guess I'm curious, but I also don't want to make her sad.

In a way, I am happy I don't have a father because I like having my mom to myself. And also, Mrs. Morgan says that I am "more independent" and have a "stronger character" because I have not been "influenced by the patriarchy." Mrs. Morgan talks about the "patriarchy" a lot. She is very against the "patriarchy."

I am helping my mom "prep" for the debate against Wesley West. I read questions for my mom off of my phone. The questions are like:

1. If the town has a surplus, how do you spend it?
2. What is the biggest problem our town is facing, and how would you address it?
3. How would you secure our borders and keep terrorists out of Allison Springs?
4. Towns like Allison Springs are soft targets for terrorism. How do we keep violence and terrorism out of public buildings, like schools, the city pool, the library, and the post office?
5. The statue of Captain Allison was hit by a car and destroyed last winter. Some have proposed that we don't rebuild the statue but instead establish a farmer's market. How do we keep terrorists out of the farmer's market?

Et cetera.

So many of the questions had to do with terrorism that I said to my mom, "Should I be worried? Is Allison Springs a MAJOR terrorist target and not just some tiny town in Maine? People seem to be VERY WORRIED about terrorism here."

My mom said, "The truth is, Ruby, if you know your neighbors and they know you, you don't have to worry about terrorism nearly as much as people think. Not in a place like Allison Springs. But the other truth is, that's not what people want to hear during an election."

Still . . . my mom may have been trying to get me not to worry. I am "neurotic." "Neurotic" means "I think about things until I am sick."

I googled how to avoid terrorism, and it said you should (1) always be aware of your surroundings, and (2) if you see something, say something, and (3) remember that terrorism can occur in places where you LEAST expect it, places like Allison Springs.

So now when I go out, I'm trying not to blink very much, and I'm making sure to scan in all directions for signs of TERROR. Do they have a lot of terrorism in Indonesia?

Your Meaning Twin,
Ruby

To: "Fatima" shes_all_fatima@yahoo.com.id
From: "Ruby"
Young_Ruby_M@allisonspringsms.edu
Date: October 1
Re: Re: Re: Re: Re: Re: Re: Re: Re: Your American Pen Pal, Friends
Around the World Pen Pal Program

Dear Fatima,

EUREKA! I went to the Allison Springs Public Library and I asked Mr. Allison to help me figure out what percentage of mayors were event planners. I tried googling so many combinations of words ("mayors, by occupation," "mayors, by *former* occupation," "mayors—what did they do before they became mayors?" "number of mayors

who worked in event planning," et cetera), but I couldn't get an answer for you. Mr. Allison said we would have to do our own research.
He said that we could take a "sample of Maine." I asked him, "What
is a sample?" He said, "Sometimes when you can't see everything,
you look at a small piece of something instead, and you can draw
conclusions about the larger piece from the smaller piece. The smaller
piece is the sample." I said, "What if you are looking at the wrong
piece?" He said, "That is true, Ruby. That is a danger. At the very
least, though, we can learn about mayors in Maine. Are you ready for
some painstaking research?" An interesting fact about "painstaking"
is that it is pronounced "pain-staking" when it should be pronounced
"pains-taking" because what you are doing is "taking pains."

We found out that there are 432 towns in Maine, and none of
the mayors are former event planners. So, the answer is 0 percent of
current mayors in Maine come from an event planning background!
My mom would be the first. Mr. Allison said we could increase our
sample to the rest of the country some other time but it would have
to be another day, because the library was closing.

Mr. Allison is the town librarian and the town historian. He is
a descendant of Captain Allison, who founded Allison Springs. He
went on a date with my mom once. Mr. Allison looks like a pencil.
He is very skinny, and his hair is reddish pink, like a pencil eraser.
He has long, blondish red eyelashes, and his Adam's apple is very
"pronounced." "Pronounced" means "I sometimes can't stop looking at it when he talks." My mom said the fact that he looks like a
pencil is not the reason she did not go on a second date with him.
I like Mr. Allison *A Lot* because he is even better at finding things
out than me. I do not know much about boys, but I think superior
research skills would be a Very Good Thing to have in a boyfriend.
I asked Mom what was wrong with him. She said "no chemistry."
"No chemistry" means "a person doesn't make you feel excited in

your heart and other organs." My mom says "no chemistry" about everyone, though.

Can I tell you something, Fatima? Maybe it's because you asked about it or maybe it's because my mom has been so busy with the campaign, but lately, I have been thinking a lot about my dad. I know he is dead, but I would like to know what he was like, and what he looked like, and am I like him, and do I look like him? Is he like Mr. Allison? Or is he like Ms. Reacher, back when she was "presenting" as a man? Who knows? I don't even know his name. If I knew his name, I would google him. I don't want to make my mom sad but I also would like to know. Is it wrong that I would like to know?

Your Friend and Meaning Twin,
Ruby

P.S. Please don't mention any of the "personal" stuff in the Skype chat on November 2. I know you wouldn't.

To: "Fatima" shes_all_fatima@yahoo.com.id
From: "Ruby"
Young_Ruby_M@allisonspringsms.edu
Date: October 5
Re: Re: Re: Re: Re: Re: Re: Re: Re: Re: Re: Your American Pen Pal, Friends Around the World Pen Pal Program

Dear Fatima,
I may have done a Very Bad Thing. I'm not ready to tell you about it yet, because you'll think I'm a terrible person. I don't want you to think I'm a terrible person. The Very Bad Thing part comes at the end of the story, so I don't have to say it right now anyway.

Thank you very much for the advice. It was hard finding a good time to talk to Mom because she is Very Busy with the election and always with Mrs. Morgan or the people (mostly volunteers) who work on her campaign. Late Friday night, everyone ate pizza, which took forever. Finally, they left, and I said, "Mom. We need to talk," like you told me to. "I want to know more about my father."

She said, "Ruby, why do you want to know about this now?"

I said, "Because I'm getting older."

She said, "You are. It's true."

I said, "And I'm lonely." I didn't know I felt lonely until I said this.

She made a :(I pretty much live my life to avoid seeing my mom make that expression. I quickly said, "Not 'lonely.' But I am 'alone' more often, with the campaign."

Mom said the story I have heard before. She said that she "loved him," but in a way, she didn't "know him" very well. (That makes no sense to me. How do you love a person you don't know?) She said that he died in a car accident, and he didn't know she was pregnant. She said that she came to Maine because she couldn't bear to be around the places she'd been with him. She said it was a long time ago and she was a different person.

I said, "What was his name? You never say his name, and you don't have any pictures either."

She said, "It's too painful."

"Then just tell me his name," I said.

"His name is . . ." She sighed. "Why does it matter?"

"Why is it a secret?"

"It's not a secret," she said. "You never asked. His name was Mariano Donatello."

I repeated the name, "Mariano Donatello." It felt so beautiful on my tongue, like licking a Creamsicle® in summer. I said it again. "Mariano Donatello . . . Mom, I'm Italian?"

"Yes," she said. "I guess so."

"I'm Italian," I said. Fatima, it turns out that your pen pal is ITALIAN and GERMAN-JEWISH, which is almost as good as being INDONESIAN-MUSLIM.

I googled "Mariano Donatello" the next morning, and there weren't many hits, except a few things in Italy, so I added, "Miami," which is where my mom is from. And I still didn't get anything. And I googled "Mariano Donatello, obituary" and still nothing. An "obituary" is like a "book report on a dead person."

Mr. Allison said it wasn't that weird. Mr. Allison said, considering the year Mariano Donatello died (I was born in 2003, so he must have died in 2003 or 2002), he might not have had that much time to establish an "online presence." An "online presence" is "all the true things and all the lies about a person on the Internet." My "online presence" is very pathetic. If you google my name "RUBY YOUNG" and "ALLISON SPRINGS," the main thing you will find is a "fake" Instagram account called "RUBY YOUNG IS A LOOZER SPAZZ," which someone made when I was in sixth grade and which my mom can't get anyone at Instagram to take down.

The next day, Mr. Allison sent me a link to a genealogy website, and he said I should try using this website if I wanted to build a "family tree." To start researching, you had to give the website $49.95 in the form of a credit card payment, and this is where the Very Bad Thing comes in. I went downstairs to ask my mom if I could use the business American Express card, even though this wasn't really business, and she said, "Yes," and waved at me. She was on the phone and I could tell she hadn't really heard me. I guess I didn't want her to hear me because I think she would have most likely said, "No."

But I DID use the credit card anyway!

It's going to sound ridiculous, but I was so anxious, I ended up throwing up. I said to myself, "Ruby, don't be a spazz." That's what the kids at school call me, though you probably already figured that out. "Ruby the Loozer Spazz" or "Ruby the Spazz" or sometimes just "Spazz." "Spazz" means "I have a lot of fears and I freak out sometimes." It is NOT a compliment.

I mean, I'll pay her back. I HAVE money.

I am a very honest person. I try never to lie, and I hate the thought of lying to my mom.

By the way, there wasn't even any information about Mariano Donatello on the genealogy website.

Your Pen Pal,
Ruby the Liar

To: "Fatima" shes_all_fatima@yahoo.com.id
From: "Ruby"
Young_Ruby_M@allisonspringsms.edu
Date: October 15
Re: Re: Re: Re: Re: Re: Re: Re: Re: Re: Re: Re: Re: Your American Pen Pal, Friends Around the World Pen Pal Program

Dear Fatima,

I'm sorry it has been so long since I've written. I have disappointing news. I think my mom won't be able to do the Skype. I'm really sorry . . .

   :(

   :(

   :(

Thank you again for the advice. I created a PayPal account like you said and I transferred the $49.95 to my mom from my bank account. I explained what happened and she said it wasn't a big deal, but I shouldn't make a habit of using the credit card for "extracurricular" purposes. I think she misused the word "extracurricular," but I understood what she meant. "Extracurricular" means "outside of school, like sports, newspaper, bullying, and French club."

I think my mom was less mad than she might have been because I told her the afternoon before the debate. She was busy getting ready, even though everyone in town already knows what she looks like. When she is an event planner, she always wears black sleeveless dresses. But when you are a politician, you have to wear colors. So my mom had to buy some new clothes, and she had to have her hair trimmed.

The debate was at Allison Springs City Hall, which is only a couple of blocks from my mom's work. Usually, we would walk, but Mrs. Morgan thought we should arrive in her Town Car. It was very silly, because it took twice as long for us to ride in the car as it would have taken us to walk.

The city hall smells like the library, but less moldy. It smells like old things and paper and the radiator and wax, but I kind of like those scents.

Mrs. Morgan went backstage with my mom, and I chose a seat in the audience. No one was there yet, so I decided to sit in the second row. I did not want to sit in the first row because I did not want to distract Mom. While I waited, I read my book for language arts. The book is about a girl whose dad is a lawyer, who is defending an African American person who is falsely accused of a crime. Mr. Dower said it was his favorite book, but I was not enjoying it very much. The girl in the book was very naïve about the way the world worked and she was kind of obsessed with her father. Maybe I didn't like the book because I couldn't "relate" to it. For instance, if I ever wrote a book about my childhood, I would not have much to say about Mariano Donatello. I was still thinking about that when someone called my name. It was Franny West, Wes West's wife.

"How are you, Ruby?" she said. "I like your new glasses."

"They're about six months old," I said.

"I guess I haven't seen you in ages," she said.

I liked Franny a lot, but I wasn't sure if I should talk to her, considering that her husband was "the competition."

"What's wrong?" she said.

"Nothing," I said.

She sat down next to me. I must have stiffened because she said, "Don't worry. I'll move before the debate starts."

"How have you been?" she said. "How is school?"

"I have a pen pal," I said.

"I love pen pals," she said. "Where is your pen pal from?"

We talked about You for a while. Only good things, so don't worry.

People were starting to come into the hall. I was hoping Franny would move, but she didn't. I said, "How are you, Franny?"

She said. "Oh, the election is very exciting! I've been running around all of the time."

"Me, too!" I said.

She said, "I miss your mother. I miss having her to talk to. I know we weren't really friends . . . Tell her I miss her, would you?"

"Yes," I said.

"The truth is, Ruby, I've been having a kind of hard year," she said. She looked around to see if anyone was paying attention to us. "I was pregnant," she said, "but now I'm not." Franny's eyes began to tear, and she looked like a glum goldfish.

I did not know what to say. My mom says when you do not know what to say, you can either say "I don't know what to say" or you can say "I'm sorry" or you can say nothing and offer a "comforting gesture." I put my hand on her hand.

"Thank you for not saying 'It wasn't meant to be' or 'You can always try again,'" Franny said.

"I wouldn't say those things," I said.

"I wasn't even sure if I wanted a child, so why am I so sad?" Franny said.

"I don't know," I said. But then I did know. "Because the things we don't have are sadder than the things we have. Because the things we don't have exist in our imaginations, where they are perfect." I knew this because it was how I felt about Mariano Donatello.

"Yes," she said, "I think that's it, Ruby. You're very wise."

"Thank you," I said.

"How did you get so wise?"

"Books," I said. "And I spend a lot of time with my mom."

"Don't tell your mom about what we talked about," she said.

"Okay," I said. "Which part?"

"The thing that exists in my imagination," she said. "It's not that I don't want her to know. I'd just rather tell her myself."

"I won't say anything."

"Never mind," she said. "Tell her if you want. I don't care."

"Mrs. West," someone called. "Wes needs you."

"Good-bye, Ruby," she said.

"I'll give Mom your regards," I said.

I went back to my book. I only read about five pages, and then the debate started.

The debate was very boring for a while, and I was deciding whether it would be rude to read my book. I had already heard the questions, so I knew what she would say before she said it, most of the time. Toward the end, it got a little more exciting, because it was clear that Wes West hadn't practiced as much as Mom. He kept stumbling over his words, and no one was clapping after he talked, and sometimes people were even booing, and he was very awkward. I could tell he was getting frustrated because at one point, he said, "I'm just worried this town is going in the wrong direction!" And then I saw him say something under his breath. I was too far away to hear what he had said, but somehow the movement of his lips looked familiar to me. It was a word with THREE SYLLABLES.

1st syllable: open mouth
2nd syllable: tighter pursed lips, teeth on lips
3rd syllable: open mouth, same as the first

My mom mouthed, "Franny." Again, I was reading her lips. But even from a distance, "Franny" made sense because Franny is Wes West's wife, of course.

In the car on the way back, I asked my mom what Wes West had mouthed to her when they were onstage. She said, "I don't know what you're talking about."

And I said, "The thing you replied 'Franny' to."

She said, "I don't remember. I think I was asking if Franny had come to the debate."

That didn't make sense to me. Why would she ask that onstage in the middle of a debate?

When I was lying in bed, I made my mouth move like Wes West's had to try to figure out what he had said. UH-BEE-UH. IH-BEE-THUH. OH-TEE-OH. UH-PEE-UH. It seemed so close to me.

I couldn't sleep so I thought about my mom saying "Franny" instead.

And that made me think about the time Mom and I went with Franny to go wedding dress shopping in New York City.

And that made me think of the Metropolitan Museum of Art.

And that made me think of this weird thing that happened there. This old couple came up to my mom and said, "You look like that girl, Aviva Grossman."

And I always remembered that name, because "Grossman" is a funny last name. I remember that I was glad it wasn't *my* last name, because things are bad enough for me at school already.

And just like that, I knew that Wes had said, "UH-VEE-VUH."

I got out of bed and I googled "Aviva Grossman."

Here's what you need to know about "Aviva Grossman":

She is this dumb girl who had an affair with a married congressman. She kept a "blog" and she became a BIG JOKE in Florida.

"Aviva Grossman" was fatter than my mom and younger than my mom and her hair was curlier than my mom's.

But really, she looked exactly like my mom.

"Aviva Grossman" was my "mom."

I went to the bathroom and I threw up.

"Mom" knocked on the door, but I told her to go away. I said, "I think I have the flu. You shouldn't come in, because you can't get sick right now."

She said, "That's very thoughtful of you, Ruby. But I think I'll risk it." She put her hand on the door, and I locked it.

I said, "SERIOUSLY, YOU CAN'T GET SICK! I'm okay. I'm already done throwing up. I just want to wash my face and go to sleep."

And the next day, I told her I needed to stay home from school, and she let me because she isn't paying much attention to anything but the election these days. After the debate, Mrs. Morgan said Mom is probably going to win in a landslide.

It's been five days since the debate, and I've been avoiding her. It isn't that hard because she is always busy, lying to everyone.

That's why I don't think my mom should speak to your class. She is not a good role model. She is a BIG liar and a disgrace.

Your Pen Pal,
Ruby

P.S. I guess my last name is "Grossman."

To: "Fatima" shes_all_fatima@yahoo.com.id
From: "Ruby"
Young_Ruby_M@allisonspringsms.edu
Date: October 18
Re: Re: Re: Re: Re: Re: Re: Re: Re: Re: Re: Re: Re: Re: Re: Your American
Pen Pal, Friends Around the World Pen Pal Program

Dear Fatima,

Thank you for being so understanding about the Skype chat. It's nice of you to say that we should "reschedule" but I don't know why you would want to, considering the type of person my mom is.

I haven't confronted my mom yet. I'm reading everything I can about "Aviva Grossman" first. I don't want her to be able to tell any more lies.

"Grossman" is a pretty good name for her because she is so "gross." She did "gross" things with the congressman, who was so old, like forty, and she wrote about them on her blog. The blog is called "Just Another Congressional Intern's Blog." Even though she never used his name or her own name, of course people were going to figure it out. Even a sixth grader knows that!

For instance, I'm not going to mention any names, but I know EX-ACTLY who started the "RUBY YOUNG IS A LOOZER SPAZZ" account. The only reason I don't turn her in is because it's better for her just to be scared that she might be found out. Something I have learned about bullies is that it's good for them to have something to focus on, and that stupid account is good for that, too. Instead of putting ketchup in my hair, or locking me out of the bathroom, or putting dog poop in my locker, they can just post some dumb thing on Instagram, and it satisfies their "making Ruby's life miserable" urge. My point is, it was actually WORSE for me before the Insta-gram account.

I started thinking about "Mariano Donatello."

I know English is not your first language . . . But "Mariano Donatello" DOES NOT sound like a real person's name.

It sounds like

1. A Ninja Turtle
2. A Character in a Storybook
3. A Porno Actor
4. A Made-Up Name

And duh, my mom is such a liar. Of course, she lied about "Mariano Donatello." And I was, like, "I'm Italian!"—what an idiot!

And if she lied about "Mariano Donatello," then she must have had a reason.

And the reason must be because Congressman Aaron Levin is my REAL FATHER.

I googled "Congressman Aaron Levin," and although he is old, he looks like me. He has greenish eyes and curly hair, and I have green eyes and curly hair.

I wonder if he knows about me.

Your Meaning Twin,
Ruby

P.S. I would rather have the last name LEVIN than GROSSMAN.

P.P.S. I know you're right, and I need to talk to my mom about all of this . . . I am going to do it soon.

To: "Fatima" shes_all_fatima@yahoo.com.id
From: "Ruby"
Young_Ruby_M@allisonspringsms.edu
Date: October 24
Re: Re: Re: Re: Re: Re: Re: Re: Re: Re: Re: Re: Re: Re: Re: Re: Re: Your
American Pen Pal, Friends Around the World Pen Pal Program

Dear Fatima,

Right after I e-mailed you, I had a big fight with my mom. I told her that I know everything, that I know she's a liar and a slut, and she didn't cry and then she did, and it was awful.

I said, "You can't lie to me anymore. I need to know who my father is."

She said, "It's Mariano Donatello."

I said, "How dumb do you think I am?"

She said, "I wanted you to have a nice story."

I said, "I want the truth."

She said, "The truth is, it was a one-night stand."

I said, "I don't know what that is."

She said, "It's a person you sleep with for one night and never see again."

I said, "That is disgusting, and I don't believe you. I know it's Congressman Aaron Levin. You wrote about the 'dirty things' you did with him. He has curly hair and greenish eyes, and I have curly hair and green eyes."

She said, "Lots of people have those, and it's not him. If you found the blog, you'll know. I never had the kind of sex with him that leads to having a baby."

I said, "That is SOOOOO disgusting, and you lie to everyone, and you're a criminal."

She said, "Ruby, baby, I—"

I interrupted her. "Don't 'Ruby baby' me."

"Ruby, I am not a criminal. I committed no legal crimes. Moral ones? Yes. But legal ones? No. Where I was from, I was a laughing-stock, and my family was so ashamed, and no one would hire me. And anyone who hadn't heard of me could google me and find out everything. You know how permanent Google is. Have you ever heard of a book called *The Scarlet Letter*, Ruby?"

I said, "I don't want to talk about books, Aviva."

She said, "It's relevant. It's about this woman named Hester, and she commits adultery."

I said, "I don't know what that is!"

She said, "'Adultery' is what I did. Basically, it's what I did. It's having sex with someone you aren't married to. She commits adultery and the town votes to make her wear a scarlet 'A' on her dress so everyone will always know what she did. Being in a scandal that people can google is like that, only a million times worse."

She said, "So I legally changed my name, and I moved far away, and I built a life for us. And I've tried to be a good person, and I've tried to be a good mom to you. I did what I had to do, Ruby."

We were both crying. I said, "Our name isn't even Young."

"Yes, it is," she said. "It's the name I gave us."

She held out her arms for me to hug her, but I didn't want to hug her.

"How can you let people vote for you?" I said. "Don't they de-serve to know who they're voting for?"

She :(ed, but I didn't even care! "No," she said. "It's my business."

I said, "What if they find out?"

She said, "I'll deal with it then. But if they find out, I will tell them the truth. And the truth is, I was young and I made mistakes."

I said, "Why did you have to go and try to be mayor? It seems so stupid for a person who has so many secrets."

"I don't know, Ruby," she said. "I *do* know, but it won't make sense to you until you're older."

I yelled, "F**K OFF, AVIVA!" I'm very sorry for the curse, Fatima. I know FAW-PUH-PUH says we should try not to "use vulgarities." I am NOT sorry for telling my Mom to "F**K OFF" because it is so rude to (1) lie for thirteen years and (2) then tell a person she'll understand when she's "older." I ran into my room and I slammed the door. I slammed the door so hard, it knocked my lamp off the nightstand. My lamp looks like a porcupine, and it has a ceramic body and gold quills, and Mrs. Morgan gave it to me for my eleventh birthday. It broke into about one hundred pieces. That is an estimate.

Mom opened my door, and she said, "Oh no, not Charlie!"

I said, "It's just a lamp." But my stupid lip was quivering. I'm probably getting too old for it, but it was the best lamp. Mrs. Morgan ordered it especially for me online because porcupines are my favorite animal. It is UH-MAY-ZING that you can find out your mom is the Olympic Champion of Slutty Liars and still have any leftover feelings for your porcupine lamp.

The thing is, I do not have many friends:

1. My mom
2. Mrs. Morgan
3. Mr. Allison
4. Ms. Reacher
5. You
6. Charlie the Porcupine Lamp

It's not like Charlie was high on the list, but still . . .

I went to sleep without brushing my teeth or taking off my clothes. I did not have to turn off my lamp, because it was already broken.

In the morning, Mom was gone. She had to go to a campaign breakfast. She left me a note: "I'm sorry." The note was under Charlie's foot—she must have spent hours gluing him back together. It annoyed me. It did not make me feel 1 percent more like forgiving her.

You break a lamp. You go to Target and you buy another lamp. I have $3,949.98 and I can buy a new porcupine lamp anytime I want.

Your Pen Pal,
Ruby

To: "Fatima" shes_all_fatima@yahoo.com.id
From: "Ruby"
Young_Ruby_M@allisonspringsms.edu
Date: October 25
Re: Re: Re: Re: Re: Re: Re: Re: Re: Re: Re: Re: Re: Re: Re: Re: Re:
Re: Your American Pen Pal, Friends Around the World Pen Pal Program

Dear Fatima,

I know you are trying to be helpful, but you honestly have no idea what you are talking about.

I am honestly pretty surprised that you're defending her. No offense, but don't Muslim women get "stoned to death" for doing what my mom did?

I am not "slut-shaming" my mom, though you have to admit what she did was pretty "slutty." Maybe I did not explain "slut-shaming" well before. "Slut-shaming" is "when you call a woman a 'slut' just because she had 'sex.'" I don't think it *is* "slut-shaming" if the person is actually a "slut."

She is a liar.

She is committing "voter fraud" and "daughter fraud." "Voter fraud" is "lying to the voters" but it can also be "rigging an election." "Daughter fraud" is "lying to your daughter."

—Ruby

P.S. I think we should take a break from our pen pal relationship. It is okay with me if you want to get a different pen pal.

To: "Fatima" shes_all_fatima@yahoo.com.id

From: "Ruby"

Young_Ruby_M@allisonspringsms.edu

Date: October 26

Re: Re: Re: Re: Re: Re: Re: Re: Re: Re: Re: Re: Re: Re: Re: Re: Re: Re: Re: Re: Your American Pen Pal, Friends Around the World Pen Pal Program

Dear Fatima,

I'm sorry about my last e-mail. I was mad at my mom and I took it out on you. There is NO WAY I want you to get another pen pal. You're the best pen pal, and you're the only person I can talk to.

I had to do a campaign event with my mom yesterday. It was the Allison Springs Businesswomen's Association Mother-Daughter Leadership Luncheon so there was no way I could get out of it. I told my mom I didn't want to go, because I am no longer supporting her candidacy. She asked me to please come because it would be "awkward" if I didn't.

I told my mom I would go but that I wasn't going to put on a dress for her or for anyone else. I wore my plaid pants and a T-shirt that Mrs. Morgan gave me that said, ASK ME ABOUT MY FEMINIST AGENDA. This T-shirt is a joke, but it's hard to explain, and honestly, I'm not even sure that it's all that funny of a joke.

Mom didn't argue about my outfit. She said, "You look cool."

I said, "It was what I was sleeping in."

The luncheon was in the ballroom of a Holiday Inn, and it was like a crappy wedding basically. Delilah Stuart from my class was there, and she pretended to be nice to me, because adults were around.

Delilah Stuart said, "Nice T-shirt."

I said, "Thank you." She said "nice" but she meant the opposite.
Delilah Stuart is the worst.

Delilah Stuart said, "What's it supposed to mean?"

I gave her EYES OF DRAGON FIRE. I said, "It means that I am
a girl and a human and I care about women's rights. You can borrow
it sometime if you want."

My mom was busy, and I sat down at the long banquet table, and
I ate a dinner roll. The dinner roll was hard but I still ate it. I tore it
apart with my teeth and imagined it was Delilah Stuart's face. Mom
gave a speech, and I periodically rolled my eyes, but I tried not to
make it too obvious. But come on! She kept saying dumb politician
words like "honesty" and "integrity."

After the speeches were over, I went to the bathroom, and when I
left, Mrs. Morgan was waiting for me. "Ruby Young, what is wrong?
You seem sour as curdled milk today."

"I'm tired," I said. I DID NOT want to lie to Mrs. Morgan. That
was the crappy thing about having a liar for a mother. It was turning
me into a liar, too.

Mrs. Morgan petted me on the head, like I was a dog. She said,
"Do you want to talk about it?"

I said, "There isn't anything to talk about."

Mrs. Morgan said, "Campaigns can be hard."

I said, "It's a dumb little mayor's race, in a dumb little town. It's
not president. What difference does it make who wins?"

Mrs. Morgan said, "That's a very cynical point of view, and I
know there are some people who feel that way. But I don't think that,
and I know your mom doesn't think that. I've lived here my entire
life, just like you, and I love this dumb little town, and even if it's not
a presidential race, I think it matters very much who wins it. That's
why I'm backing your mother."

I didn't say anything.

Mrs. Morgan said, "May I guess what's bothering you?"

"It's a free country," I said.

"It's been you and your mom against the world for a very long time, and now there are so many other people in your lives. Maybe you don't want to share her?"

I shook my head. I hated that Mrs. Morgan thought I was so petty. I wanted to tell her what I knew, but I couldn't betray my mom that way. "That isn't it," I said.

"It's something though?"

I bit my lip. "It's nothing."

"All right, Miss Ruby. You come and see me if you ever want to talk. You wouldn't know it to look at me, but I'm very old and I'm very wise."

I've been thinking about it, Fatima. Maybe I should tell Mrs. Morgan the truth? I know it would be betraying my mom, but I also think Mrs. Morgan's right. If it does matter who runs Allison Springs, maybe people should know who my mom really is.

Your Friend (I Hope),
Ruby

To: "Fatima" shes_all_fatima@yahoo.com.id
From: "Ruby"
Young_Ruby_M@allisonspringsms.edu
Date: October 28
Re: Re: Re: Re: Re: Re: Re: Re: Re: Re: Re: Re: Re: Re: Re: Re: Re: Re: Re: Re: Re: Your American Pen Pal, Friends Around the World Pen Pal Program

Dear Fatima,

I decided to ignore your advice. I think a friendship doesn't mean that you have to always agree with a person or always do what they say, do you?

I told Mrs. Morgan.

It was hard to get Mrs. Morgan alone. When she is at our house, she is always with my mom. I couldn't take an Uber to Mrs. Morgan's mansion, because she has five corgis, and I am allergic to dogs. A "corgi" is a "very fluffy dachshund." A "dachshund" is "a stretched out version of a regular dog." The queen of England also has corgis and that is why some people call Mrs. Morgan "the queen of Allison Springs."

I went to go see her at the *Allison Springs Cryer*, which is the newspaper she owns and which is three streets over from my mom's office. She has an office there, but a man with a mustache said, "Ha! Mrs. Morgan never comes into the office." I realized at that moment that I had a new pet peeve. My new pet peeve is people who say "ha" instead of "laughing."

I did not like his "tone." I answer the phones for my mom, and I would never say something like that to a client or to a stranger or to anyone else. You would think a grown-up man would understand how to greet people. I said, "Mrs. Morgan is your boss, and you shouldn't say things like that to strangers."

The man said, "You're not a stranger. You're the kid of Jane Young, the future mayor of our fine burg."

I said, "What you should say is, 'Mrs. Morgan isn't here right now. Would you like me to tell her you stopped by?'"

The man said, "Well, sure, I was going to get to that. Also, I'm not her assistant. I'm the editor in chief."

"But Mrs. Morgan is still your boss," I said.

"Technically, yes," he said. He reshaped the ends of his mustache.

"What's an editor in chief?" I said.

"It's someone who comes into the office every day," he said.

I do not like when someone answers a perfectly good question that way.

Finally, I sent Mrs. Morgan a text message (*We need to meet ASAP and IN PRIVATE. This Text Is for Your Eyes Only*), and she said we could meet at her office in an hour, which means the man with the mustache was wrong. Mrs. Morgan does sometimes go to her office.

At her office, Mrs. Morgan said, "What's so urgent, Rubes? What's so secret?"

I opened my mouth and then I closed it. It was hard to say the words.

Mrs. Morgan said, "I'm starving. Do you want to go to Clara's? Confessions go down better on a full stomach."

Clara's is my favorite restaurant, and Mrs. Morgan is one of the owners. My favorite thing to eat at Clara's is the corn chowder. My other favorite thing to eat at Clara's is the chicken pot pie. I was hungry, but I was also a little sick. I said, "I would rather do it right here."

"Do what?" Mrs. Morgan said. Her eyes grew very wide and interested. "What are we doing?"

I said, "I need to tell you something."

Mrs. Morgan said, "Yes, I gathered that."

Then, I said it. I told her that my mom was Aviva Grossman. I said, "I don't want you to lose all your money trying to get my mom elected when she is a liar."

Mrs. Morgan sighed and then her eyes grew soft and she smiled. "Ruby, I already know."

I said, "What?"

Mrs. Morgan said, "Your mom and I have worked together for years. We've planned more than a dozen fund-raisers. Do you think I wouldn't have looked up some information about her? It wouldn't be good business for me not to know. I'm very rich and the way a person stays very rich is by protecting her interests."

I said, "Why did you push her to run for mayor then?"

Mrs. Morgan said, "Because, my Ruby, I don't think any of what happened matters."

I said, "But, Mrs. Morgan! Have you read the blog?"

Mrs. Morgan said, "I have."

I said, "Won't the people of Allison Springs think you lied to them?"

Mrs. Morgan said, "We haven't, Ruby. Choosing what to reveal is not the same as lying. Your mom is Jane Young now—"

I interrupted her. "No, she's not."

"Yes, she is, Ruby. And that's all there is to it."

I said, "I don't think it's right that you should decide what the people get to know."

Mrs. Morgan said, "That's leadership, Ruby. But if people find out, your mom won't deny it, and we will deal with it then."

I said, "So Mom knows you know?"

Mrs. Morgan said, "Not in so many words. But we have an understanding."

I had to sit down on Mrs. Morgan's couch. I said, "I'm so confused."

Mrs. Morgan said, "You were brave to come to me. I know what a lot of guts it took." She put her hand on my hand.

I looked at her wrinkled fingers. She was wearing a ring in the shape of a leopard. He was gold and had green eyes made from emeralds, and he probably cost more money than I have in my entire bank account, and that is disgusting. I bet she didn't even like the ring that much when she bought it. I pulled my hand away. "DON'T TELL ME ABOUT GUTS!" I yelled. "I don't care what you think of me because you are a liar, just like my mom. I never want to see you again."

I ran out of the office, past that stupid editor in chief with the mustache, and I went to our town house, and now I'm writing this e-mail.

I'm so disappointed in Mrs. Morgan.

How can she NOT care that my mom was a totally other person? What is wrong with everyone?

Your Pen Pal,
Ruby

P.S. I went to bed without eating and now I am starving and the only thing I can think about is corn chowder. I probably should have gone to Clara's with Mrs. Morgan, since I am never eating there again in protest.

P.P.S. Mrs. Morgan is wrong. People have a "right to know" who they are voting for.

To: "Fatima" shes_all_fatima@yahoo.com.id
From: "Ruby"
Young_Ruby_M@allisonspringsms.edu
Date: October 31
Re: Re: Re: Re: Re: Re: Re: Re: Re: Re: Re: Re: Re: Re: Re: Re: Re:
Re: Re: Re: Re: Re: Re: Re: Your American Pen Pal, Friends Around the World Pen Pal Program

Dear Fatima,
I've come up with a plan of action. It's happening so don't try to "write" me out of it.

1. I am going to Miami to meet Congressman Aaron Levin. If he's my father, I want to see him and talk to him. If he's my father, he should know that he has a daughter. If he's my father, he probably won't mind if I move to Miami. There is NOTHING for me in Allison Springs.
2. I am going to leave an "anonymous" note for the *Allison Springs Cryer* about Aviva Grossman. Maybe Mrs. Morgan is right and it doesn't matter. I think VOTERS deserve to know.

I spent last night researching flights and hotels. It is a little bit harder to travel when you are thirteen.

Luckily, you can do almost anything with a smartphone and a business American Express card and a personal PayPal account and Google and a printer. For example, the airline website has their policies for "unaccompanied minors," and I had to write a note that said it was "OKAY for me to fly alone and not be met at the gate," and then I had to forge my mom's signature. I have been forging my mom's signature for years, but I have never forged it without her knowing about it.

For the record, I am not stealing money from my mom. I have been very carefully budgeting my trip so that I will not exceed the amount remaining in my bank account, which is $3,770.82.

I also wrote the note for the *Allison Springs Cryer*. I wrote many drafts, but I decided on:

To the Editor in Chief, Allison Springs Cryer—
GOOGLE "AVIVA GROSSMAN"
—A Concerned Citizen

I thought the part with "a concerned citizen" was very good.

I printed my note, and then I put it in a security envelope, and on the way to the airport, I had my airport taxi stop at the newspaper, and I put it in the mail slot there. I tried not to feel like a terrible person, though it was probably the WORST THING I HAVE EVER DONE.

But then I decided I didn't care. I felt cold as Maine in January. I felt cold as an ice cream brain freeze. Maybe I am a terrible person. Maybe I am a terrible person because that's what happens when you are LIED to your whole life.

The taxi driver said, "You're a little young to be traveling alone."

I said, "I'm older than I look."

"How old are you?"

I said, "I'm fifteen."

The taxi driver said, "I would have guessed eleven."

I said, "Most people think I look thirteen."

The taxi driver said, "Hmm. You're going to miss Halloween."

I said, "I'm not that into Halloween." But actually, I LOVE HAL-LOWEEN. I love dressing up in costumes, and every year my mom and I do a "joint costume." Last year, for example, my mom and I were Zombie Bride and Groom. And the year before that, we were Hot Dog and Bun. And the year before that, we were the people from *Portlandia*, which is our favorite show except for *The Walking Dead* and *House of Cards*. And the year before that, we were Zombie Bridesmaids. And the year before that, we were an iPhone and an iPad. And the year before that, we were Willy Wonka and the Golden Ticket. And the year before that, we were a waffle and a pat of butter. And I don't want to tell you any more costumes because I'm almost crying as I type this already. Anyway, with everything that has been happening, I totally forgot it was Halloween and I guess Mom had, too. Do they have Halloween in Indonesia?

"They still have Halloween where I'm going," I said to the taxi driver. "I am going to South Florida to see my father."

"Lucky you," he said. "Weather's a lot nicer there."

I said, "I like the weather in Maine."

"Even in winter?"

I said, "It's so pretty in winter. Everything is so bright it hurts your eyes. The air is so crisp, your throat feels like straws of ice. My mom . . . My mom's an event planner, and she says the winter weddings always have the best pictures."

"You're a Maine girl is what you are," he said.

I'm at the airport now. I got through security, no problem. My forgery worked just fine.

Hold on.

Mom just sent me a text: *ARE YOU ALREADY AT SCHOOL? WHAT ARE WE GOING TO DO FOR HALLOWEEN TONIGHT?!?!?*

I replied, *2 Late.*

She replied, *You can't be mad at me forever.*

I replied, *Teacher says to put my phone away.*

She replied, *I love you, Ruby.*

Then I blocked her number from being able to text me again. I'll unblock her when I get to the hotel in Miami. Once I'm there, she can't try to stop me from going. That is a "tautology," but it is also "true." A "tautology" is "when you say the same thing in different words." Ms. Reacher says they should be "avoided whenever possible."

The plane's about to take off, so I actually do have to shut off my phone.

Don't worry if you don't hear from me for a while.

Thank you for trying to help me and for listening to me. I've learned so much about Muslim people from Indonesia, and I hope you've learned something about nonpracticing Jewish people from Maine. Actually, I don't know that I would make a good "sample." Maybe you're not a good "sample" either. Maybe it is silly to try to learn about cultures from "pen pals." All you can really learn about is the specific person you're writing to. I don't mean to sound down on the "pen pal" program. I've loved having you as my pen pal! I couldn't have asked for a better pen pal than You.

Love,
Your Meaning Twin,
Ruby

P.S. If you give me your address, I will send you an ACTUAL PAPER postcard from Miami Beach.

IV

Angel in the House

EMBETH

It had been folly to have an anniversary party a week before Aaron's reelection. When Aaron had suggested it a year earlier on their twenty-ninth wedding anniversary, Embeth had been in the middle of her second round of chemo and had spent most of the evening with her head over a toilet. "Next year will be different," Aaron said, lingering in the doorway, trying not to breathe too deeply. He was not the type of man to hold back your hair, but by God, he would bear witness to your suffering. He would try to cheer you, with promises of a party for *you* and not for donors. Had she ever once said she craved such an event? Her cancer had made him sentimental. That was the only explanation. No, he had always been sentimental. She had known well before she married him that sentimentality was his weakness. "Come on, Em. We deserve a bash for our thirtieth," he said. "We'll do it at the Breakers. We'll invite people we actually like for once. We won't give a darn who we offend."

I'm not going to be alive next year, Embeth thought. "We can't have a party in November," she said. "You'll be campaigning." Embeth retched over the toilet and nothing came out. Worse than throwing up was *not* throwing up.

"I won't be," Aaron said. "I mean, I will be, but who cares? I've been a congressman for ten terms. If they don't want to reelect me because I take a night off for our thirtieth anniversary, screw the goddamn people. I'm going to do this, Em. I don't care what you say. I'm texting Jorge right now to clear the schedule."

He must have really thought she was going to die.

But here she was, a year later, alive. Frizzy hair, fuzzy brain, scarred chest, beating, beating, dumbly animal beating heart, alive, alive.

It was 4:55 a.m., and Aaron was wearing a suit and no tie. He had to fly to D.C. for the day. He would be back for the party at 8:00 p.m. The trip could not be avoided. His opponent, Marta Villanueva—blond, boobs, Republican—was putting up a bigger fight than anyone had anticipated based on the size of her coffers (not a euphemism for those boobs), and he couldn't afford to miss the vote that was happening in the House. Why in God's name the House had scheduled such an important vote days before an election he did not know. The optics were impossible. Not just for him, but for everyone who was up for reelection. What an altogether, unprecedentedly lousy year this had been. He was sorry to leave the last minute preparations to Embeth. He was sorry to leave her, on this, their thirtieth anniversary. Thirty years! Can you imagine? They must have been babies. They must have not even been born yet. He kissed her on the head.

"Go," she said. "Godspeed. Everything's planned. There's not much to do anyway. Nothing I can't easily do myself."

"You're an angel," he said. "I'm so lucky," he said. "I love you," he said. "Happy anniversary," he said.

She offered to drive him to the airport, but he said she should stay in bed. He had already called a car anyway.

Embeth rolled over in bed and she tried to go back to sleep, but sleep would not come.

If he was going to wake her, she might as well have driven him to the airport. She did not sleep well since the cancer. She was lucky to get three hours a night. In the daytime, she was exhausted.

Embeth closed her eyes.

She had almost drifted off to somewhere near sleep when she heard the flutter of wings, like cards being shuffled.

She opened her eyes.

An emerald parrot with a crimson head flew straight at her and just as its hooked beak was about to hit her in the forehead, the bird alighted on the pasture where her breasts used to be.

"Señora, señora," the parrot said. "Wake up, wake up."

Embeth said she needed to sleep, but the parrot knew she wasn't sleeping. She rolled onto her side and the parrot repositioned himself so that he was sitting on her waist.

"Much to do, much to do," the parrot said.

"Scat, El Meté," Embeth said. She did not know how the parrot had gotten this name or what it even meant. Was it Spanish? Why hadn't she ever learned Spanish? God knows, it would have come in handier as a politician's wife in Florida than three years of bloody high school Latin had. She was not even sure that El Meté was a he. Her eyes still closed, Embeth swatted at the air, making a windmill with her arm. The parrot flew to the windowsill. "If I don't get some sleep, I'll be useless today. And I need to be sharp."

"El Meté help. El Meté help."

"You can't help," Embeth said. "You can help by going away. You can help by letting me get some effing rest."

The parrot flew over to Aaron's nightstand, where he began grooming his feathers. The process was a reasonably quiet one, but it was too late. Embeth was awake. To pretend to sleep was more tiring than to resign herself to the day.

Embeth got out of bed, and she washed her hair in the shower, and when she got out of the shower, the parrot was perched on the towel rack.

"I'd love it if you gave me a little personal space," Embeth said.

El Meté flew onto her head and pecked her with his pink beak. "Moisturize! Moisturize!"

SHE WENT TO the kitchen to pour herself some coffee. She was meant to have given up coffee, but what was the point of living without coffee? Living, it seemed to her, was the acquiring of bad habits. Dying, the process of rescinding them. Death was the land without habits. Without coffee.

El Meté alit on her shoulder. "I don't want you to come with me today," Embeth said.

"El Meté come. El Meté come."

"Seriously, I have to go to the doctor, the salon, the dry cleaner, the florist, the seamstress, the jeweler, and I have to speak at that stupid lunch, and there's the party—"

"Party! Party!"

"I don't even like parties—"

"Party! Party!"

"You cannot come to the party," Embeth said.

"Party! Party!"

"You can be incredibly thick, El Meté. And repetitive. And also, you think you're light but you're enormously heavy on my shoulder. I think you're gaining weight. Your claws dig into me now. You're worse than a bra strap. You're worse than a Birkin bag. I'm going to need to get a chiropractor."

Margarita the part-time housekeeper came into the kitchen,

carrying a large box. "Ms. Levin, good morning! Happy anniversary! This was on the steps." Margarita set the box on the counter.

Embeth looked at the return address. It was from her most faithful friend, Shipment Fulfillment Center. Embeth got a chef's knife and opened it. Inside the box, entombed in an infinity of bubble wrap, was a tacky-looking statue. The statue was about the size of a large penis and made from resin and garishly hued like a black-and-white movie that had been colorized. A winged, rosy man wore a pink toga and carried a bronze Star of David, like a shield. He must have been some kind of Jewish angel. Were there Jewish angels? Yes, of course there were. There were angels in the Old Testament, so there must be Jewish angels. Wasn't everyone in the Old Testament Jewish? She turned the base over. An accompanying certificate of authenticity indicated that this was Mattatron, which sounded like the name of a robot. Who would have sent her such an object? Embeth was not the type of woman to whom anyone would send an angel.

"Oh, very nice," Margarita said. Margarita appreciated kitsch. Her look was a bit kitsch, too. She wore her glossy black hair like a burlesque queen. She paraded around the kitchen in shoes with cherries on them, her young breasts pushed up to her chin. Jorge, who was Aaron's right hand, had taken one look at Margarita and said, "Are you sure you want this in your house?"

"What do you mean?" Embeth had asked.

"I mean, she looks like T-R-O-U-B-L-E."

"Aaron's old. I'm old," Embeth had said. "I'm home more than he is, and it's sexist not to hire someone because she's cute. She's very smart, too. She's getting an MFA in sculpture."

"Trouble," Jorge had repeated.

"Would you like it?" Embeth said now to Margarita as she dug through the bubble wrap for a note. She supposed people sent her this kind of crap because they thought the cancer had made her soft.

"I couldn't," Margarita said. "The angel is meant for you."

"Or perhaps it was meant for me *to give* to you," Embeth suggested.

"It is bad luck to take another woman's angel," Margarita said.

"If you don't give him a home, he's going in the trash," Embeth said.

"It is bad luck to throw your angel in the trash."

"What isn't bad luck?" Embeth said. She picked the angel up by the head. "I don't believe in bad luck." She opened the trash can and then paused. "Is he recyclable, do you think?"

"Don't do that," Margarita said. "Maybe he'll grow on you?"

"He won't."

"Maybe the congressman?"

"Aaron would loathe this."

"Fine," Margarita said. "Give him to me." She took the angel and set him by her purse.

"Are you going to be able to come to the party tonight?" Embeth asked.

"Yes," Margarita said. "Of course I am, Ms. Levin. I would not miss it! I sewed my dress myself. It is a red corset on top and a black hoop skirt on the bottom, and I will wear small black lace gloves without fingertips, and my hair up, pulled back tight, and a small veil over my face. It will be so dramatic."

"Sounds it," Embeth said. "You can wear it again to my funeral."

"Do not be morbid, Ms. Levin. The dress is very festive."

"Margarita, what does *meté* mean in Spanish?"

"A child having a tantrum might yell it to get someone to put something down. *Meté! Meté!*" Margarita said.

"But what if there's an *el* in front of it? *El Meté.* Does that make a difference?"

"Ah," Margarita said. "Then, it means nothing at all."

. . .

THE RECEPTIONIST APOLOGIZED. The doctor was running behind schedule. Behind schedule was the schedule, Embeth thought.

Embeth took out her phone and searched for mentions of Aaron's congressional race online. She decided she wouldn't care if he lost. Despite what people said about her—that she was the ambitious one, that without her, he would most certainly be a high school English teacher, not that there's anything wrong with that—she would almost welcome his defeat.

"Embeth Levin, is that you?"

She turned, and it was Allegra. Allegra was so old. She looked like she was in her late forties. Oh God, Embeth thought, she doesn't look old. She *is* old. She is in her late forties, because I'm in my late fifties. Allegra had worked with Embeth, back when Embeth had worked for the hospital. They had been so close. People had jokingly referred to them as "work wives."

"Allegra, it's been too long," Embeth said.

Allegra kissed her on the cheek. "I hope you're well."

"I was sick last year, but I'm better now," Embeth said. "I'm only here for a checkup."

"Well . . . ," Allegra said. "Well, you look good."

"Don't lie. I look like shit," Embeth said.

"You do look good . . . A little tired maybe. I hate when people say I look tired."

"We're having an anniversary party tonight," Embeth said. "And after this, I'm going to the salon. I've got to figure out something with these useless feathers."

"I like your hair. It's very chic," Allegra said. "By the way, I know about the party. I mean, I'm coming to it," Allegra said.

"Why?" Embeth said without thinking.

"Well, I was invited," Allegra said. "I assumed by you?"

I should goddamn remember a thing like that, Embeth thought.

"Of course," Embeth said. "Of course." What state of mind must she have been in to invite Allegra?

"You sound surprised."

"I'm not. I'm . . ." The truth was, she couldn't remember anything lately. Probably chemo brain.

"Mrs. Levin," the receptionist called.

"I was happy to get the invitation," Allegra said. "Surprised, but happy. But if you don't want me to come . . . If it was some sort of accident, I mean."

"I *do* want you to come." Embeth squeezed Allegra's hand. The hand was cool and soft, and Allegra smelled of frangipani and something spicier and earthier, like sandalwood or pure cocoa powder. "Sometimes, my brain works better when I'm barely thinking."

Allegra smiled. "I don't know what that means."

"I want us to have an impossibly long lunch next week," Embeth said. "Can we promise to do that?"

"I wish I'd known you were ill," Allegra said.

"I wasn't any fun to be with," Embeth said.

"Still, I would have done something . . ."

What would she have done? Walked a 5K? Worn a ribbon? Brought chicken soup for Embeth to throw up? Posted a sympathetic tweet? "Why are you wearing cat ears?" Embeth asked. "Am I imagining them, or are you actually wearing cat ears?"

"Oh!" Allegra laughed coyly, a bit embarrassed, and patted down the hair beneath the black cat ear headband. "It's my costume. Yesterday was Halloween."

"I forgot," Embeth said.

"But the party at Emory's school is this morning. Something to do with testing. I'm in charge of punch. One of the moms sent me a text last night, *Don't put nuts in the punch!* Who puts nuts in punch? I'm the oldest mom there, and they think I'm a flake."

"Mrs. Levin!" the receptionist repeated.

"The ears suit you," Embeth said as she went through the doors into the doctor's office.

"How's Embeth today?" the doctor asked. English was not his first language, and he seemed frightened of pronouns.

"Embeth has found a new lump," she said brightly.

ON THE WAY out of the doctor's office, Embeth felt stupidly cheerful. The promise of future tests! The promise of another round of chemo! The promise of death! These were not reasons to be cheered, and yet, cheered she was.

It was certainly not the promise of the evening's festivities.

Perhaps it was the relief of revelation. When she'd found the knot in the shower, she had felt like a failure, though she knew that was a trick of her brain, pure foolishness. It was not her fault that her body had continued to grow anomalous clusters of cells. Embeth had been raised to believe that everything was her fault. She was enormously powerful and couldn't do anything right. Embeth, Creator of Anomalous Clusters. Embeth, Destroyer of Worlds.

Perhaps her cheerfulness was a result of the day itself. It was a dry, cool morning after what had been a dry, cool October. The late-season hurricanes did not arrive. Her hair, what there was of it, obeyed more than it usually did.

Perhaps it was seeing Allegra.

If *It* wasn't back, if Embeth had but time, she would have that lunch with Allegra, and then she would have another lunch with Allegra, and at that second lunch, when everyone was more relaxed, they would order two desserts and split them and let their fork tines intertwine and lightly clang against each other and they'd eat those desserts down to the last crumb, and then Embeth would say to the waiter, *Yes, actually, I will have an espresso*, and Allegra would suggest they take a yoga class together ("It's hatha, Em; anyone can do it"), and at yoga, one of them would suggest starting a book club, and Embeth would somehow organize her life so that she might see Allegra every, every day until one or both of them were dead.

Why had Allegra been at Dr. Hui's office? She should have asked. How self-centered she was. She sometimes forgot that she was not the only person in the world with cancer. Conversely, she often forgot that everyone in the world did not have cancer.

She had convinced El Meté to wait near the car—one couldn't bring fowl to the doctor's. El Meté perched on the hood of her Tesla. His nails clicked happily against the car's paint job. He flew up and landed on Embeth's shoulder. "The blouse is silk," she said. "Be gentle."

"Gentle! Gentle!" he said. "Good night! Good night!"

Embeth got into her car, and her cell phone rang, and she was careful to use the speaker, because the last thing you wanted was cancer of the brain on top of all the other cancers you already had.

It was Tasha, one of Aaron's assistants in Miami. Tasha was new. She said they had an emergency at the office. Aaron's assistants were always given to dramatics, though. The new ones especially. They didn't have the experience to separate a situation from an emergency, a crisis from a tragedy. A week before an election, what wasn't an emergency? "Can't Jorge deal with it?" Embeth said. "I'm pretty booked with the party tonight. Why in God's name we are having this ridiculous party . . ." Embeth performed an apologetic laugh.

Tasha said, "Maybe emergency is the wrong word. I'd call it a situation."

"Fine," said Embeth impatiently. "I trust Jorge to deal with all situations."

"Fine! Very fine!" said El Meté.

"Shh!" said Embeth.

"Oh, I'm sorry," Tasha said.

"No, not you. I was talking to someone else," Embeth said. "Call Jorge."

"Okay. The thing is . . ." Tasha lowered her voice, and Embeth could not hear what she said. She asked her to say it louder. "It's a girl."

"What?"

"There's a girl here," Tasha said. "She says she's Aaron's daughter," she whispered.

"Daughter! Daughter!" said El Meté.

"That's not possible," Embeth said. "We only have sons."

"I'm looking at her. She's about four feet eleven inches tall and she has braces and curly hair. I'd guess she's about eleven or twelve—"

"No, Tasha, I do not need you to describe a girl for me. I know perfectly well what a girl looks like, having been one myself, though you probably find that hard to believe, and I do not dispute that you are looking at a girl! The point is, you are not looking at Aaron's daughter because my husband and I only have sons," Embeth said.

"Sons! Sons!" said El Meté.

"Would you kindly shut up?" said Embeth.

"I wasn't talking," said Tasha.

"Not you. Someone else. Call Jorge and tell him that there's some crazy kid at the office, and he'll tell you what to do. I don't have time for crazy people today."

"Okay," said Tasha. "I can do that. But one other thing—"

"*What?*"

"She says her last name is Grossman."

How Embeth loathed that name! "Gross," she said.

"No, Gross*man*," said Tasha.

"I heard you the first time." She would have loved to go the whole rest of her life without ever having to hear that name again.

"The election's next week," Tasha continued.

"Yes, Tasha, I am aware," Embeth said.

"I know you're aware," Tasha said. "I meant, there are a lot of people in the office and a lot of people coming to the office today.

Campaign staff. Media. It might be a good idea to move her to a different location while things sort themselves out. Jorge's in D.C. with the congressman. I can't get either of them on the phone. I didn't want to text it, in case someone saw. There might not be time for me to reach him. I don't want to cause any trouble."

And what if there were trouble? What if Embeth didn't come? What if Embeth just hung up the phone and went to the salon and continued on with her day as she had planned? What if Embeth didn't intervene and fix things for Aaron? How irritating that people always assumed that Embeth was the person to call when Aaron had caused a crisis. Weren't there some wives who were protected from the truth at all costs? Why did no one ever think that Embeth was that kind of wife? The kind of wife who should be left in the dark when it came to her husband's shortcomings?

Once, many years ago, Embeth hadn't intervened, and look how that had worked out.

"Fine," Embeth said. "I'll come get her."

"What should I do with her in the meantime?"

"Stick her in a broom closet! I don't really care."

"Broom! Broom!" said El Meté.

"Shut it," Embeth whispered.

"You want me to shut the door of the broom closet?" Tasha asked.

"I wasn't talking to you," Embeth said.

"Who *are* you talking to?" Tasha said. "I'm sorry. It's none of my business."

Indeed, it was not her business. "I'm with El . . . ," Embeth said. "Friend."

"Friend? Friend?" said El Meté.

"Yes, I'd call us friends," Embeth said.

The bird nuzzled the nook of Embeth's neck and cooed.

"I don't even know if we have a broom closet, Mrs. Levin," said Tasha.

"Tasha, honestly! In this world, to be overly literal is a profound weakness. It doesn't have to be a broom closet. Just put her somewhere out of the way until I get there. It could be a basement. It could be the roof. It could be a neglected cubicle. The location of your motherfucking choosing!" Embeth hung up the phone. This girl was hopeless.

"Hopeless," said El Meté.

Before Embeth drove to the office, she looked in her phone for Rachel Grossman's number. Rachel Grossman, otherwise known as the Worst Neighbor Ever. Yes, this—and who knew what this was?— *this* should definitely be Rachel Grossman's problem, not Embeth's.

Embeth dialed the number, but the number no longer worked. She started the car.

AT THE OFFICE, phones rang. Some rings were answered enthusiastically; some rings had been ignored for weeks and would always be ignored. A girl in a dress composed a tweet, and a girl in a cheaper version of the same dress wrote yet another memo—"Re: pros and cons of Snapchat for incumbent political candidates"— concluding that at this stage in the campaign it was too late for the congressman to join. Everyone was being careful about what they put in e-mail or in texts because you never knew who was watching/ hacking, and you could mean something to be funny, but nothing was funny without context, nuance, and, oh God, the vagaries of tone. Still, a text was preferable to an e-mail. An e-mail was preferable to a phone call. A phone call was preferable to a sit-down. A sit-down was to be avoided at all costs. But if you had to sit down, drinks were better than lunch was better than dinner. Everyone hated his or her phone and couldn't imagine functioning without it. A girl in jeans shot a nasty look at the girls in dresses and told a boy in jeans that the girls in dresses didn't really do anything important. (But everyone knew the girls in dresses ran the show.) A girl in a skirt and a boy in a tracksuit discussed whether Up Ticket would help Down Ticket this year. Someone tossed an old imitation Nerf football with LEVIN 2006 on the side, and someone yelled, "Quiet down, the vote's on C-SPAN!" and someone else yelled, "No one cares!" and someone else yelled, "I care!" Two boys in blazers took lunch orders, and a girl in a dress said she wouldn't take coffee orders so don't even think about asking. A boy in a tie revised his résumé (but everyone was always doing that), and a girl in a dress said, "Can someone please explain to the congressman again that you need to put a period at the beginning of a tweet that starts with an '@'?" and then she muttered something about "working with old people." A different girl in a dress sent an e-mail to someone she knew at CNN: "Out of curiosity, how does one become a surrogate?" A boy in a tie flirted with another boy in a tie, and a boy in khakis stole office supplies and told himself he was stocking his own eventual campaign larder. A girl in a dress cried on the phone to her mother and quietly moaned, "I have to stick it out or I won't get credit!" And everyone was very important, and very underappreciated, and very underpaid, and in the way of all campaign offices, very, very young.

Embeth had known prior versions of these boys and girls, though she did not know any of the current versions personally, and her arrival was not noticed. Through years of tepid celebrity, Embeth had learned the art of entering a room. When she wanted to be noticed, she was noticed. When she didn't want to be noticed, she almost never had to be. The trick was in looking as if she knew where she was going while putting out a benign and boring, if slightly unpleasant, energy. The trick could sometimes be her phone, her (and everyone else's) fortress of solitude, and a practiced absorption in it. The trick could involve an unpretentious hat, but never sunglasses. Whatever method she used, the older she got, the easier it was to flip that particular switch to the invisible setting. Someday soon, she supposed, the switch would stick there, and Embeth would never be seen again.

Embeth arrived at Tasha's desk, which was in a separate reception area outside her husband's personal office. Across from her desk sat the girl. She wore a seersucker blazer and blue jeans with cheerful designs painted on them (a rainbow, a heart, the sun, clouds), and a T-shirt that said, WOMEN'S RIGHTS ARE HUMAN RIGHTS, and pink running shoes. Her hair was frizzy with humidity and pulled into an awkward half ponytail. She had on circular frames, which emphasized the roundness of her face. Beneath those glasses were soft green eyes and Embeth could tell from looking in those eyes that school—nay, life—must be hard for her. She looked less guarded than was optimal for survival. She reminded Embeth of a turtle on its back, a porcupine born without quills. Either her mother had done a very good or a very bad job raising her. Very good, because the girl did not look as if she cared what anyone thought of her. Very bad, because the mother had not prepared her for the world. To Embeth's eye, yes, the girl did resemble Aaron—the curly hair, the light eyes, though Aaron's were more blue than green. But then again, Aviva Grossman's features were quite similar to Aaron's, so who was to say? What the girl mainly looked was Jewish, Embeth supposed. The girl looked peaceful and nerdy. She had on headphones and was reading something intently on a tablet.

If she was Aaron's daughter, it would be completely out of character for Aviva Grossman to have kept such a secret for so long. That girl was the most indiscreet person Embeth had ever encountered. Have an affair with my husband, if you must, but don't write about it on the Internet! Certainly don't write about having anal sex with him, for the love of God. Even if you changed the names, it was only a matter of time.

"Mrs. Levin," Tasha said, jumping out of her desk chair. "I told them to tell me when you were coming up."

"I'm slippery," Embeth said.

"That's her," Tasha said.

"Yes, I assumed a second girl hadn't shown up," Embeth said.

"I couldn't find a closet, so I left her here," Tasha said.

"I'm going to speak to her. Would you give us a moment? And Tasha, please. I'm counting on you not to breathe a word of this to anyone."

Tasha left the office, and Embeth sat on the love seat next to the girl.

"We're wearing the same sneakers," Embeth said.

The girl took off her headphones. "What?" she said.

"We're wearing the same sneakers," Embeth said.

"Yours are black," she said. "Mine are the pink ones, which I had to wait two extra weeks to get. Some people I know don't like pink."

"It's not my favorite color," Embeth admitted. She would love to die without ever having to see another pink ribbon for breast cancer, for instance.

"Me neither," she said. "It's my *second* favorite color. Mrs. Morgan says that not liking pink is a way of saying you don't like women. Because women are so associated with pink."

"I see Mrs. Morgan's point," Embeth said. "But, it's worth remembering that pink is forced on women from a young age—the ubiquity of pink for girls and blue for boys in baby stores, for example. So to resist the wearing of pink is to reject old-fashioned ideas about what it means to be a woman."

"Hmm," the girl said. "But it's not pink's fault that people do that. And no one feels about blue the same way they do about pink. And the blue is forced on the boys as much as the pink is forced on the girls, so I think the issue is complicated. I think the issue is nuanced, which is one of my new favorite words. Nuanced means—"

"I'm Embeth," Embeth managed to interject. "Embeth," she repeated. "The congressman's wife."

"I know. I googled the congressman. I'm Ruby. I'm here to meet the congressman, but Tasha told you that when she called. Sorry, I heard her side. And I'm also sorry I didn't make an appointment," she said.

"Yes, you probably should have made an appointment, but we are where we are. Let us not be Lot's wife, looking back toward Sodom."

"You're hilarious," Ruby said.

This comment momentarily disarmed Embeth. She hadn't meant to be funny, and also, no one had ever thought Embeth was hilarious. Occasionally, Embeth's dry wit was noted. "I can possibly arrange a meeting for you with the congressman, but you need to answer a few questions first."

Ruby nodded.

"Your mother is Aviva?" Embeth asked.

"Yes. She calls herself Jane now," Ruby said.

"Why does she do that?" Embeth said.

"Because she's a liar," Ruby said.

Embeth had to admit that the girl had an appealing directness.

"Because she's ashamed of herself, I think," Ruby said in a gentler tone. "And because she's scared people will judge her because of what she did with your husb—— congressman."

"She's probably right. Why are you here?" Embeth said.

"I want to meet my father. I'm not sure if the congressman is him, but I want to know if he is," Ruby said.

"And no one's encouraged you to come here this week, of all weeks?"

"I don't know what you mean," Ruby said.

"For instance, your mother? Might she have put you up to this?"

"My mom doesn't know where I am," Ruby said. "I left her a note."

"You seem rather young to travel alone," Embeth said.

"I am, but I'm very mature for my age. I've always had a lot of responsibility. My mom is an event planner, and I've been working for her for years."

Embeth sighed. "You seem like a good person, Ruby—"

"I'm not," Ruby said. "I've done terrible things."

Embeth paused. "What have you done?"

"I don't want to say. It wasn't illegal, but it was possibly immoral," Ruby said. "Maybe it wasn't immoral, but it was definitely disloyal. Maybe—"

"Never mind, this seems terribly complicated," said Embeth. "Let's put a pin in that. You must admit, the timing of your visit is somewhat suspicious. Do you know what an election is?"

"Yes, of course I do," Ruby said.

Embeth could tell she had insulted her. In her defense, it was difficult to know what any given child knew. "Congressman Levin is up for reelection next week, and your presence could be less than ideal for him. Whether you turn out to be the congressman's daughter or not, there are many people who would love to dredge up the ancient scandal between him and your mother. I don't know how much you know about that?"

Ruby averted her eyes.

"Well, yes. Well, my point is it could be very bad for the congressman the week before an election."

Ruby considered this. She took off her glasses and she wiped them on her T-shirt. "It's so hot here," she said. "My hair has never in my whole life been this frizzy."

"Tell me about it," said Embeth. "This can't be your first time in Florida?"

"It is," Ruby said. "We live in Maine, which is the Pine Tree State."

Maine. For whatever reason, the thought of Aviva Grossman in Maine amused Embeth. Damned to eternal winter.

"Did you have cancer?" Ruby asked casually.

"Why? Do I look like I have cancer?"

"My mom does a lot of benefits for people with cancer. You look like you have cancer, or you had cancer, I guess. You don't have any eyebrows," said Ruby. "You might have overplucked them. That sometimes happens with brides."

"No, I'm not a bride. I haven't been a bride for a very long time. I do have cancer," Embeth said. "Usually I draw my brows on, if I think of it. They say they'll grow back, but mine seem determined not to."

"It's weird that you call your husband 'the congressman,'" Ruby said.

"It probably is," Embeth said. "But I've been doing it so long, I don't even know I'm doing it. He is my husband, but he is also the representative for my district. So he is actually my congressman and my husband." There had been times when Aaron had let her down as a husband, but she could honestly say he had never let her down as a congressman. As a politician, he was honest and he never made promises he couldn't keep.

"I never thought about it that way," said Ruby. "Have you voted for him every time he ran?"

"Yes," said Embeth.

"Would you ever not vote for him?"

"Probably not," said Embeth. "We feel the same way on all of the most important issues, and I believe in his judgment and his vision."

"What do you mean by 'judgment'?"

What *did* Embeth mean by 'judgment'? She had been saying the same lines for so long she barely knew what she meant. "He's careful about who he takes money from, and he cares about his constituents more than his donors, and he cares about his conscience even more than his constituents. This is to say, he cares about doing the right thing more than getting elected. That's what I mean by judgment."

Ruby nodded slowly, but she did not look convinced.

Embeth tried to read Ruby's expression. She imagined Ruby was thinking about Aaron's judgment when it came to sleeping with young women like Ruby's own mother. Embeth's special power was what Jorge referred to as "negative empathy"—she could always imagine the worst thing a person might be thinking.

Ruby put her iPad in her backpack. "You asked me if I knew what an election was. I do. I mean, I have for years. Since I was little. My mom took me to Washington, D.C., to see Barack Obama get sworn in. I know about elections. It's not the reason I'm here, but it is the reason I found out about the congressman."

Embeth asked her to clarify.

"My mom's running for mayor of Allison Springs. That's my town. It was named for Captain Eliezer Allison, who was a great captain but a bad husband and father. Isn't it interesting how people can be good at some things and bad at others?"

"So, how did you find out about the congressman?" Embeth tried to conceal her impatience.

"My mom is running against Wes West, who is a Realtor. Wes West whispered 'Aviva' at the debate, and that made me google some things, and that's when I decided to go to Miami."

"Wes West sounds like a douchebag," Embeth said.

Ruby laughed. "Mrs. Morgan says people shouldn't use 'douchebag' in a negative way, because it turns a feminine hygiene product into a bad word. She says there's nothing wrong with a douchebag except that douching itself creates an unhealthy climate for a vagina."

"Who's Mrs. Morgan?" The alarm on Embeth's phone went off. She dug through her purse to find it.

"Mrs. Morgan is a woman who is now my enemy. Why do you think Wes West is a douchebag?" Ruby asked.

"When the congressman and I are running against someone, we decide what we're going to use against him or her, though usually it's a him, and what we aren't. We never *half* use a thing, because that's cheap. That's what Wes West did when he whispered 'Aviva.' He did it to bother her, to silence her in the moment. And that shows a weak and undisciplined candidate who probably wouldn't be a good mayor, even of some podunk town like Allison Springs, no offense." Embeth silenced her phone. "Damn it," she said. "I have to go speak at this luncheon thing in about twenty minutes. And Aaron's in D.C. right now."

The girl's face looked hopeless. "I should have thought of that."

"He'll be back tonight. It isn't as bad as all of that, but I'm not sure what to do with you in the meantime."

Ruby picked at a string on her cuff. "I could come with you?"

"It's going to be intensely boring," said Embeth.

"I know. I go to a lot of luncheons. The bread is always stale, but the salad is sometimes edible. The meal is usually pretty bad, except for dessert. A good dessert is meant to trick you into forgetting about the bad meal that came before."

"Is that something your mom taught you?"

Ruby shrugged.

"I wish I didn't have to go," Embeth said.

"What would you do if you could skip it?" Ruby asked.

"I'd go to the movies," Embeth said. "I'd buy a huge tub of popcorn, and I'd call my friend, Allegra, and after the trailers, I'd fall asleep. I love sleeping at the movies, and I haven't slept much for months. But that is not going to happen. Okay, say you come to the lunch. What if someone asks who you are?"

"I'll say I'm shadowing you for the Future Girls' Leadership Initiative."

"That was a most deft improvisation, Ruby," said Embeth. "Have you considered a career in politics?"

"No," said Ruby. "I don't think I'd be good at it. People don't tend to like me. People my own age, I mean."

"People don't tend to like me either," said Embeth. "I like you, though. I am finding you very likable, and we've only just met, and trust me, I have many reasons not to like you, which must mean you are remarkably likable. Okay, you're coming with me, but we need to call someone first. Your family will want to know you aren't dead. Do you have your grandmother's number? She lives pretty near here, I think."

Ruby said she didn't know her grandmother.

"You don't know Rachel Grossman?"

Ruby shook her head. "I don't know any of the Grossmans. Grossmen. You're not going to call my mom, are you?"

"Are you kidding me? Your mom is about the last person in the world I would ever want to call," Embeth said.

Embeth left a note on Tasha's desk, asking her to please track down a number for Rachel Grossman.

IN THE PARKING lot of the Allen Library, Embeth hastily drew on eyebrows with a pencil.

"One of them's a little high," said Ruby.

"Shut up, El Meté," said Embeth.

"Sorry," said Ruby. "Just trying to help."

"Oh jeez," said Embeth. "Not you. I thought you were someone else."

"Someone called El Meté," Ruby said. "I like that name. Is it Spanish? I'm interested in languages. I have a pen pal from Indonesia."

Embeth rubbed out and redrew her left eyebrow. "Is this better?"

Ruby looked at her. "It is." Ruby looked at her some more. "It looks like you are raising one eyebrow, as if you are slightly disapproving of something."

"Sounds about right," said Embeth. "Let's go in."

"Is your friend a boy? 'El' means masculine, usually."

"I'm not sure," Embeth said.

"My teacher at school is like that," said Ruby.

"Like what?" Embeth said.

"Transgendered," said Ruby.

"No, it's not like that," said Embeth. "My friend is a parrot."

"Oh, wow, you have a pet parrot! Can I meet him?"

At that point, they had reached the entrance, and Jeanne from Embeth's alumni association approached them. "Mrs. Levin, greetings! Thank you so much for agreeing to do this!" Alumna Jeanne called.

Jeanne, in her shapeless black cardigan and shapeless black dress, the shapelessness providing a kind of bulwark. Jeanne, her hair long and unkempt and undyed and washed in coconut oil. Jeanne, in sensible Swedish clogs. Jeanne, who smelled like expensive soap but never used perfume. Jeanne, who splurged on quality glasses and overpriced trips with her alumni association. Jeanne, who had two whippets or perhaps two cats or perhaps raised turtles. Jeanne, who only bought fair trade chocolate. Jeanne, who belonged to a book club where no one ever finished the book. Jeanne, whose primary workout was swimming. Jeanne, who didn't wear jeans, just loose organic cotton pants. Jeanne, who admired the congressman but would never quite forgive him for what he had done with that intern. Embeth had met many Jeannes. How she envied the Jeannes.

"Jeanne, wonderful to see you again!" It was always better to assume you had met someone before, though, in fact, Embeth had no specific recollection of having met this particular Jeanne. For whatever reason, it gave less offense to be remembered falsely than to be forgotten.

"What a wonderful day that was," Jeanne said.

"Wonderful, wonderful," Embeth agreed.

"The weather!" Jeanne said.

"The weather!" Embeth said, with a laugh.

"The weather!" Ruby repeated, and then she threw her hand over her mouth. "Sorry," Ruby said. "The way you guys were describing that day, I almost felt as if I had been there, too."

Alumna Jeanne looked over at Ruby. "And who are you?"

"She's my mentee in . . ." Embeth tried to remember it.

"Future Girls' Leadership Initiative," Ruby filled in.

"The FUGLI," Embeth added.

"Does that spell *fugly*?" Alumna Jeanne asked. "That seems unfortunate."

"Well, we don't say it that way. Technically, it's the FGLI," Ruby explained. "But at FGLI, our motto is 'Embrace the fugly.' For too long, the threat of being called ugly has been used to silence and disempower women. By embracing the fugly, we say we don't care if you think we're attractive. We're powerful and we're smart and that's what matters."

Ruby stuck out her hand, like a pro, and Alumna Jeanne shook it.

"This is a very impressive young woman," Alumna Jeanne said.

WHAT AN HONOR *to be here with you this afternoon* . . .

With few alterations, Embeth's speech was the same one she had given for the last fifteen years. She could do it without notes. She could do it in downward-facing dog. She could do it while making love to her husband, though that happened pretty rarely. She was called upon to give the speech far more often than she was called upon to make love to Aaron.

. . . never occurred to me not to work. My father was the Sturgeon King of Millburn, New Jersey. My mother built bridges. Literally. She was a civil engineer.

[Pause for laughter.]

She savored the quiet time alone at the podium. Alone, but with people. She looked into the audience, a sea of soft, shapeless neutrals, and she wondered how many of those women loved their husbands as much as she loved Aaron. Yes, the irony to end all ironies! Embeth *loved* Aaron.

. . . I am proud that I was a working mother. It's interesting, that term, "working mother." Working becomes the adjective; mother, the noun. We don't say "worker-mother," and we certain don't say

"mothering worker" . . . *People expect you to put the emphasis on the mother part at the expense of the worker part. I was proud of my children, but I was equally proud of my work . . .*

How many people had called it a "political marriage" over the years? Yes, it was a political marriage, but that didn't mean she didn't love him. She wondered how many of them had been cheated on. She wondered how many of them had forgiven their husbands after they were cheated on.

. . . the first topic that comes to mind is often a woman's right to choose or sexual assault, but I believe the most important women's issue is the wage gap. I believe this is the root issue from which all other inequalities stem . . .

The truth was, being cheated on was not that bad. It was being cheated on *in public* that was hard. It was wearing the ill-fitting shroud of the wronged woman. It was standing next to him, meekly, when he apologized. It was figuring out where to cast your gaze, and choosing the right suit jacket. What suit jacket would say "supportive," "feminist," "unbroken," "optimistic"? What one effing suit jacket could possibly accomplish that? She still, fifteen years later, wondered if they judged her for staying with him after Avivagate.

. . . But you all know the statistics . . .

She wondered if the summer-weight cashmere sweater she had been eyeing at J.Crew was still on sale.

She wondered if her eyebrows were sweating off.

She wondered what to do about Ruby.

. . . proud we have sons. And they are exceptional, strapping young men in every way. Not that I'm biased. [Pause for laughter.] But do I think they deserve twenty percent more money than a comparably qualified young woman? I do not!

She liked the girl, but she knew that she could not have Ruby meet Aaron today, or this week, or this month. Aaron needed to keep his head in the game. The best thing to do would be to dispatch the girl to her grandmother's, that idiot Rachel Grossman. With any luck, Tasha would have found her number by now.

. . . True conviction is believing something to be right even after it becomes disadvantageous to you. This is what I tell my sons. This is what . . .

Also, Aviva Grossman was running for mayor? In a way, Embeth had to admire the girl's chutzpah. She hadn't thought about her in years, not in a future way.

. . . as a mother, my greatest accomplishment will be to have raised sons who are feminists . . .

When she did think of her, Aviva was locked in a perpetual 2001. Twenty-two years old and slutty and needy forever. She had not conceived of her as a mother, let alone as a candidate for public office.

. . . I was a woman before I was a mother. I was a feminist before I was a politician's wife. I was . . .

She had known that girl was trouble from the first time she had laid eyes on her. The first thing Embeth remembered was her mouth. The big mouth, with the slight pout. The red punch of lipstick. She was holding a can of Diet Coke, lipstick traces around the tab. The way those curves taxed the seams of that good-quality, sales-rack suit. Many of the interns dressed like that, though. Their professional wardrobes came from big sisters, mothers, friends, neighbors, and the fit betrayed these origins.

That couldn't have been the first time she saw her, though. They'd been neighbors.

Applause.

Applause indicated the speech was over. Alumna Jeanne thanked Embeth and announced the start of a Q&A. Why had Embeth agreed to a Q&A? All she wanted was a nap.

A gray-haired woman in a shapeless gray cardigan and shapeless gray pants stood up. These clothes, Embeth thought. These women look like they are dressed for a funeral at an insane asylum. In fact, Embeth dressed this way, too.

The gray woman asked, "Listening to you talk, you're so intelligent. When are you going to run for office? Can't there be two politicians in a family?"

Embeth laughed her public laugh. Inside, a private joke: *There may already be two politicians in this family.*

Once upon a time, a question like that might have flattered her. A long time ago, she had harbored such ambitions. She burned with them. She had pushed Aaron forward and then resented him when he actually succeeded. As a politician's wife, though, she had had her fill of politics. But then, there was no worse job in politics than politician's wife. Literally, there was no job that paid less—which is to say, nada—and demanded more. At the peak of Avivagate, she'd once attended a women in politics panel on human trafficking, and they'd had a PowerPoint presentation with screening questions to determine if a person was being trafficked. The questions were: (1) Are you paid for your work? (2) Are you never alone? (3) Do other people answer questions for you? (4) Can you leave your house when you want? Et cetera. Based on her answers, Embeth had determined that she was a likely victim of human trafficking.

"I'm not Hillary Clinton," she told the crowd. "I don't have the stomach for another election. I don't have the desire to travel. These days, my interests don't extend much past leaving my house. I'll be voting for her, by the way. Who else would I be voting for?"

THE LIBRARY DIDN'T have a green room, so they had stowed Embeth's belongings in someone's dumpy office. As soon as Embeth turned her phone back on, Jorge was calling.

"How was the speech, beautiful?" he asked.

"Fine," she said. "The vote?"

"Still happening," Jorge said. "He'll be back late—only an hour or so."

"Shocking. Remind me why we're having this party again."

"He'll have to go straight from the airport to the hotel, so if you could bring his tuxedo. I'll be on the originally scheduled flight," Jorge said.

"Why?" Embeth asked. Jorge and Aaron usually flew together.

"Why pay two change fees? And I don't want to miss the start of the party," Jorge said. "Also, I wouldn't mind a word with you alone, if you have a moment."

Embeth knew what this was about. The election was next week, and Jorge wanted to leave them. Embeth knew it was time—he had been with them for almost twenty years; no one had served Aaron more loyally—but still, she feared a post-Jorge world. She knew there would be a new Jorge, but she dreaded the opening of her inner circle to a stranger.

"Is the girl with you?" Jorge asked in a low voice.

"Yes, she's having lunch," Embeth said.

"What's she like?" Jorge asked.

"She's thirteen. She's a girl. She has curly hair and light eyes. She talks a lot," she said. "She doesn't seem like a liar and she doesn't remind me of Aviva."

"Thank you, Em. You're a trooper to take her, and on your anniversary, no less. I can't imagine what that's like."

"Yes, I am a trooper," she said wearily.

"Trooper! Trooper!" said El Meté.

"I don't mind the company, actually. Did you tell Aaron?" Embeth said.

"Not yet. Do you want me to?"

"No. Let's wait and see what this is first. Why upset him if this is nothing?"

Another call came in.

"I should take this," she said. "It's Aaron."

"How's your day going?" Aaron asked.

"Fine," she said.

"Any good stories for me?"

"Someone sent us an angel," Embeth said. "Like an effeminate, incredibly tacky Jewish angel boy. I guess it's an anniversary present, but I don't know who it's from."

"How weird," Aaron said.

Yet another call came in. Tasha.

"I should take this," Embeth said to Aaron.

"I need to get back to it anyway. I just wanted to hear your voice. Love you, Em."

"Love you."

Embeth flipped to Tasha.

Tasha said she had found Rachel Grossman's number. "She's Rachel Shapiro now."

Embeth hung up and dialed Rachel Shapiro's number, but she did not press call. She put the phone in her bag, and she went out to find Ruby.

Ruby was speaking to Alumna Jeanne.

"Oh my, Embeth, the FGLI program sounds marvelous!" said Alumna Jeanne. "Ruby was telling me about it. I have a niece who would be perfect for it."

"They're not doing it next year," Ruby said.

"Funding," Embeth said with an exaggerated sad face.

"Maybe I could help with that?" Alumna Jeanne said. "My expertise is not-for-profits."

"Definitely send me an e-mail," Embeth said.

The women thanked her for her speech, and Embeth "you're welcome"-ed until her throat was hoarse and her face hurt from smiling. If a speech had gone well, it always took longer to leave an event than she thought it would. Someone wanted a picture. Someone wanted to tell a story about her own mother. Someone cried. Someone invited her to dinner. Someone pressed a business card into her hand. Someone wondered if her sons were married. The distance from the hall to the parking lot could be a few hundred feet that lasted an hour. Embeth couldn't be brusque because she needed these women to vote for Aaron, after all.

By the time Embeth and Ruby arrived at the car, Embeth was exhausted. She was not shy, but she was not a natural extrovert either.

"I've been thinking, Ruby," Embeth said. "What if we both played hooky today? I mean, it's your first time in Miami. Let's do something. Do you like the beach?"

"No," said Ruby.

"Me neither," said Embeth. "I only said it because it's something people like to do when they come to Florida."

"I'm kind of a nerd," Ruby said.

"Me, too," said Embeth. "What *would* you like to do?"

"Well, I'd like to meet your parrot," Ruby said. "I've never met a talking bird before."

"El Meté's shy. He/she doesn't always like to come out."

"Okay . . . then, what if we went to the movies?" Ruby said.

"Don't say that because you think it's something I want to do," Embeth said.

"That *is* why it occurred to me," Ruby admitted. "But it is also something I want to do. Mrs. Morgan says, 'A woman should never please other people at the expense of pleasing herself.'"

"Mrs. Morgan is correct," Embeth said. She started the car.

The only movie that was playing at a convenient time was a superhero movie. They bought the largest size of popcorn and the largest drink. Embeth fell asleep before the trailers were even over. She had a strange dream. She was an enormous tree with many branches, perhaps an oak, and woodsmen were trying to cut her down. She should have been in a panic about being cut down, but she wasn't. It was almost pleasant. It was almost like a massage. The feeling of being hacked into with tiny axes. The feeling of being felled.

Ruby nudged Embeth when the movie was over. "What did I miss?" Embeth said.

"They saved the world," said Ruby.

"I thought it might turn out that way," said Embeth.

As they left the movie theater, a policeman in tight shorts with tanned legs and a carpet of black curly leg hair stood in the lobby. Ruby observed discreetly, but with Christmas morning glee, "Police officers in Florida wear shorts!"

"They do," Embeth said.

The police officer was showing the manager a photograph on a phone. The manager pointed toward Ruby. "That's her!"

Ruby began to back away.

"Are you Ruby Young?" the police officer said.

"I thought your last name was Grossman," Embeth said.

"It is," Ruby said. "My mom changed it."

"Your mom is very worried about you," the police officer said.

"How did she find me? I had my phone off."

"She tracked you down using Find My iPad."

"There's a Find My iPad? That's . . ." Ruby threw what was left of her popcorn toward the police officer, and then she began to run. But instead of running outside, she ran toward the bathroom.

Embeth and the police officer both headed toward the bathroom. The policeman brushed popcorn from his hair. "What's your role in all of this?"

"I'm no one," Embeth said. "I'm irrelevant."

"You're the adult who is with the child who was reported missing," the cop said. "I would say that seems somewhat relevant."

"I'm not some pervert," Embeth said. "My name is Embeth Bart Levin. I'm an attorney and I'm Congressman Levin's wife. This young woman came to my husband's office, wanting to meet him, and he's in D.C. until tonight."

"So you took a thirteen-year-old girl to the movies?" the police officer said. "Is that how you treat every random child who shows up at your husband's office?"

"You're making it sound tawdry, but it isn't like that. She's a friend of the family," said Embeth.

"You didn't say that before."

"We've only just begun talking," said Embeth. "Ruby's the granddaughter of an old neighbor of mine. Rachel Shapiro. Call her and ask, if you'd like."

"I'll do that," the police officer said.

They had reached the movie theater bathroom. "I'm going in," said the police officer. "You wait out here."

"You're going into the women's room?" Embeth asked.

The police officer paused. "It's not illegal, and this is an active crime scene."

Embeth rolled her eyes. "Let me go in first," she said. "Seriously, the kid likes me. I'll get her to turn herself over. Why have a big scene?"

Embeth went into the bathroom. She didn't see legs under any of the stalls.

"Come on, Ruby. Just come out. The jig is up," said Embeth. "I know you're on a toilet seat. Don't make me touch all the doors. Public bathrooms are basically the dirtiest places on earth, and I'm immune compromised."

"I can't come out. I haven't met the congressman yet," said Ruby.

"Well . . . you've met me. We're friends now, and that means you can meet the congressman later. I can make that happen for you. But you have to go with the police officer."

"How do you know I'm on a toilet seat?" Ruby said.

"Because I've spent a good portion of my life hiding from people in bathrooms, okay? Squatting on the toilet is the way it's done."

"Who do you hide from?" Ruby asked.

"Oh, Christ. Everyone. Donors. My husband's staff. Even my husband sometimes. Everyone. I literally hate everyone."

The door swung open. Ruby's face was sticky with tears. "I haven't even met El Meté yet," she said.

"Ruby, if I let you in on a secret about El Meté will you do something for me?" Embeth said.

"Maybe," Ruby said.

"Good girl," said Embeth. "You should never agree to something before you know what it is."

"HOW'S IT GOING IN THERE?" the police officer yelled.

"ONE SECOND," Embeth yelled back.

"I'll tell you what I need you to do, and then I'll tell you the secret about El Meté, okay?" Embeth said quickly. "It's not something I've ever told anyone."

Ruby nodded.

"You know how that election is next week? I need you to not tell the police officer that the congressman might be your father. We don't know for sure if he is yet. Your mom hasn't said for sure that he is. And if it got out that you were here, it could be a lot of trouble for him and for me. Can you do that? It would be an enormous favor to me."

Ruby nodded again. "I understand," she said. "What should I say instead?"

"Say you came to Florida to meet your grandmother, Rachel Shapiro."

"Okay, enough time! Come on, Ruby." The police officer came through the door and put his hand on Ruby's shoulder. Ruby wrested herself away.

"What's the secret about El Meté?" Ruby asked.

"I'm almost ninety-three percent sure that he's not real," Embeth said.

"It's okay," Ruby said. "I used to have a friend that was a lamp."

The police officer turned to Embeth. "I'm not done with you. Let's all take a ride to the police station, shall we?"

She could have argued—Embeth was excellent in an argument—but an argument might have led to her getting arrested, and that was the last thing Aaron needed.

THEY TOOK RUBY to the policeman's office, and Embeth sat in the waiting area. She called Jorge, but it went straight to voice mail. "Jorge, I'm at the police station. I may be late to the party. It's a long story. Can you get Aaron's tuxedo from the house? And if Margarita's there, have her pick out a dress from my closet. If she's not there, just pick out anything that looks appropriate. Anything but the navy. I never want to wear the navy again. Also, I need you to bring my wig. I didn't have time to get to the salon today. I'll meet you at the party."

The policeman came out of his office and walked over to Embeth. "You're free to go," he said.

"What happened?" Embeth said.

"The mother, Jane, vouched for you. The grandmother's coming to pick up the girl." The police officer sounded slightly incredulous. "In the future, I'd avoid going on impromptu field trips with thirteen-year-old girls without checking in with their parents first."

"I'd like to speak to Ruby," Embeth said.

"I'm not stopping you," he said.

Embeth went into the office. "I guess this is good-bye," Embeth said. "I thought I'd slip out of here before your grandmother showed up."

"But I haven't met the congressman yet!" Ruby said in an urgent whisper.

"I know," Embeth said. "I'm sorry about that. I just talked to him.

His flight is late, and then it's our anniversary party tonight. We've been married for thirty years. Did you know that?"

"What about after the party?" Ruby said.

"The party won't be done until midnight, or later. Maybe we could do it tomorrow afternoon?" Embeth said.

"My mom's making me fly back tomorrow morning!" Ruby said. "I'm in huge trouble, and I've spent half of my savings, and I haven't done anything I came to do."

Embeth made a sad face "I'm sorry, Ruby. It's a busy week for us."

Ruby began to cry—snotty, messy tears. "Were you ever going to let me meet him?"

"I . . . ," Embeth began. "Honestly, I don't know. I needed to talk to him first."

"If I told the police officer that you kidnapped me, then the congressman would have to come down to get you," Ruby said.

"Please don't do that," Embeth said.

"If I told the police officer that you were some big pervert . . ."

"Ruby!"

"I wouldn't do that," Ruby said. "I just wanted to meet him. I just wanted to see for myself." Ruby put her head in her lap. "Everyone hates me," she said. "If I was related to him, then I would be someone, and maybe they wouldn't hate me so much."

"Ruby," Embeth said. "That's not how life works. I'm married to him, and everyone loves him, and no one seems to like me at all."

"My mom said he wasn't my dad," Ruby said. "She said it was a 'one-night stand.' That's when you sleep with someone for *one night*—"

"I know what it is," Embeth said. "Ruby, your mom's right. The congressman told me. He's not your father, and I'm sorry to say this, but he doesn't want to see you."

Ruby nodded solemnly.

"But I thought he looks like me. He looks so much like me. It has to be true."

El Meté flew through the open window and landed on Embeth's shoulder.

"True! True!" El Meté said.

"Shh!" Embeth said.

"Party! Party!" El Meté said.

"Shut up, would you!" Embeth said.

"He's here, isn't he?" Ruby said. "El Meté."

The bird flew over to Ruby, and he alighted on her forearm.

"Can you see him?" Embeth asked.

"No," Ruby said. "But I can feel him. What color are his feathers?"

"He has a red head, and a green body and wings, and there are blue tips at the end of his wings. He has green eyes and a pinkish beak. He's very handsome and a little bit vain."

El Meté nuzzled into Ruby's breast.

"I wish I could see him," Ruby said.

"I wish I couldn't," Embeth said.

"What do you think he means?"

"I try not to think about what he means. I guess he means I'm crazy or lonely or both."

The police officer came into the office. "Your grandmother's outside."

Ruby wiped her eyes on her sleeve. "You know her," she said to Embeth. "Will you introduce us?"

"We're not exactly great friends," Embeth said.

In the waiting area, the former Rachel Grossman stood with her friend, Roz Horowitz. Rachel Grossman, who was tough as they came, had tears in her eyes. Those women had never liked me, Embeth thought. But maybe this idea that people didn't like her was as much of a delusion as El Meté? Embeth put on her brightest politician's wife smile. "Roz! Rachel! How wonderful to see you both. This is my friend, Miss Ruby Young."

Ruby stepped forward—her chin stuck out, her shoulders back. "Hello," she said. She squeezed Embeth's hand and whispered, "Fugli forever."

EMBETH TOOK AN Uber to the hotel where the party was being held. She would get her car from the movie theater parking lot in the morning. The driver eyed her in his rearview mirror.

"You look familiar," the driver said.

"I get that a lot," Embeth said. "I have one of those faces."

The driver nodded. "Yeah, but you're someone, aren't you?"

"Not really," Embeth said. She checked her phone. A text from Jorge said, *Don't worry. I'm on my way and I've got everything. See you at the hotel.* The text warmed her enough to try to make conversation with the driver. She had recently read that the drivers rated the passengers, too, which seemed ridiculous to her. Embeth always tried to be polite to waiters and drivers and the like, but she wasn't always in the mood to put on a show. Did everything and everyone and every act require a review? "I'm not someone," she said, "but I'm married to someone."

"Yeah?" he said. "Don't leave me in suspense."

"My husband is Congressman Levin," Embeth said. "From the Twenty-Sixth Congressional District of Florida."

"I don't follow politics. He been in Congress long?" the driver asked.

"Ten terms," Embeth said. "He's up for reelection this year, and I know my husband's very concerned about making sure that Uber pays employment taxes for all of its drivers."

"Not registered to vote. Don't care who gets elected." The driver checked her out in the mirror. "That's not why I know you. You look just like my ex-wife's sister. Such a bitch, but what a great lay."

Embeth didn't know what to say. Did he expect her to thank him? She considered lecturing the man about what was appropriate language and narrative for a customer and a woman he didn't even know. Embeth had no feelings, but she didn't like the thought of someone like Ruby being exposed to such casual misogyny. But in the end, it had been a long day, and it was easier to stare at her phone for the next twelve minutes than confront a driver, IRL. When she reached her destination, she rated him one star.

JORGE WAITED FOR her in the parking loop in front of the hotel. She could see him, standing beneath a palm tree, conspicuously not sweating in his tuxedo, carrying a garment bag.

"No one's here yet," he said. "You've still got plenty of time to change."

"Is Aaron on his way?"

"His flight was delayed. He should be here by nine thirty."

"An hour and a half late? Not bad," said Embeth. "How do you never sweat?" she asked.

"Um . . . I do sweat," he said. "Inside, I'm filled with toxins and rage."

They went up to her hotel room, and Embeth went into the bathroom, where she threw on some makeup, taking special pains with her eyebrows. She called out to Jorge, "Did you pack Spanx?"

"You don't need them. Just put on the pantyhose," Jorge said.

"Foundation garments are everything, Jorge," Embeth said.

Embeth hiked up the pantyhose, which were not as good as Spanx but would have to do.

She donned her wig as if it were a hat. Then she put on a cold-shouldered black jersey gown.

"I've had this dress forever," she called.

"It's back in style," Jorge said. He always knew such things. "Everything old becomes new again."

She put on a white-gold necklace that Aaron had bought her for some occasion or other and a pair of shoes that had a two-inch heel, which was all she could manage these days. She looked at herself in the mirror.

Despite the fact that he had omitted essential foundation garments, Jorge had done a fine job picking out this ensemble. He could be counted on to do anything.

When she left the bathroom, she found him asleep and snoring on the bed. She felt sentimental looking at Jorge's restful face. He reminded her of Aaron, only he was better than Aaron. He was better than Aaron because he had never let her down. How she would miss Jorge!

Embeth nudged him awake. "I'm ready."

"Apologies!" Jorge said. "I dozed off."

"You wanted to talk?" Embeth said. "It seems we still have a few minutes."

"Yes," he said. "I'm still half asleep. One second." Jorge sat up. The sleep made him seem younger and almost bashful. "This is hard to say . . . ," he said.

"Let me help you," Embeth said. "After the election, you want to leave Aaron and me. It's time, Jorge. It's time for you to run for your first office. It's time for you to make a killing in the private sector, if that's what you want to do. It's time for you to have something of your own. We'll miss you, but we'll support you all the way. We'll help you raise money if you run. We'll stump for you. We'll help you find staff. You're like a son to us. You must know that."

"Em, that is very kind, but that's not—"

"It is necessary," said Embeth. "No one has been more loyal to Aaron than you."

Embeth was an awkward hugger, but she pulled the still boyish man close to her. "Was there anything else?"

"How did it go with the little girl? What's her name? Ruby?"

"Oh, fine. I don't think Aaron's the father. Ruby—that's her name—wanted him to be, but Grossman said it was a one-night stand. Nothing to worry about after all."

IT WAS A party largely determined by negation. Two hundred fifty guests, because that was the fewest number of people they could invite without offending anyone. A celebrated chef prepared dishes with foams, because it was the season of foam, the season of flavor without substance. No one would overeat and everyone would go home hungry. A DJ because a DJ was tacky, but badly played covers were even tackier. Centerpieces made from herbs and succulents because Embeth didn't want anything—even a flower—to have to die unnecessarily for this party.

It was a party. Indistinguishable from a fund-raiser except that Embeth felt certain Aaron would have managed to be closer to on time if a roomful of checkbooks had been waiting.

Of course, there were donors in attendance. The most loyal and biggest donors had had to be invited. The biggest folly was to have thought Embeth and Aaron could possibly have a party without them. Who was more near and dear than a loyal donor?

"I know it's your night off and I hate to ask you, but might you have a word with the Altschulers?" Jorge said. "They look restless."

Embeth went over to the restless Altschulers. "Embeth," said Mrs. Altschuler. "How wonderful you look. What a spectacular night this is."

"There was a time we thought the two of you wouldn't make it," Mr. Altschuler said.

"Jared," Mrs. Altschuler scolded.

"What? There's nothing wrong with me saying that. Marriages aren't for the weak or the fainthearted. Emmy knows that."

"I do," Embeth said.

Out of nowhere, Molly the party coordinator urgently grabbed

Embeth's hand. Molly's special skills seemed to be invisibility and sneak attack. "We can't possibly hold the food any longer," Molly whispered. "Chef José is freaking out."

"Excuse me," Embeth said to the Altschulers. "Chef José is freaking out." Embeth kissed Mrs. Altschuler on the cheek. "We'll have you over soon."

Dinner was served. But every time Embeth was about to sit down to eat it, Jorge would ask her to have a word with a different guest. By the time Embeth had completed the rounds, all of Chef José's magical foams had dissolved and her plate had been cleared.

Chef José came by to check on her.

"Did you enjoy the food, Embeth?"

"It was amazing," she said. "Thank you so much for doing this, Chef José. You're too good to us."

"Anything for the congressman. I'm only disappointed that he himself did not get to eat it."

"The vote. It couldn't be avoided," Embeth said for the hundredth time that night. "I'll make sure to tell him how delicious it was. He'll hate to have missed it."

"Describe it in great detail. Make him suffer," Chef José said. "What was your favorite part?"

"The foam," Embeth said.

"Which one?" Chef José asked.

"Mine was the wasabi vanilla," Molly said, suddenly at Embeth's side again. "Embeth, I know we were going to make a thing of cutting the cake, but I think we should just serve it. You and the congressman can do a champagne toast before you do the opening dance."

"Let them eat cake," Embeth said.

By 9:30 p.m., his revised ETA, Aaron was still not there, and there was no choice but to open the floor to dancing. At 9:33, he sent a frenzied, typo-filled text that his plane had arrived and he was only a brief forty-five minutes away. Molly told Embeth that they should revise the plan yet again. It was getting late, and Embeth should speak.

"It seems odd," Embeth said. "It's an anniversary party, and I'll be the only one speaking?"

"When the congressman arrives," Molly said, "we'll tell the DJ to play your song, and we'll clear the dance floor for you and Aaron. Have you decided on a song, by the way? I have 'Stand by Your Man' at the ready."

"Jorge and I were *joking* about that," Embeth said.

"I know," said Molly. "What song?"

"'Crazy Love' by Van Morrison," said Embeth. "Yes, we're old."

Molly sent a text to the DJ.

Embeth delicately reached under her wig and scratched the back of her scalp. "I still think it seems odd for me to speak alone."

Molly poured Embeth a glass of champagne. "I'm a professional. Trust me. Nothing is ever odd at a party unless the host makes it odd," she said. "But I'm sure you already know that."

"I'd like to come out to the song 'It's My Party (and I'll Cry If I Want To),'" Embeth said.

"Irony. I get that," said Molly. "I'll make it happen."

"How does one become a party planner anyway?" Embeth asked.

Molly looked momentarily confused at the introduction of a personal question.

"I know a girl who is a party planner and I wondered how one got into that field," Embeth said.

"I studied hotel management as an undergraduate at Cornell," Molly said. "I should go talk to the DJ now."

EMBETH MADE HER entrance to the plaintive teenage wails of Lesley Gore. She walk-danced. She half-assed aerobic cha-chaed. She tried to look jaunty. She tried to look like she had no fucks left to give. El Meté was on her shoulder, but he stayed very quiet. The music came down, and the DJ said that Mrs. Levin would like to say a few words.

Embeth looked into the crowd. It was dark, and she couldn't see Allegra or Margarita or Jorge or Dr. Hui or anyone else. "I'm told Aaron is on his way," Embeth began. "Ah, the life of a politician's wife! Your husband is always on his way."

The crowd laughed warmly at the joke that was barely a joke.

A moment later, the crowd magically divided. Aaron came down the aisle, like Moses parting the Red Sea.

"I'm here," he bellowed. His gray curly hair bounced in the spotlight. "I'm here, Embeth Bart Levin, love of my life!"

The crowd awwwwed.

Embeth grinned stupidly. How handsome he still was. How ready to forgive him she felt. How she loved that man.

And maybe that was what her life came down to. For him, she had lied, cheated, eaten dirt, blinded herself. She had shielded him from unpleasantness as much as she could. She had protected him from Ruby, Destroyer of Worlds. When they wrote the Book of Embeth, the only thing to be said was that she had loved Aaron Levin as well as any woman could.

He finally reached the microphone. He squeezed her hand. He leaned in, and El Meté flew away. He kissed her, and then he whispered in her ear, "What did I miss?"

V

Choose

AVIVA

1

Your name is Aviva Grossman. You are twenty years old, a junior at the University of Miami (Go Hurricanes!), and today is your first day as an intern for Congressman Levin, the Democrat from Miami, the Twenty-Sixth Congressional District of Florida.

You are super pumped. You believe in the possibility of government to effect positive change! You believe in the congressman! He's such an inspirational speaker. He's so young-looking and handsome, not that these things matter. But hey, it doesn't hurt that he looks like a Jewish John F. Kennedy, Jr.

You are standing in your dorm room, contemplating your wardrobe. You have spent the last year in sweatpants and Birkenstocks. All of your "good" clothes are tight, because you gained twenty-two pounds your freshman year. You are still not fat, but you don't know this at the time. You could have asked your mother to buy you new work clothes, but then she would have lectured you about your diet. She would have said, "Are you drinking enough water? Are you eating after ten?" You don't want to hear it. You want to concentrate on your new job. You put on black tights even though it's ninety degrees out.

Turn to page 2.

2

They haven't invented Spanx yet, and in the fall of 1999, tights are the next best thing. You squeeze your flesh into your chosen sausage casing.

You lay three options on your extralong twin bed: a black stretch crepe cocktail dress, a navy blue summer-weight wool dress that you fear might be snug as you haven't tried to zip it up in more than two years, and a white blouse and gray kilt combo.

If you choose the black dress, turn to page 4.

If you choose the blue dress, turn to page 5.

If you choose the white blouse and kilt, turn to page 11.

11

You choose the white blouse because you think it's the most professional, but then, when you put it on, the buttons strain across your breasts, creating eye-shaped gaps. You don't have time to change. You don't want to be late. If you hunch your shoulders forward, the eyes mainly close.

"Whoa," your roommate Maria says, "sexy mama!"

"Should I change?"

"No way," says Maria. "Put on some lipstick, though."

You sloppily apply red lipstick to your mouth. You are not good with makeup because you rarely wear any. When you went to your prom, your mom put on your makeup for you. Yes, you know how that makes you sound. You and your mom are close. She's probably your best friend though you are not hers. Her best friend is Roz Horowitz, who is funny and, in the way of many funny people, occasionally mean.

You arrive to the new intern orientation. The other female interns are wearing simple black and navy shift dresses, and you regret that you did not wear such a dress. The boys are wearing khaki pants and blue dress shirts. You think they look like they work for Blockbuster.

You feel conspicuous. After the orientation, you go to the bathroom and try to wipe off the red lipstick with a scratchy brown paper towel of the variety only found in public restrooms. It does not wipe off the lipstick. It just spreads it around, and now you look like a tragedy. You look like Bette Davis in *What Ever Happened to Baby Jane?*, which is one of your mom's favorite movies. You splash water on your skin, but it

12

doesn't help. You can't get a decent stream of water because the taps are set to run for five seconds at a time, and the quick splashes seem to tattoo the lipstick stain onto your face.

Back in the conference room, they are training the interns to place and receive phone calls to and from constituents. One of the boys raises his hand and asks, "When do we get to meet the congressman?"

The training person says that the congressman is in Washington, D.C., right now but will be flying back in the evening. You'll all be gone by the time he gets here.

"The congressman is personable, but at this level, you won't have much direct interaction," the training person says.

Later that morning, the boy who had asked the question sits next to you at the call bank. He is skinny and tall, though his shoulders slump like an old man's. He uses Yiddish phrases, which seem to go over well with the callers. He's the same age as you, but he reminds you of your grandfather.

He introduces himself, "I'm Charlie Greene," he says.

"Aviva Grossman," you say.

"Since we're going to be interns together, do you want to have lunch with me?" he asks.

You go to lunch with him because he seems nice enough and because it beats eating alone and because he reminds you of the boys you went to high school with. The other interns seem to have already made friends with one another. How did friendships form so quickly? You wonder if you had worn one of the dresses whether things would have been different.

"What do you want to do when you graduate?" he asks over French fries.

13

"I'd like to run campaigns for a while. Then, I'd maybe like to run for office myself," you say

"Me, too. That's what I want to do!" he says. "High-five!" You smack palms.

"What's your major?" he asks.

"Political science and Spanish literature," you say.

"Me, too!" he says. "Double high-five!"

You smack palms twice.

"Minus the Spanish literature part," he says. "But that's smart. I should get on learning Spanish. Who's your favorite president?" he asks.

"This is going to sound weird," you say, "because, you know, Vietnam. But other than Vietnam, I really like Lyndon Johnson. He was an excellent dealmaker and legislator. And I like that he started out a schoolteacher. And I like that every person in his family had the initials LBJ."

"Even the dog was LBJ," Charlie says. "Little Beagle Johnson."

"I know!" you say. "Who's yours?"

"Despite everything, Bill Clinton," he says. "Please don't shoot me."

"I like him, too," you say. "I think he got a bad rap. I mean, isn't it on Monica Lewinsky, too? People talk about the power imbalance between them, and I guess that matters. But she was a grown-up and she pursued him. And whatever, people make their own choices."

"I like you, Aviva Grossman," Charlie says, "and I think you should be my official Phone-a-Friend." The show *Who Wants to Be a Millionaire* is at the peak of its popularity. "For the internship, I mean."

14

"What does that entail?" you ask.

"Oh, you know, if either of us gets access to the congressman or gets in trouble or whatever, we vouch for the other one."

"Okay," you say.

He gives you his phone number and his e-mail address, and you give him yours.

After lunch, you spend the rest of the afternoon on the phone bank, which is fun at first, like playing at grown-up work, but gets boring fast. At the end of the day, the supervisor of the interns calls you into her office.

You go into the office, wondering why you are being singled out.

"Aviva, sit down," the supervisor says.

You sit, but your skirt is so tight, you can't cross your legs. You have to mash your thighs together. You cross your arms over your breasts.

"How was your first day?" the supervisor says.

"Good," you say. "Interesting. I learned a lot."

"Well, I wanted to talk to you about something potentially awkward," the supervisor says. "The thing is, there's a dress code for the interns."

You had read the dress code. It had only mentioned "professional work attire." You feel yourself begin to blush, but you aren't embarrassed. Mostly, you are angry. The only reason the clothes aren't professional is because of your fat ass and your inconveniently enormous tits.

Okay, you are somewhat embarrassed.

"I thought it would be best to nip this issue in the bud," the supervisor says.

15

You nod and try not to cry. You can feel your chin begin to stupidly quiver.

"No," the supervisor says. "It's not as bad as all of that, Aviva. Take tomorrow off. Get yourself something nice and appropriate to wear, okay?"

You go out to the interns' room, and you gather your things. The other interns have left, and your eyes are beginning to spill over.

The hell with it, you think. No one's here. It's better that you cry before you drive. Miami's confusing to navigate at night, and they haven't invented Google Maps yet.

You weep.

There is a knock on the window. It's Congressman Levin. You knew him when you were a little girl. He smiles at you.

"Are we treating our interns that badly?" he asks kindly.

"Long day," you say. You wipe your eyes on your sleeve.

"Aviva Grossman, right?" he says. "We used to be neighbors in Forestgreen."

"No, I don't live there anymore. I'm in college now. I live in a dorm."

"You're all grown up," he says.

"I don't feel very grown up," you say. "You just caught me crying in the break room."

"How're your folks?" he asks.

"Very well," you say.

"Good, good. Well, Aviva Grossman, I hope your second day is better than your first."

You had heard about the congressman's charm. You must admit: his presence is warming.

16

You are leaving when Charlie Greene calls your name. He had been waiting for you in the love seat by the elevator banks.

"Hey," he says. "Phone-a-Friend! Where'd you go?"

"I had to call my mom," you lie.

"Well, I had a thought. What if we watched *Conan* together? You strike me as a Conan person. Maybe you're a Letterman, though? You're definitely not a Jay."

"You can be a Conan and a Letterman person at the same time," you say.

"That's how it's done, Grossman," Charlie says. "Finish Letterman, flip to Conan. It's how the ancient Romans did it."

You laugh. You like Charlie Greene. He feels as comfortable as your Birkenstocks.

You both look up to see the congressman running toward the elevator. He has long legs. You think you read that he used to be a pole-vaulting champion and you can believe that. You imagine him in tight track shorts. "You left your keys," he says. "Cute keychain."

Your keychain is a spinning cloisonné globe, which was a gift from your father to commemorate a trip you took to Russia with your high school history class. The congressman spins the globe, and it strikes you how large his fingers are compared to the tiny world your father gave you.

"Thanks," you say. When he hands you the keys, your fingertips touch the congressman's, and through a curious feat of human circuitry, you feel his touch directly between your legs.

"Since I caught you, I was thinking," the congressman says. "I don't like the thought of one of my interns crying on the

17

first day. I definitely don't like the thought of Dr. Grossman's daughter crying on the first day. I mean, I have a lot of stress in my life. I might need a quadruple bypass someday. Let me take you for a falafel or something. There's a café downstairs. They do other things, too, but I'd go with falafel or frozen yogurt."

If you introduce the congressman to Charlie and then tell the congressman you already have plans, turn to page 20.

If you don't introduce the congressman to Charlie—indeed, you forget Charlie is even there—and immediately leave with the congressman, turn to page 22.

22

You forget Charlie is there. You're about to leave with the congressman when the congressman holds out his hand to your Phone-a-Friend. "Aaron Levin," he says. "You must be one of the new interns."

Charlie manages to say his name, and then he says, "An honor to meet you, sir."

"Thank you for coming to work for us, Charlie," the congressman says, looking deep into Charlie's eyes. "I appreciate it."

The congressman suggests that Charlie come to the café.

"We actually had plans," Charlie said.

"Nothing solid," you say.

"What plans?" asks the congressman. "I like to know what the young people are up to."

"We're going to watch Letterman and then Conan," Charlie says.

"Let's do that," the congressman says. "But let's get something to eat first. It's only ten thirty. We have time."

"Whoa. What?" Charlie stammers. "My apartment's pretty dirty. I have roommates. I—"

"Don't worry, kid. We can eat downstairs and watch up here," the congressman says. "There's a TV down the hall."

You go downstairs to the café, and the owner bows when the congressman comes into the restaurant. "Congressman!" he says.

"Where have you been? We've missed you!"

"Farouk, these are my new crackerjack interns, Charlie and Aviva," the congressman says.

"Don't let him work you too hard," Farouk says. "He works all night long, six nights a week."

23

"You only know that because you keep the same hours," the congressman says.

"When anyone asks me, I say, no one works harder than my congressman . . . except me," Farouk says. "I don't know when you see those boys or that pretty wife of yours."

"I see them all the time," the congressman says. "In my wallet. On my desk."

The congressman orders a plate of falafel balls for the table and a side of hummus. Farouk brings baklava, on the house.

"So let me pick your brains," the congressman says. He has a spot of hummus on his upper lip. You don't know if you should mention it, but you can't stop looking at it. "I'm supposed to give a speech for the National Organization for Women about the leadership gap and what we can do about it, especially thinking about the next generation. You're a young woman, Aviva."

You nod too eagerly.

"You must know a few young women, Charlie?" the congressman says.

"Fewer than I'd like," Charlie says.

The congressman laughs. "So, any thoughts, kids?"

Charlie says, "I think it's the same thing with late night television. I'm really into late night . . ."

"Yes," the congressman says, "I'm gathering that."

"The person who hosts the late night show always wears a dark suit," Charlie says. "The person who becomes the president always wears a dark suit. Maybe if a lady put on a dark suit, the problem would be solved."

The congressman looks at you. "What do you think?"

24

"I think he's right-ish." You can feel yourself blushing.

"Ish?" the congressman says.

"Ish," you say. "I'm not, like, a feminist."

"You aren't?" The congressman looks amused.

"I mean, I'm not *not* a feminist. I mean, I believe I'm a human before I'm a woman." You say this because you are young, and because you have the wrong idea about feminism. You think feminists are your mom and Roz Horowitz. You think they're middle-aged women with fond memories of 1970s-era marches and ancient trunks filled with buttons and message tees. "But I think—I mean I know—women are judged on their appearance. If a woman wore a dark suit, they wouldn't make her president. They would say she was 'trying to be a man.' She can't win."

The congressman excuses himself to the restroom. Charlie says, "How do you know him?"

"We used to be neighbors," you say. "And my dad operated on his mother's heart."

"Wow," Charlie says. "Go me for picking an awesome Phone-a-Friend. I can't believe he wants to hang out with us! Seriously, he's so earnest. He really seems interested in what we have to say."

You agree.

"Man, I kind of wanted to work for a senator or in the White House, but this is turning out great."

You all go back to the office where the congressman puts on *Letterman*. Halfway through the show, he removes his tie and dress shirt and then he is only wearing a white undershirt.

25

"Sorry, kids," he says. "Avert your eyes. It's damned hot." You suddenly become glad that Charlie is with you. You have heard that the women staffers have crushes on the congressman, and you would rather avoid that particular cliché.

When you get back to your dorm that night, your roommate, Maria, isn't there, but that isn't anything unusual. She sleeps at her girlfriend's apartment most nights. You wish you had a girlfriend's apartment to go to. The novelty of dorm life has worn off. You are tired of the cinder block walls and your roommate's *Pulp Fiction* poster that will never stick to the wall for more than five days straight. You are tired of shower shoes and communal bathrooms and the dry-erase board on the door that doesn't quite erase. You are tired of objects going missing and not being entirely sure if they have been stolen or just misplaced. You are tired of the smell of body odor, of sex, of dirt, of football fields, of socks, of weed, of week-old pizzas and ramen, of moldy towels, of bi-semesterly changed sheets. You will die if the guy across the hall plays "Crash into Me" one more time. It's his hookup song. The worst. All this seems particularly intolerable when you have put in a full day at work.

You aren't physically tired, though, and you wish you had someone to talk to about everything. You think about calling your mom, but you don't. It's late, and there are things she wouldn't understand.

It's late.

You check your e-mail on your roommate's computer. She has left her browser opened to a blog, written by a woman who works in fashion. Lately, everyone has a blog. You read a

26

little. The woman puts up pictures of her outfits, with her head cut off, and rants about her boss and the sexist practices of her industry.

You could do that.

You lie down on your bed and you take out your laptop, and you decide to start a blog.

You decide to make your blog anonymous, because you want to be able to speak candidly about your experiences. You don't want this blog to affect you later in life. It's a way to blow off some steam.

You write:

Just Another Congressional Intern here.

First day on the job and I'm already in trouble. Did I steal from the campaign? Did I throw a tantrum in front of a constituent or the congressman? Did I arrange a Watergate-style break-in and then try to cover it up?

No, Imaginary Readers, I BROKE THE DRESS CODE.

Congressional interns have a dress code, and I thought I was following it. But my Big Boobs had other ideas . . .

And I guess this is my point. If a less well-endowed intern had worn the exact same outfit I wore, would she have gotten in trouble? Methinks not. This means there are double standards, based on body types, implied by the congressional intern dress code. This smells rotten to me, Imaginary Readers.

27

And also, what am I meant to do? I gained twenty-two pounds my first semester at U. Am I supposed to buy an entirely new wardrobe? Did I mention INTERNS ARE PAID NOTHING? The guy interns are dressed like tech support slobs, so maybe I'll get myself a pair of khakis and a denim shirt and call it a day.

On other fronts, met the Big Kahuna tonight. You know Gaston in the cartoon version of Beauty and the Beast? He looks like that, only more muscular.

Is it weird that I have always been, like, "Belle, choose Gaston. He's not that bad. He's good-looking. He's rich. He's into you. A bit egotistical, but who isn't? Seriously, Belle, do not go with the Beast. That guy lives alone in a castle and he has anger issues and his closest friend is a servant who also happens to be a fucking candelabra. Major warning signs ahead, babe. Also, did I forget to mention? He's a BEAST!"

XO,

J.A.C.I.

28

You finish writing the blog, and then you read it through.
You think you're pretty funny.
You locate the Publish button.

If you save it to your draft folder and then wait until morning to decide whether you want to publish, turn to page 30.

If you delete it, turn to page 32.

If you publish it, turn to page 33.

33

You publish the blog before you chicken out. You refresh the browser several times to check and see if there are comments. There aren't. You brush and floss your teeth, and when you come back, there is one comment—a spam that reads "Ginuine $$$Louise Vuittone$$$ purses—What All the Super Classy Women Want—Just Click Here." You erase the comment and strengthen your spam filter settings. You laugh. Who did you think was going to comment on your blog? No one knows about your blog. You consider deleting the blog, but you leave it there. You can use it the next time you have something to complain about.

In the morning, you drive up to Boca to see your mother.

When you think of your mother, the word that occurs to you is *too*. She hugs you too hard, kisses you too long, asks you too many questions, worries too much about your weight/your love life/your friendships/your future/your water consumption. She loves you with an almost religious fervor. She loves you too much. The love makes you feel embarrassed for her and almost guilty—other than be born, what have you done to deserve such love?

She is happy to buy you new work outfits. Of course she is. What is within her power to provide, she always happily provides. She doesn't explicitly mention your weight. She says things like, "The next size up might look more fashion forward" or "You don't want the skirt to ride up in the back" or "That jacket is cute, but it pulls a teeny bit across your boobs" or "Maybe we should go up to lingerie to look at bodysuits?" You feel too defeated to argue. The purpose of these clothes is to avoid a future confrontation with the supervisor.

34

You wonder how much of your mother's disapproval of your body is in your head and not based on anything she actually says. It cannot be denied that your mother is very slender. She has long dancer legs, perky boobs, and even at forty-eight years old a waist nearly as trim as Audrey Hepburn's. She works out religiously. The only thing she loves more than her job as a vice principal is the gym.

In return for the shopping, your mother grills you about your new job.

"So you like working with the congressman?" she says.

You laugh. "I don't work with him directly, not really."

"What do you do, then?"

"It's boring," you say.

"Not to me! Your first real job!"

"I don't get paid," you say. "So it's not a real job."

"Still, this is exciting stuff," she says. "Tell me, my daughter. What do you do?"

"I answer phones," you say. "I get coffee."

"Aviva, come on, give me one good story to take back to Roz."

"I didn't take this job so you'd have stories for Roz Horowitz."

"Something about the congressman."

"Mom," you say impatiently. "Thank you for the clothes, but honestly, there's nothing to tell. I should get back to Miami."

When you return to work, you are more acceptable to your hypocrite supervisor. "Looking good," she says.

You thank her and you hate yourself for thanking her. You want to say something sharp like, "I'm glad you no longer have to be repulsed by the sight of my flesh straining cheap fabric,"

35

but you don't. You want to do well at this job. You don't want to screw this up. You want to have a good story for your mother to tell Roz Horowitz. You cross your arms in front of your chest, and the suit jacket doesn't pull at all, and it feels like your mother is hugging you, and you could almost cry for gratitude. You wonder what girl interns who don't have doting, wealthy mothers do when they are caught in such a situation.

You settle into life as an intern. Sometimes, you read the mail from the public. Sometimes, you get coffee for the office. Sometimes, you fact-check and research the congressman's speeches. The year is 1999, and you seem to be the only one in the office who knows how to perform an Internet search properly. "You're a wizard, Aviva," says the supervisor.

You become known as the "Fact-Check Girl." You become the official Young Person in the Office, expert on youth-related matters. You become invaluable. You have heard the congressman himself say, "Put Aviva on it." You suggest that the congressman start a blog to talk to the younger voters, and your suggestion is adopted. You love being important. You love your work.

Charlie Greene asks you to come to his grandparents' house for his birthday. You agree because, despite your relatively meteoric rise, Charlie is still your only friend in the office.

On the night of Charlie's dinner, your supervisor asks if you could do some research for the congressman.

"What kind of research?" you say.

"Something for his speech on the environment this weekend," the supervisor says. "It's super important that this speech go well as I'm sure you know."

36

"No problem," you say, "I'll get to it first thing tomorrow." You explain about Charlie's birthday.

"Could you stay just a little longer? I know the congressman wanted it tonight. He'll tell you exactly what he needs when he gets here."

"I can come back as soon as the dinner is over," you say. You don't even want to go to Charlie's house, but you said you would.

"The congressman specifically asked for you. You've made a real impression on him," the supervisor says.

"That's nice to hear," you say. You look at your watch. If you don't leave in five minutes, you'll never make it to Century Village on time. You look at Charlie's present, which is sitting on your desk: a collection of Letterman top ten lists.

"Charlie's a great kid. He'll understand. And we're all in this together, aren't we?"

If you tell the supervisor to screw himself, you're going to dinner and you'll be back at ten, turn to page 40.

If you call Charlie and tell him you're going to be late, turn to page 43.

If you don't call Charlie (you don't want him to talk you out of staying) and you stay at work (you'll get there when you can), turn to page 45.

45

You fall asleep in your cubicle. You miss Charlie's dinner, and the supervisor must have gone home, and the congressman hasn't even asked you for whatever it is he wants.

You feel a hand on your shoulder.

It's the congressman.

"Hey, sleepyhead," the congressman says, "what are you still doing here?"

You take a moment to orient yourself and then you say, "They told me you needed me so I stayed!"

"No, they shouldn't have done that. I'm not anywhere near done," he says. "I'll be able to tell you what I need tomorrow."

You shake your head, and you take a deep breath, and you say more harshly than you mean to, "Well, I guess I'm going home then."

"Wait," he says. "Aviva, what is it?"

"It won't matter to you, but I missed my friend's birthday to stay here. My only friend, and he probably hates me."

"I'm sorry about that," the congressman says.

"No," you say. "It's not your fault. I should have left. I'm an adult. I should have read the situation better."

The congressman nods. "That's an admirable attitude," he says.

"I stayed because I wanted to stay. I really like working here," you say.

"Everyone thinks you're doing a great job," the congressman says. "We've had excellent feedback on the blog. Very forward thinking. Embeth and I were both impressed with the response."

46

For a second, you forget what blog he is talking about. You are drowsy, and you wonder if he's read *your* blog and how he knew it was yours, and then you remember that he's talking about *his* blog, the official blog of the congressman. "Great," you say. "I'm glad."

He watches you gather your things—your floral JanSport backpack, your cloisonné keychain, your pen that looks like a flamingo—and you wonder why he hasn't left yet.

"Cute keychain," he says.

You wonder if he remembers he said that to you before.

What a lousy night.

You can't stop thinking about Charlie.

You don't like Charlie that way even though you know he likes you that way. Nonetheless, he has been a good friend to you. You are amused by the same things and you enjoy his company and you have a lot in common. You have spent hours talking about the campaigns you would run for yourselves, and whether you should get master's in public policy degrees or go to law school, and whether it was better to do higher-level internships or try to get promoted within a lower-level internship (like you consider the one you are currently in), and which cities would be the best ones to establish yourselves in, and what your campaign slogans would be. You particularly love coming up with good, bad campaign slogans with him, like *Politics Is a Dirty Business. Sometimes You Need a Grossman to Do the Job.*

The fact is, you have spent more time talking about the future with him than with anyone else in the world.

47

When you were twelve, you threw a birthday party, and you invited everyone in your class, and only three people came because another girl in your class had a party the same day. Granted, Charlie is turning twenty-one, but still. You can imagine Charlie and his grandparents, sitting around the table. *Should we eat without her?* Charlie says, *No, let's wait.* He keeps saying it, until finally, he gives up on you. You feel like a heel.

You need to do something to blast the guilt out of your brain.

If you call your roommate to see if she wants to go clubbing, turn to page 48.

If you call Charlie to apologize profusely and to ask him if he wants to watch Letterman/Conan, turn to page 50.

If you eat your feelings, turn to page 53.

If you kiss a handsome congressman, turn to page 54.

54

You don't think about his unpleasant wife—you have heard the marriage is a political one, whatever that means. You don't think about his sons. You don't think about your mother the vice principal or your father the cardiac surgeon and how hard they both work so that you can work at an internship for no money. You don't think about your grandmother Esther and your great-aunt Mimmy, who both survived the Holocaust. You don't think about the only time you had sex, with a boy who was your boyfriend but who definitely did not ask permission. You don't think about the summer you spent at fat camp when you were fourteen. You don't think about how much you hate your body, which has never done a thing to you really. You don't think about your body at all. You certainly don't think about sweet, funny Charlie Greene. You don't ask yourself whether you would even want a man like the congressman.

The point is, you don't think. You didn't want to think, and you don't think. You wanted to feel something other than guilt.

You walk over to him, and you press your lips up against his lips, and you push your tongue into his mouth. You are bold and fearless and reckless. You like being this kind of girl.

His tongue meets your tongue for a second, and then his tongue propels your tongue out of his mouth with a muscular force. He pushes you away from him and then he holds you at arm's length. He looks around to make sure you're alone.

"I understand your impulse," he says. "But this is inappropriate. This can't happen again."

You nod and you grab your backpack and you run out to your car.

55

That night, you consider the phrase, "I understand your impulse."

Does he mean:

A. I, too, had an impulse to kiss you.
B. I understand why someone like *you* would want to kiss someone like *me*, though I do not, in fact, share your impulse.
C. In general, I understand that people have impulses to kiss other people.

You decide that it is impossible to know what he means. Still, you pose the choices to your roommate, who is having a fight with her girlfriend. The roommate thinks the answer is A.

The next day, Saturday, Charlie Greene calls you on the phone.

"What happened to you?" he says.

"They held me at the office."

"I thought it was something like that. Next time, like, call or something. Anyhow, my grandmother still wants to meet you," he says.

"Okay," you say.

"She thinks she knows your grandmother," Charlie says.

You get a call on the other line. You don't recognize the number, but you flip over anyway.

"Aviva," the congressman says. "I'd like you to come into the office today."

Usually, the supervisor calls with the schedules for the week.

56

Part of you wonders if the congressman is going to fire you, and part of you wonders if the congressman is going to kiss you again.

You don't take a shower. You slept in track pants and a T-shirt and you don't bother changing. You don't want to look special. You don't want to look like you care.

You drive to the office, and your hands are freezing, which is what happens when you are nervous.

You take the elevator up, and when you arrive, Aaron Levin calls you into his office. "Leave the door open," he says.

He says, "I want you to find out everything you can about the government's involvement in the redigging of the Kissimmee River."

"Yes, sir," you say.

The Internet search takes twenty minutes. The Kissimmee is the longest river in Florida, and like any river, the Kissimmee started its career as a series of irregular, undulating curves. In the middle of the twentieth century, a time of optimism and fool-hardiness, the U.S. Army Corps of Engineers decided that the Kissimmee could help with flood control and be a useful navigational tool for planes if it were straight. Win-win! They dug out the sides of the river, killing innumerable species of flora and fauna and damaging the river practically beyond repair. From an environmental standpoint, the Kissimmee River is a disaster.

You go into the congressman's office and you describe this for him and you add some facts about what the continued costs of restoration will be.

"Tragic," he says.

57

"Tragic," you agree.

"Close the door," he says.

You close the door. "I can't stop thinking about you, but I'm married and I have children and I'm an elected government official, and so this cannot be," he says.

"I understand," you say.

"But I'd still like us to be friends," he says.

"Yes," you say, though you don't have any friends his age, except for your mom.

He offers you his hand to shake.

If you shake his hand and then you try kissing him again, turn to page 60.

If you shake his hand and then leave the office, turn to page 94.

If you don't shake his hand and offer your resignation, turn to page 95.

60

You shake his hand.

You shake it, and you don't let go. You pull him toward you, and then you kiss him again.

If you think you're having fun, turn to page 62.

If you think you're in love, turn to page 65.

65

You have never been in love before and so you don't know for certain if you are.

He is not like anyone you've ever known.

He's not like the boys your age, like Charlie Greene.

He's smart and he's powerful and he's sexy as fuck.

It's easy for you to find reasons to stay late.

No, you're remembering that wrong.

It's easy for him to find reasons to *have you* stay late. "I need Aviva," he'll say. "Put Aviva on it."

Sometimes, that means he wants actual work from you. Sometimes, that means he wants *you*.

You never know what he'll want until he says, "Close the door." There's an excitement to this arrangement. It's like you're a contestant on a game show. What can possibly be behind door number one?

You wonder if anyone suspects.

You progress to saying, "I love you."

And he says, "I love you, too."

No, you're remembering that wrong. He never says those words. He says, "Me, too."

You say, "I love you."

He says, "Me, too."

But maybe he isn't demonstrative.

You look for evidence of love.

Exhibit 1: If he didn't love you, why would he be spending all this time with you? Why would he be risking so many things—his marriage, his family, his work? You conclude that he must love you.

66

Exhibit 2: Once, without any prompting from you, he says, "As soon as I'm reelected, I'm going to leave Embeth. We haven't been happy for some time."

Upon further consideration, maybe that isn't actual evidence. All he said was he was unhappy with his wife. Maybe that has nothing to do with you? How can you know if you caused the unhappiness or if you are a symptom of it?

You can't even come up with a decent third piece of evidence. The first time he saw you without a bra, he said you had "the sexiest tits [he'd] ever seen." You're not so dumb that you think evidence of lust is the same as evidence of love. Still, the lust is intoxicating and appreciated. You have always felt lumbering, misshapen, and bulky. He looks at you like you're butter and he's a hot knife.

You decide it doesn't matter if he loves you. You love him. You know what you feel.

You know what you feel, but there are still a few things that bother you.

He doesn't want to have vaginal intercourse with you. You have every other kind of sex that a man and a woman can have, but not that kind. You want to have it with the congressman, but you don't press him. You are still a virgin, in a way, and you're slightly scared of what will happen. It hurt so much when you did it with that boy who didn't ask permission. You haven't done it since.

Another thing that bothers you is the fact that he says he will end his marriage after the next election. You know that congressmen run for office every two years. As long as he's a

67

congressman, will there ever be a good time to end his marriage? He's always in the middle of a campaign.

If he becomes a senator or a governor, which you know he would prefer, then there would be more wiggle room. This isn't outside the realm of possibility. He is very ambitious, and his constituents in Miami love him. He's Jewish and good on Israel. He speaks Spanish, which goes a long way in South Florida. He served in the military and is always fighting to expand veterans' benefits. He was a teacher and came out against testing as a sole measure of a school's progress. He photographs like a model. Babies love him. They are almost obsessively drawn to him. The point is, he ticks a lot of boxes for people. Even outside Florida, the congressman's getting to be a star. It's only his second term, but he broadly caucuses, and he's already serving on several committees and subcommittees. No one thinks Aaron Levin will be a "lifer" in the House, although there's already talk that he might make a good Speaker of the House someday. Considering all this, you believe his career would survive his marriage ending, assuming it was all handled properly.

You need someone to talk to about all of this.

If you talk to Charlie, turn to page 68.

If you talk to your mother, turn to page 70.

70

You tell your mom about the affair, and she begs you to end it. She literally gets on her knees. You have to tell her, "Mom, please get off the floor." Once you've told her, she won't talk about anything else. You regret telling your mother. You had told her because you had wanted to discuss the relationship with her, as two adults. You had things you wanted to know—why doesn't he want to have vaginal intercourse with you, for instance? But she is so hung up on the morality of it that she's useless. She rails on about your good name—"It's all you take to the next life, Aviva!"—and your grandmother who survived the Holocaust and whatever else she can think of. Finally, you cry and tell her that you'll end it even though you know that you won't.

You accept that you have no one to talk to. The congressman has been pretty adamant that you need to keep your relationship a secret. "None of the other interns," he says one night, "not your roommate, no one." And maybe he's right. The only person you would have even trusted to tell was your mom, and look how that turned out. Because you have no one to talk to, you begin to write about the relationship in your blog. Just a little. You're coy with details. You've been watching a lot of *Sex and the City*, and you think of yourself as a younger, more political Carrie Bradshaw.

Data analytics tell you that you have about six regular readers of your blog. They occasionally leave supportive comments. One even asks if you're based in Florida. You do not reply.

Maybe you thought having an affair would be exciting, but mainly what it is, is lonely. Your days are spent waiting for the

71

nights, which is the only time you ever see him. And it's not like it's every night, or every other night, or even once a week. It's when he has time, usually late. Less generously, it sometimes feels like he is a toddler with many toys and you are a doll he occasionally remembers to play with. Sometimes, he is in D.C. for weeks at a time, and this is almost better because at least you know there isn't a chance you will see him. But those weeks are bad, too. You miss him constantly. You miss him even when you're with him.

You never argue with him, because you know—in the part of yourself that knows—that he will end your relationship if you put up any kind of fuss. You have no power, and he has all the power. And this sometimes frustrates you. But you kissed him. That was your power, right? You asked for this. And this, you believe, is the price you pay for being with an extraordinary person.

The holidays are coming.

If you buy him a present, turn to page 72.

If you don't buy him a present, turn to page 74.

72

You buy him a Chanukah present even though Chanukah is a children's holiday. He doesn't get anything for you, but you don't expect it. You buy him a leather-bound edition of *Leaves of Grass*.

"This must have cost you two weeks' salary," he says, kissing you.

"You don't pay me anything," you remind him.

"We should do something about that," he says. "I love it. This is the best gift I've ever received." He kisses you again. "Did you have to rob a bank?"

"I'm a camp counselor during the summer," you say.

"Oh God, your camp counselor money? Now I feel terrible."

"I've got some bat mitzvah money left, too," you say.

"Stop!" he says. "You're killing me."

"It wasn't that much money," you tell him. "Anyway, I'm glad you like it."

"Do you know what the title means?" he asks.

You realize you have no idea. "Something to do with nature?" you say dumbly. He often says that you are mature for your age, wise, and you always want to impress him with the things you know. (But you are young and there is still so much you do not know!) "We studied 'Song of Myself' in school, but I'm not sure that we ever talked about the title of the collection," you say.

"In Whitman's time, 'grass' referred to cheap or low quality literature. So, he's making a little joke. 'Leaves' like the pages of a book. It sounds pretentious, but actually, it's the opposite of pretentious."

73

He was an English teacher before he went into politics. He often gets in teacher mode, which is adorable and annoying at the same time.

You are in a Days Inn fifty miles outside of Miami. You don't even know the name of the town. The bedspread is made of gold and green polyester. There is a reddish stain on the wall beneath the air conditioner. The air conditioner produces a meager, moldy cool and has a steady drip. You love him. You tell him you love him.

He says, "I will always treasure the time we spent together."

~~If you take his words as a sign to break up with him and then you actually break up with him, turn to page 74.~~

If you wait for him to break up with you, turn to page 76.

76

Maybe sensing the rhythms of the school year, he breaks up with you just before summer. He does it at the office, which you find appropriate. In the part of you that knows the truth, you didn't think it would be forever. Still, it comes as a shock. He says, "We've had a great time, Aviva, and in another life, maybe. But the timing is wrong."

You start to cry, and you feel like a dope.

"No," he says, "don't cry. It isn't you. I like you more than I probably should. I think your future is enormously bright. But the more I think about it . . . I think I'll sleep better if . . . I think we'll all sleep better if . . . I'm not comfortable being the kind of man who sleeps with a subordinate. I know I'm not your immediate supervisor, but still . . . It's selfish of me, and it's wrong. I wouldn't like it if someone treated my own children that way."

"We're just having fun," you say. You're starting to ugly cry.

"You sure don't look like you're having much fun, kid," he says.

"Do you want me to quit?"

He wipes your tears on his sleeve.

"Of course not," he says. "You're one of the best interns we've ever had. Now that the school year's over, Jorge wants to promote you to a paid staff position. I'm not supposed to be the one to tell you. Act surprised when you hear, okay?"

You nod.

He pats you on the shoulder. "We're lucky," he said. "We got to have this time, and we didn't ruin anyone's life in the process. It doesn't feel like it right now, but one day, you'll look back and think this was a very good outcome."

77

An outcome, you think. When I was young, I had this affair, and wow, what an outcome!

"You're smiling about something," he says.

You're a big girl, and you pull your shoulders back, and you don't put up a fuss. Later, you yell at your mother, but you know it isn't her fault. You yell at her because she's there and because she's your mother and she'll take it.

If you continue working for the congressman, turn to page 78.

If you stop working for the congressman, turn to page 98.

78

You continue working for the congressman. You are good at this job, and your discretion when you were still having the affair means you don't have any reason to leave. You congratulate yourself on your maturity. In the past, you have had trouble seeing things through.

You occasionally date, but you don't meet anyone you like as well as the congressman. Charlie Greene has lost interest in you. In the years to come, he runs a presidential campaign, and then he becomes chief of staff, and then he semiretires from politics and moves to Los Angeles to become a consultant on an award-winning political soap opera. Sometimes you still see him as a commentator on news channels. He never changes. You will wonder, How is it that he gets to do so many things and he never changes? How is it that you have done so little and you change like a second hand on a clock? Why is he allowed to be constant, the eternal Charlie Greene? Why are you the protean Aviva Grossman?

Roz Horowitz sets you up with her nephew, Archie, who has recently passed the bar and has just begun practicing human rights law. "It's the 'good person' kind of law, not the scumbag kind of law," Roz says. "You'll have a lot in common. And he's not bad looking, Aviva. Trust me, he's your type." You wonder how on earth Roz Horowitz would know what your type is.

You ask your mother if she told Roz Horowitz about the congressman. Your mother says, "Aviva! Of course not! I'm a vault!"

Ultimately, you go on the date because your mother wants you to go and because it has been four and a half months—you

79

have pined enough. Archie is handsome—in the looks department, he does remind you of the congressman—and funny
and passionate about his work. (Maybe you should apply to
law school after all?) You can't fault his taste in restaurants
(Japanese-Cuban fusion) or in clothes (conservative, but his
socks have lobsters on them). Still, you don't sense much chemistry there.

"I had a great time," Archie says over dessert. "And we could
definitely hang out again. But you should know, I'm gay. I'm not
entirely out to my extended family. I should have told Aunt Roz,
but once you tell her anything, you might as well have made a
press release."

"I can't ever tell who's gay and who's not," you say. "My old
roommate used to say I have no gaydar."

"Well, thank God for that. I loathe people who have gaydar.
It's just a kind of prejudice, but it's got that funny word, so
people think it's funny. You know what people who have great
gaydar usually are? Bigots."

"Maybe we can start a campaign against gaydar?" you say.

"Let's do it," Archie says.

"It's not as hard as you think," you say. "You publish a few
op-eds in prominent places, or you know, whatever places will
have you. The first pieces can be of a more humorous bent.
Anything to raise awareness. Maybe you get lucky and people start blogging about the issue. You call local TV stations.
They'll probably ignore you, which is why you try to recruit
a gay-friendly politician—maybe it's a city councilman rep-
resenting South Beach or any area with a fair number of gay

80

constituents—to introduce a piece of legislation or even just a proclamation about 'casually homophobic hate speech, particularly the use of the word *gaydar*.' You go online and you try to find a message board of like-minded individuals to come out with signs and rally against gaydar."

"Gaydar, get yar ass out of here!" Archie suggests. "Out of har?"

"Yeah . . . ," you say, smiling and wrinkling your nose. "Or something better even?"

"I'll work on it," Archie says.

"At the hearing, you get a photogenic high school kid to tell a story about how he or she has been negatively impacted by use of the word *gaydar*. You call the news stations again. This time, they come. You've got a politician, a high school kid, and a mob of people with signs. You've got the mayor or the head of the city council having to say the word *gaydar* awkwardly over and over—"

Archie makes his voice sound square and conservative, "So, what precisely is the gayyy-darrrr?"

"Exactly. I mean, it's great footage. Like, how can they resist us?

"Even if you fail to get *gaydar* officially banned—which you won't because no one's going to ban a word—by the time you're done, you've at least raised awareness, maybe, one percent. And maybe some of those people will pause before they say gaydar."

"They'll pause and say, 'Now I know this isn't PC . . .' and then, they'll say it anyway," Archie says.

81

"But think how validated you'll feel by that clause. It's a win!"

"I don't know if this is depressing or inspiring," Archie says.

"It's definitely inspiring," you say. "Lots of drops in the bucket."

"Would you call all of this politics or press?" Archie jokes.

"Press," you say, and then you think better of it. "Maybe they're the same thing."

"Hmm. Is this what they're teaching the interns these days?" Archie asks.

"I'm not an intern anymore," you say. "By the way, no one even knew what a blog was when I got there. They're all so old."

"I know," Archie says. "There's this ancient lawyer in my office, and he's asked me to show him how to turn on his computer five times. I'm like, dude, there's a switch. It's not that hard."

Archie drops you off at your apartment. You're living off campus this year. You're about to unlock your front door when the congressman calls your cell phone. "I'm in your neighborhood," he says.

"Why?" you say.

"I thought you could show me your new place," he says.

If you invite him over, turn to page 84.

If you make an excuse ("I'm in Boca" or "I'm tired"), turn to page 100.

84

"Come on over," you say. If you're honest with yourself, one of the reasons you moved into an off-campus apartment and didn't get any roommates is because you hoped something like this would happen. You set the stage, and you knew the player wouldn't be able to resist the call of the theater.

"We missed you tonight," he says.

The election is in a month, and there had been a town hall meeting that night and you hadn't gone.

"I had a date," you say.

"Oh yeah? Someone I should be jealous of?"

"No," you say, as you take off your blouse.

"It's good," he says. "It's good you should date. I want you to meet someone nice."

You take off your skirt.

"You look pretty," he says. He goes into your bathroom and he turns on the faucet.

You put your hair into a topknot. You had it blown out for your date with Archie, and you don't want to mess it up.

"Your absence was noted tonight," he calls.

You turn on the television. A rerun of *Who Wants to Be a Millionaire* is on.

The question on the screen is:

Henry VIII split from the Roman Catholic Church after it refused to grant him an annulment so he could marry which woman?

85

a. Anne Boleyn

b. Jane Seymour

c. Anne of Cleves

d. Catherine of Aragon

"Anne of Cleves," he says, as he leaves the bathroom.

The answer is Anne Boleyn.

"Darn," he says. "I always get the Annes confused."

You set a pillow on the floor. You lower yourself to your knees, and he unzips his pants.

If you continue seeing him, turn to page 86.

If you tell him it's over, turn to page 150.

86

You slip back into seeing the congressman. Once a week. Sometimes, twice. It's a bad habit, you know. You know, you know, you know. You end up feeling like the congressman's garbage can or his suitcase. You feel functional, if not beloved.

You consider quitting your job even though you still love it, even though you're good at it, even though you derive self-esteem from the fact that you're good at it. You liked being Aviva, the girl who could find anything.

If you quit the job, maybe you'll be able to quit him, too.

If you don't quit the job, turn to page 87.

~~*If you quit the job, turn to page 160.*~~

87

You know you should quit your job, but you decide to wait until after the election. You start taking steps, though. You put together a new résumé; you put out feelers.

In November, he is reelected.

He doesn't end his marriage, not that you ever thought he would.

Turn to the next page.

88

You don't see him for a while, and you don't even miss him.

You decide you will leave your job in January. It's the last semester of your senior year. This seems as good a reason as any to leave.

You go to your supervisor. You tell her you'll stay until the end of the month to train someone new. "I'm sad to see you go. We've really liked having you," she says. "Is there anything I can say to convince you to stay?"

"No," you say.

She takes you downstairs for a frozen yogurt. Farouk says, "Hello, Aviva!"

"She's leaving us," the supervisor says.

"No one works as hard as me, except Aviva and the congressman," Farouk says. He brings you and the supervisor a plate of free baklava.

"I have to say," your supervisor says, "I never thought you'd be such a success that first day. You've really opened my eyes about some of my own prejudices about interns."

You feel irritated even though you know she's trying to be nice. "Why?" you say. "Because you didn't like my outfit?"

"Yeah. It sounds shitty when you put it that way. I guess so. We get a certain kind of girl, from time to time. Pretty girls who think it'll be fun to have a political adventure, because they saw, like, *Primary Colors* or something. But once they find out how boring it is here, they don't want to work."

"Well, maybe they *would* want to work if you made them feel more welcome," you say.

89

The supervisor nods. "I'm a douche. Officially, a douche."
She holds up her iced tea, and you clink your Diet Coke to it.

Turn to the next page.

90

At the end of January, just before your last week, he is briefly back from D.C., and he asks you if you want to "hang," which makes him sound like one of the kids from your old dorm. You don't want to "hang," but you go with him anyway.

You are in his car—the whole point of quitting your job was so you wouldn't end up in his car—but there you are! You are in his car and you are thinking about Houdini. You have recently read a book about Houdini, and you are thinking how having an affair with your boss is kind of like being in a strait-jacket and in chains and submerged in water. You feel like you will need to be an emotional Houdini if you are ever going to extricate yourself.

You did this to yourself.

You have only yourself to blame.

For argument's sake, who else might you blame?

A. The Congressman

B. Your Father, Whom You Love and Who Thinks You Don't Know About His Mistress

C. The Supervisor at the Congressman's Office for Making You Cry That First Day

D. Your Mother for Interfering Too Much in Your Life

E. That Boyfriend You Had When You Were Fifteen

F. Your Boobs for Making Everything Look Slutty

No, you decide, none of the above. It's me.

In the future, you will have interns of your own. And the thought of sleeping with any one of them will seem insane and

91

wrong to you. But at this moment, you are in the passenger seat of the congressman's car, and he is stopped at a traffic light, and you are thinking, Maybe I should just open the car door and get out. No one is stopping you, Aviva Grossman. You are a free person. You may be an adult, but you can still call your mother to come get you and no matter what she's doing, she will come. You put your hand on the interior handle, and you're about to jerk it open when the light changes to green and the congressman starts driving again.

"Why are you so quiet?" he asks.

Because, you want to say, I am a person with an interior world that you know nothing about. But to say such a thing would violate the terms of your relationship. That is not the key in which your relationship is played. If he wanted a person with an interior world, he could just deal with his wife. You are the garbage disposal. You are the golf bag.

"Tired," you say. "Classes, work."

He turns up the music. He likes hip-hop, but it always seems like an act. He is somewhat obsessed with staying young.

The song that plays is "Ms. Jackson" by Outkast. You've never heard it before. At the beginning of the song, the first-person narrator/singer apologizes to a girl's mother for how he's treated her daughter. You cannot think of anything you want to hear less.

"Can we listen to something else?" you ask.

"Give it a chance," he says. "Seriously, Aviva, you have to open your mind about hip-hop. Hip-hop is the future."

"Fine," you say.

92

"Outkast is our Walt Whitman. Outkast is—"

You hear the sound of breaking glass, crumpling metal.

The car's air bags deploy.

The driver's side window's glass is cracked, and through it, the outside world looks like a surreal version of a stained glass scene in a church. Through it you see palm trees and the wind-shield of the other driver's car, a petal pink Cadillac, and an old woman with her head slumped over—she might be dead.

"Looks like stained glass," you say.

"More like cubism," he corrects you.

The woman will turn out to have Alzheimer's disease. Her license had been suspended three years ago. Her husband didn't even know she still had keys. "How she loved that car," is what he'll say when he hears the news that she's dead.

The congressman sprains his wrist. You end up with a neck injury, nothing serious, but you don't know that at the time. In the moment, it's terrifying.

"Are you okay?" he asks, his voice sounding remarkably calm.

You feel light-headed, but you know you need to leave the scene. You want to protect him from what will happen if the cops find out that he is having an affair with a former intern. You think he's a good man. No, you think he's a good congress-man, and you don't want him to suffer through a scandal.

"I should go," you say.

"No," he says. "You stay here. If the woman is dead, there will be an investigation, and you are my witness. If you leave and your presence is later discovered, it will seem as if we were

93

trying to cover up something. It's the difference between a scandal and a crime. It's the difference between a storm that will pass and the end of my career. When the cops come, you are an intern who I am giving a ride home. You can say this confidently because it's true."

You nod. Your head feels heavy and light at once.

"Say it, Aviva."

If you run, turn to page 96.

If you stay, turn to page 110.

110

"I am an intern," you say. "Congressman Levin is giving me a ride."

"I'm sorry, Aviva," the congressman says.

"For what?" you say numbly. "She drove into you. It wasn't your fault."

"For what's to come."

You wait for the police. It starts to rain.

Turn to the next page.

111

You are in a storm.

You are pelted by rain, and your clothes are soaked through.

Your house floats away.

There goes your dog, but there's no time to mourn.

Your photo albums are lost or damaged and waterlogged beyond repair.

Your insurance doesn't work.

You are clinging to a mattress.

You have no one to call for help.

Your family and friends have perished in the storm.

The ones who are still alive are angry that you have lived.

You think the rain will never stop.

But eventually, the rain stops, and when the rain stops, the newspeople arrive.

The newspeople *love* the story of the GIRL ON THE MATTRESS IN THE STORM.

"Who is this girl on the mattress?"

"Where did she go to school?"

"Was she popular at school?"

"Why is she wearing so few clothes?"

"She should wear more clothes if she's going to end up washed up on a mattress!"

"Why didn't she know better?"

"I heard the girl on the mattress was basically a psycho. She was a stalker. She was a storm chaser."

"Does she suffer from low self-esteem?"

"You'd think the storm would prefer someone thinner and better looking."

112

"I consider myself a feminist, but if you decide to cling to a mattress in the middle of a storm, that's on you."

"Oh my God, the girl on the mattress kept a blog!"

"Stay tuned for an exclusive with the ex-boyfriend of the girl on the mattress! Says Grossman was 'always pretty needy and clingy.'"

It's odd, you think, how everyone loves (hates) the girl on the mattress, but no one seems that interested in the storm.

Turn to the next page.

113

It seems as if people will never tire of news of the Girl on the Mattress, but then a bigger storm hits, one with flashier elements, like Terrorism and Apocalypse and Death and Destruction and Mayhem.

And they forget about you, more or less.

If you decide to never leave your house again and become a Boo Radley–style shut-in, turn to page 114.

If you decide to go on with your life, turn to page 118.

118

You continue with your life. Of course you do. What choice do you have really? You get out of bed. You do your hair. You get dressed. You put on makeup. You make sure to eat salads. You make conversations with waiters. You smile when someone looks at you. You smile too much. You want people to think you are a nice person. You go to the mall. You buy a black dress. You buy makeup remover. You read magazines. You work out. You avoid the Internet. You read books. You tire of salads. You eat frozen yogurt. You make jokes with your dad. You never talk about the thing that happened with him or with anyone else. You masturbate a lot. You don't call the congressman.

You go to your grandfather's funeral, your father's father. You weren't close to him the way you were to your mother's father, but you cry anyway. He once brought you a puppet from Argentina. You don't have any grandfathers left now. You cry. You cry too much. You suspect you aren't even crying about your grandfather.

You go to the synagogue's ladies' room. You go into the stall, and you hear two old women enter the bathroom behind you. You can hear them spraying perfume on themselves. The synagogue's bathrooms are always stocked like drugstores: perfume, but also gum, hair spray, lip balm, moisturizer, mouthwash, hair bands, combs.

"This scent is delicious," the first woman says. "What is it?"

"I don't know," the second woman says. "I don't have my reading glasses, but I think it's a knockoff of something else."

"It's not a knockoff," the first woman says. "There was an uproar last year. Shirley—"

119

"Which Shirley?"

"Hadassah Shirley. Hadassah Shirley said it was immoral for the synagogue to stock imitation perfumes in the bathrooms, so now they're all bona fide."

"Hadassah Shirley is ridiculous," the first woman says.

"But she does know how to get things done," the second woman says. "And keep your voice down. Hadassah Shirley is everywhere."

"She didn't come today," the first woman says.

"I noticed," the second woman says. "Poor Abe Grossman."

"How much do you think Abe knew?" the second woman says. Abe is your grandfather. These women aren't related to you, so they must have been his friends. Maybe they're just busybodies from this synagogue though.

"His mind was gone," the first woman says. "They didn't tell him what had happened. It's a mitzvah."

"A mitzvah," the first one agrees. "If he'd known, it would have killed him."

You are aware that they have transitioned into talking about you.

You are no longer curious about where such a conversation will lead.

You leave the stall and you step between them. "Might I borrow this?" you say. You take the perfume and you spray it all over yourself. You look at the bottle. "It's Jo Malone," you tell them. "Grapefruit."

"Oh, we were wondering," the first woman says. "It's delicious."

"How are you, Aviva?" the second one says.

120

"Great," you say.

You smile at them. You smile too much.

You graduate from college a semester late.

You apply for jobs in your field—jobs in politics mainly, but a few in PR and not-for-profits.

Your most significant work experience is for the congressman, but no one from his office can write you a letter of recommendation for obvious reasons.

Still, you are hopeful.

You are twenty-two years old.

You polish up your résumé and it's not bad. You speak Spanish fluently! You graduated with honors! You worked for a congressman in a big city for two years, and by the end of it, they were paying you and you even had a job title, Online Projects and Special Research. You once kept a blog that had more than one million hits, not that you can point anyone to this.

And people in New York City, in Los Angeles, in Boston, in Austin, in Nashville, in Seattle, in Chicago, people can't have *all* heard of Aviva Grossman. The news story could not have spread that far. This was a regional story, like when you were a kid and Gloria Estefan and Miami Sound Machine were in a tour bus crash. That story was on the news every day in South Florida. Sure, it might have been picked up nationally, too, but the obsession with Gloria Estefan and her road to recovery was regional.

You receive almost no replies to your job applications.

Finally, someone calls you! It's an entry level position at an organization that helps children from around the world get

121

access to health care. They are based out of Philadelphia. They do a lot of work in Mexico and they LOVE that you speak Spanish.

You arrange to have a phone interview, and if that goes well, you will fly to Philadelphia to speak with the team.

You are imagining your new life in Philadelphia. You browse winter coats online. The stores in Florida rarely stock them. How nice it will be to be somewhere with winter. How nice it will be to be somewhere where no one knows your name or the stupid mistake (series of mistakes, if you're being completely honest) you made when you were twenty.

It is June. You make your mom leave the house, and you sit in your bedroom, and you wait for the phone to ring at 9:30 a.m. It is summer, and your mom's school is on break, and she is hovering around you like flies around raw meat.

The phone does not ring.

At 9:34, you begin to worry that you missed the call, or that you screwed up the time. You check your e-mail again to confirm the details. Yes, 9:30.

If you wait for the phone to ring, turn to page 124.

If you call (even though the interviewer said she would call you—who cares if you look "too eager"?), turn to page 126.

126

The interviewer picks up on the first ring.

"Oh Aviva," she says, "I meant to call you."

You can tell she is not referring to the interview.

"We've decided to go in another direction," she says.

Normally, you wouldn't ask for details. But you've had enough of being ignored, so you say, "Can you level with me? What happened? I really felt good about this one."

The interviewer pauses. "Well, Aviva, we did an Internet search on your name, and the stuff about you and the congressman came up. It didn't really bother me, but my boss felt that since we're a not-for-profit, we need people of impeccable character. His words, not mine. But the truth is, we live and die on donations, and some of those people can be super conservative and weird about sex stuff. I argued for you. I truly did. You're great, and I'm sure you'll find something great."

"Thanks for being honest," you say. You hang up the phone.

This is why no one is calling you.

Because even if no one has heard of the Aviva Grossman scandal in Philly, in Detroit, in San Diego, they only have to search your name, and they can find every last ugly detail. You should know. Internet searches were your specialty.

Want to know about the shady past of the Kissimmee River? Want to know which city councilmen are homophobes? Want to know about that dumb girl from Florida who had anal sex with a married congressman because he wouldn't put it in her vagina?

The discovery of your shame is one click away. Everyone's is, not that that makes it any better. In high school, you read *The*

127

Scarlet Letter, and it occurs to you that this is what the Internet is like. There's that scene at the beginning where Hester Prynne is forced to stand in the town square for the afternoon. Maybe three or four hours. Whatever the time, it's unbearable to her.

You will be standing in that square forever.

You will wear that "A" until you're dead.

You consider your options.

You have no options.

Turn to the next page.

128

You are depressed.

You read every Harry Potter that has been written.

You swim in your parents' pool.

You read all the books on your childhood bookshelf.

You read a series of books called Choose Your Own Adventure that you liked when you were young. Even though you're not the intended age for them anymore, you feel obsessed with them that summer. The way these books work is you get to the end of a section, and you make a choice, and then you turn to the corresponding page for that choice. You think how much these books are like life.

Except in Choose Your Own Adventure, you can move backward, and you can choose something else if you don't like how the story turned out, or if you just want to know the other possible outcomes. You would like to do that, but you can't. Life moves relentlessly forward. You turn to the next page, or you stop reading. If you stop reading, the story is over.

Even when you were a kid, you were aware of the fact that the Choose Your Own Adventure stories were pretty bald morality tales. For instance, one of your favorite ones, *Track Star!*, involves a runner deciding whether or not to take performance-enhancing drugs. If you take the drugs, you'll win for a while, but then something horrible will happen to you. You'll be a victim of your poor choices.

You think that if your life were a Choose Your Own Adventure story—let's call it *Intern!*—this would be the point where it would say THE END. You would have made enough poor choices for the story to have had a bad ending. The only

129

redemption would be in going back to the beginning and starting again. This isn't an option for you, because you are a person and not a character in a Choose Your Own Adventure.

The rub of the Choose Your Own Adventure stories is that if you don't make a few bad choices, the story will be terribly boring. If you do everything right and you're always good, the story will be very short.

You wonder if the congressman ever read Choose Your Own Adventure stories. He's probably too old, but you think he would get a kick out of them and what a good metaphor they are for life.

If you call him, turn to page 130.

If you don't call him, turn to page 146.

130

You decide to call him even though you know you shouldn't. In fact, you've explicitly been told not to. You haven't been alone with him or even spoken to him since the night of the crash.

He doesn't answer his phone so you leave a message. As you are babbling abut Choose Your Own Adventure stories, you realize that the thought that seemed deep sounds incredibly lame over the phone.

A few days later, Jorge Rodriguez shows up at the house. He's important in the congressman's organization. You don't know exactly what his title is now, but he used to be the head of fundraising. You've spoken to him a few times, but you've never had much interaction. He's charming, and very handsome. He looks like the congressman, but he is shorter, Cuban, younger. He's maybe five years older than you.

He knows your mother because of an event she did for the congressman at the school. "The beautiful Grossman women," Jorge says. "Good to see you, Rachel. How are you? How's BRJA?"

"I was fired," your mother says to him, in an odd, spiky, almost confrontational way.

"Sorry to hear that," Jorge says. "Well, Aviva, I'm actually here to see you."

You go out to the back patio, and you sit under the bougainvillea, and your mother brings you both iced teas. Jorge waits for her to leave before he says genially, "You can't contact him anymore, Aviva. It's best for everyone that you move on."

"It's best for him," you say.

131

"Everyone," he insists.

"I'd move on if I had anywhere to move on to," you say. "My whole life is ruined," you say. "No one will ever hire me. No one will even fuck me."

"It seems that way," Jorge says, "but it's not that bad."

"Respectfully," you say, "how the hell would you know?"

Jorge doesn't have an answer.

"You know about politics. You know about PR. What would you do if you were me?"

"I'd go back to school. Get a degree in law or a master's in public policy."

"Okay," you say, "let's assume I can get a single teacher to write me a recommendation letter. Let's assume I can manage to get accepted to a school. I incur an additional one hundred thousand dollars or so in student loan debt, and then I apply for jobs again. How is it different? You search my name, and everything's still there, fresh as the year it happened."

Jorge drinks his iced tea. "If you don't go back to school, you could do volunteer work. Make a new name for yourself—"

"Tried that," you say. "They don't want me either."

"Maybe what you need is witness protection," he jokes. "New name. New town. New job."

"Probably so," you say.

"I honestly don't know what you should do," Jorge says. "But I do know something . . ."

"Yeah?"

"You said no one would fuck you. That's not true. You're a beautiful girl."

132

You are not a beautiful girl, and even if you were, you know that is not related to how much sex a person has. Plenty of ugly people have sex. Plenty of ordinary people have sex. Plenty of beautiful people spend their nights alone.

You are not beautiful. You are interesting looking, and your large breasts signify to men that you are sexy and easy and a little dumb. You know exactly what you are, and since the scandal and its ensuing coverage, you know exactly how people see you. There is nothing that anyone could say about you or to you that is surprising. You have not spent the summer in your parents' pool and suddenly turned beautiful. And again, there are always people to have sex with, if you set your standards low enough. What you'd meant is, *No one I'd want to sleep with will want to sleep with me.*

This is to say, you know that Jorge is flattering you.

If you decide to sleep with Jorge anyway, turn to page 133.

If you ask him to leave, turn to page 148.

133

You walk over to where he is sitting, and you kiss him. You don't want him, so much as you want anyone. You take him upstairs, and you decide you'd rather have sex in the guest room than your childhood bedroom, surrounded by high school yearbooks and framed drama club ephemera.

You go in the guest room, and you lock the door.

You can tell he's experienced, which is fortunate. You, despite being the star player in a sex scandal, remain as inexperienced as can be.

When he touches you, you shiver with pleasure. You feel like a blade of grass, and he is a warm summer wind.

"So much lusciousness," Jorge says.

Turn to the next page.

134

You miss a period, but you don't even notice.

Turn to the next page.

135

You miss another period.

A few days later, you find yourself with your head over the toilet.

"Aviva," your mother calls. "Are you sick?"

"Perfecting my eating disorder," you reply.

"That's a repulsive thing to say," your mother says.

"Sorry," you say. "I think I am getting sick."

Your mother brings you soup, and you pull the covers over your head.

You've seen movies, you've read novels, and you have a pretty strong inkling what this might be.

You had been on the Pill, but maybe you'd gotten sloppy with taking the prescription. What was the point? You weren't having sex.

You take a pregnancy test.

Blue line, but it looks smudged.

You take another pregnancy test, just to make sure you did it right.

Blue line.

You consider having an abortion. Of course you do. You know there is no earthly reason you should bring a child into this mess you call your life. You have no job, no prospects, no partner. You are profoundly lonely. You know that this is not a reason to have a child.

You believe in a woman's right to choose. You would never vote for someone who didn't believe in a woman's right to choose.

136

If you decide to have an abortion, turn to page 138.

If you continue with the pregnancy, turn to page 141.

141

Your last semester of college, you took an advanced political science seminar called Gender and Politics. The seminar was led by a silver-haired woman in her late forties, who had recently had a baby. She would bring the baby—a boy—to class in a papoose. Despite the fact that he was the only male in the seminar and the discussions sometimes got quite heated, the baby never cried and almost seemed soothed by the discussion. You were jealous of that baby. You wished you might be brand-new, male, and in a papoose on a political scientist's back.

The class, however, was something of a wash. Maybe it wasn't the class but the mood you were in at the time. The scandal had passed, but you were filled with bile and rage. Around the middle of the semester, the professor stopped you after class.

"Don't give up on us feminists," the professor said.

"I haven't," you said.

"I'm going to go out on a limb here. Your paper—'Why I'll Never Be a Feminist: A Gender-free Approach to Public Policy'—perhaps that suggests otherwise?" She looked at you with kind but mirthful eyes.

"It's Swiftian," you said. "It's satire."

"Is it?" she asked.

"Why should I be a feminist? When everything happened, none of you exactly rushed to my defense," you said.

"No," she said. "We probably should have. The power imbalance between you and Levin was obscene. I think, on some level, it was in the greater public interest to *not* defend you. He's a good congressman. He's good on women's issues, too. It's not perfect."

142

"The *Miami Herald* wrote that I had set the feminist cause back fifty years. How exactly did I do that?"

"You didn't."

"She stood by him. Didn't she set feminism back more than me? Isn't it *more feminist* to leave your cheating spouse? Honestly, I've been sitting in this class for five whole weeks—not to mention, I've been a woman my whole life—and I don't even know what a feminist is," you say. "What the hell is it?"

"From my point of view as a political science professor, it's the belief that all sexes should be treated equally before the law."

"Obviously I know that," you said. "So what's wrong with my paper?"

"The problem with it is that gender exists," she said. "Differences exist, and the law must acknowledge that or the law isn't fair."

"Fine," you say. "You held me after class. Is there something you want?"

"You didn't ask me the next logical question," she said. "What is feminism from my point of view as a woman and as a human being?"

Who fucking cares? you thought.

"It's the right every woman has to make her own choices. People don't have to like your choices, Aviva, but you have a right to make them. Embeth Levin has a right to make them, too. Don't expect a parade."

You tried not to roll your eyes.

143

"I'd like you to give that paper another think," she said.

The next week, you *chose* to drop the seminar.

You want this baby, even though it defies logic.

You do not expect a parade.

You must change your life.

The clock is ticking. You have seven months to change your life.

You need to find employment, but you are Internet infamous. There is nowhere you can move that is far enough away.

You could stay home and let your parents support you and the baby. But the baby would still be the daughter of "Aviva Grossman," and who wants to do that to a kid?

You could go back to school, but what would that solve? As you told Jorge, you would still be "Aviva Grossman" at the end of it.

The problem is your name.

If you stay home, turn to page 144.

If you change your name, turn to page 146.

146

Everything is online. Maybe *they* can find out about you, but there's some justice in the fact that *you* can find out about anything. You google "legal name changes, Florida." In less than five minutes, you find out everything you need to know: how long it will take, where you'll have to go, what it will cost, and what documents you will need.

You pay for a background check to prove that you have committed no crimes. You haven't, by the way.

You go to the police station to have your fingerprints taken, and you sign your name for a notary.

You file a Legal Change of Name form at the courthouse.

The clerk reads through your paperwork. She says, "Everything looks in order."

"Is that it?" you say.

"That's it," she says. There's a long line, and she doesn't care who you are or what you've done. She cares that your paperwork has been filled out correctly, which it has been. You feel a swell of gratitude for bureaucracy, for government.

Still, you expect someone to try to stop you. You expect media to show up. No one does, or maybe no one cares about you anymore. You aren't, after all, Tom Cruise. You aren't famous. You are infamous, and maybe people tire of infamous people when they stop doing infamous things.

The clerk schedules a hearing.

No one objects to your petition, so the hearing is canceled.

Your name is changed.

You are Jane Young.

Turn to the next page.

You go to your grandmother to ask for money. You know she'll give it to you, but you hate to do it anyhow.

She is so tiny, tinier than your mother. She is barely larger than a child. When you hug her, you think you might crush her. She wears slacks with thin belts and flats with capped heels. She is always dressed just so. An Hermès scarf. A quilted Chanel handbag. Things well made and chosen with care. Things cared for once they were chosen. Suede shoes are brushed. Necklaces are wrapped in paper so they don't tangle. The handbag has its own bag and is stuffed with tissue paper when it is not in use. You remember pleasant afternoons passed in your grandmother's closet. "When you have little, mine Aviva, you learn to take care. When you have much, you must accept that you could someday have little," she would say. "To take care of something is to love it."

If she leaves the house, there must be earrings. Today's earrings are fruit made from jewels—jade, emeralds. They're her favorite. Her father made them, and they're one of the only things she brought from Germany. All she has from Germany is that which she brought, because she will never buy anything German as long as she lives. Someday, she promises to leave the earrings to you. But you hate thinking of "someday" because someday she will be dead. Who will call you "mine Aviva" when she is gone?

You tell her you need to go away, to start fresh. You say you're sorry for everything, for the shame you've brought on her and Aunt Mimmy and the Grossman family.

She gets out her checkbook and she puts on her reading glasses with the delicate filigree chain and she takes out her tiny polka-dot checkbook pen. She asks you how much you need.

You ask for ten thousand dollars. You're not as dumb as you once were. You know ten thousand dollars won't last very long, but it will give you enough to start over.

She writes a check for twenty thousand dollars, and then she pulls you close to her. She smells like carnations and apples and talcum powder and Chanel No. 5. "I love you, mine Aviva," she says.

You almost cry to hear the way her German accent wraps around the syllables of your name.

"That man was no good," she says, "and if Grandpa were still alive, he would cut off his balls."

YOU LEAVE YOUR mother a note, saying you're leaving town and you'll call her once you're settled.

You buy a bus ticket to Portland, Maine, and when you get to Portland, you buy a cheap car.

You drive to Allison Springs, where your parents once took you on vacation.

It's winter, so the town is empty.

You rent an apartment just outside the center of town. It's one bedroom, five hundred square feet. The walls have recently been painted to exorcise the memory of the prior tenants, and everything still smells of fumes. The apartment feels enormous because you have nothing.

You eat lobster rolls and think about jobs you could do.

You are willing to work hard, but you want something with flexible hours. You have a baby on the way.

Also, you're sick of bosses. You want to be your own boss, but you don't have much money to start a business.

You're in your apartment, weighing your options, and a movie with Jennifer Lopez comes on television. It's a dumb fairy tale, where she falls in love with the person for whom she's planning a wedding. You are through with fairy tales. You will never have a workplace romance again. However, you are interested in her business. You try not to consider what it means that you are watching romantic comedies for occupational advice.

What do you really need to be an event planner? What does JLo have?

A desk. A phone number. A business card. A computer.

I could do that, you think.

Events by Jane, you think.

You have made decisions in worse ways before.

In the early aughties, not all businesses have websites, and there's an enormous advantage for those that do. You have a certain amount of online skills, thanks to your years with the congressman, and you are easily able to build a website.

You wait for the phone to ring.

After a week, it does.

Your first potential client is a woman named Mrs. Morgan. You arrange to meet her at a coffee shop in town.

You put on a black shift dress. You still aren't showing very much, though your breasts are enormous. Nothing to be done.

Mrs. Morgan is throwing a benefit to expand English as a second language program in area schools.

"Is there a lot of need for that in Maine?" you ask.

"Oh God, yes! Mainly Spanish, but other languages, too," Mrs. Morgan says. She has a loud voice that she uses to state her many opinions. You have the sense that time is precious with her: she's just come from something, and she's on her way to something else. You like her immediately. She reminds you of a WASP version of your grandmother. "That's why I called you actually. I saw the Spanish literature on your résumé. I thought it would be marvelous to have an event planner who had an appreciation for other languages.

"Also, my regular planner has disappointed me twice. You are allowed to disappoint me once and then I will move on. Do you understand me, Jane?"

"Yes," you say.

"I see you're expecting," Mrs. Morgan says. "Is that going to be a problem?"

"No," you say. "I'm young"—you acknowledge this is so, and yet you feel so old—"and I want to work. I need to work."

"Fair enough, young Jane Young," she says. "And have you planned many events?"

"Well, this is a new career for me. I'm actually transitioning. I thought I was going to work in politics."

"Politics," Mrs. Morgan says. "How interesting. What made you change course?"

YOU GIVE BIRTH to a little girl and you call her Ruby. Ruby is a good baby, but she is still a baby. She makes copious amounts of excrement. She requires an endless supply of paper products, an endless supply of everything. She doesn't cry much, but she rarely sleeps either. You have no friends, no husband, no money to hire a regular nanny, no one to help you. You can't stop working either. You need the money. So Ruby learns to be quiet, and you learn to keep stress out of your voice when you take work calls. You find a babysitter you like. You order flower arrangements while you give Ruby baths. Ruby's first word is "canapé."

You don't always feel like you love Ruby as much as you should. Where is room for love? All you have is fear and a to-do list. But you take care of her as best as you can, and you think of what your grandmother said: "To take care of something is to love it." You, who try to regret as little as possible, regret that Ruby will not know her great-grandmother.

You think about calling your mother, but you don't. This decision is not about your mother. For a long time, for right or for wrong, you were angry at her, but you aren't any longer. You can forgive your mother, and because you have your own child, you know that she must have forgiven you. You don't tell your mother to come because you don't want to have to explain that part of your life to Ruby.

When people ask you, you say Ruby's dad was killed overseas. They assume he was a soldier, but you never explicitly say that. You drop a few intriguing details and people form a narrative of their own. *Poor Jane Young, whose husband was in the Marine Corps! Was he killed in Baghdad? Fallujah? Ah, best not to ask her too many questions. Poor Ruby Young—she never even got to meet her father!*

After a while, you have lived in Allison Springs so long that people stop asking you questions. You are an institution.

You are with Ruby nearly every one of her waking moments, and you think no two humans on earth have ever been closer. You know everything about her, and you couldn't love her more. She appreciates a good pun. She loves quotation marks and peanut butter and words. She is not emotionally guarded, which makes her seem childish. She is not childish. The girls at her school don't like her, and she doesn't even care. She won't change for them, though you know she wishes they would leave her alone. You have murderous thoughts toward those girls. She knows how to find things out and she delights in knowledge. She knows who to call for an ice cream truck in winter. You trust her with everything. She is you, but she is not you. For instance, your life is a lie, and she never lies. When she heard the story of George Washington chopping down the cherry tree, she barely understood it. "Of course he told the truth. The chopping down of a cherry tree would be a very big thing to cover up," she said.

A day will come when you catch her looking at you in a strange, contemplative way. Her head is cocked. Her expression seems to say, *I don't know you at all.*

And it occurs to you that you know your child and you operate under the principle that your watchfulness means there is no subject on which you have greater expertise. Yet there are parts of her that are not accessible to you either.

You love your daughter, but you have fewer choices than you once did. Your choices are dictated by her.

Maybe not fewer choices. Maybe it's that the answers are more obvious, so you don't pose the questions. Life unspools more inevitably. You keep turning the pages.

Something you don't predict is how your job makes you privy to the secrets of everyone in town. You are a confessor, and you know the town's sins. For instance, a bride whose wedding you planned said she was a murderer. The woman reminded you of a newborn fawn. Very slender, large eyes, a bit shaky on her feet.

When she was sixteen years old, she was driving a car that crashed into a tree, and the three girls who were her passengers were killed.

She wasn't drunk, but she may have picked up her phone to send a text message. She couldn't entirely remember what had happened. People thought she was lying when she said that, but she promised it was true. "I honestly wish I could remember," she said. "Because then I would know whether to feel guilty or not."

She tried to kill herself.

She went to a mental hospital for a while.

She recovered.

She met a man, and then she met you.

You asked her the thing she was most looking forward to about her wedding. She told you she was looking forward to having a new name.

"Is that silly?" she said. "Gosh, I think half the point of marrying him for me is that I'll officially be someone else."

ONLY ONCE, IN ten years, are you ever confronted about your past, and it's by the husband of that woman. You use this woman's secret to keep the husband quiet.

Maybe this is wrong, but he is threatening your livelihood and your and Ruby's way of life. The husband is ambitious. He has told you several times that he wants to seek political office.

You say to him, "If you tell people about who you *think* I am, what would it do to me? Maybe people would care? Maybe they wouldn't? I'm a private citizen and I don't need anyone to vote for me for anything, you know?"

. . .

THREE YEARS LATER, Mrs. Morgan shows up at your office, without a meeting. "I've decided you should be the next mayor of Allison Springs," she says.

"That's interesting," you say. "But it's not possible."

"Why? What else are you doing?"

"Lots of things. I have a business. I have a daughter. And if you haven't noticed, I don't have a partner."

Mrs. Morgan insists. "I'm never wrong about these things."

"I don't have any money for a campaign," you say.

"I'm loaded," she says. "And I have tons of rich friends."

"I don't want you to waste your money or your rich friends' money. I have a past," you say.

"Who doesn't? Did you murder someone? Did you abuse a child? Were you a drug dealer?"

"No," you say. "No, no."

"Did you go to jail?"

"No," you say.

"Then it sounds like a youthful indiscretion to me, and no one will care," she says. "Okay, I'll bite. What did you do that was so bad?"

"I had an affair with a prominent married man when I was in my early twenties."

She laughs. "Was it super steamy?"

"It was somewhat steamy."

"Do you still have hot dreams about him?"

"Occasionally," you say. "Mainly I have dreams where I calmly explain to him why he shouldn't be sleeping with a girl half his age."

"No one will care," Mrs. Morgan says. "NO ONE WILL CARE. Plus, you're not running for president, though the standards for that office seem pretty low these days, too."

"Also, I have a daughter and I'm not married," you say.

"I know," she says. "I've met Ruby. Lovely girl, Ruby."

"Why me?" you ask. "I've got baggage."

"Because I like you. You're smart. You know everyone, and people trust and respect you, and in your line of work, I bet you know where a lot of this town's bodies are buried, and that's always a good thing. And I've lived here for thirty years, paid my share of taxes here, and I'd like to see a lady mayor before I died."

You know you shouldn't run for office.

You know it will compromise Ruby.

You know it will put too much scrutiny on you and your past.

You know if you lose, and the secret comes out, it will likely damage your business and your reputation in the community.

On the other hand, you are thirty-seven years old.

You love being Ruby's mother, but loving Ruby does not stop you from wanting things for yourself.

You know it's not a national office. It's not president, or senator, or congressman.

You know it's not what you imagined when you were young.

Still, it seems like a big thing to be mayor.

You aren't so very different than when you were twenty years old. Despite everything, you still believe in the power of government to effect positive change. And you've come to love this town and the people who live in it. You don't like the idea of Wes West or a person like him becoming mayor. Wes West is a bully. He bullies his wife. He tried to bully you.

Your grandparents believed in public service. They were taken in by this imperfect country, and they believed they owed something to it in return. To take care of something is to love it.

YOUR DAUGHTER FINDS out everything, of course, and she reacts in predictable ways. She says she hates you and then she runs away. She leaves you a note, as if that is supposed to be a comfort. She is so young! She has no idea what can happen in the world.

You try to track her down using her phone, but she is savvy with technology—she is your official Young Person in the Office—and she has her phone turned off.

You remember that you can track her down using her iPad. The iPad doesn't have GPS, but when it connects with Wi-Fi, her location appears on a map.

The blinking dot pulses like your heart.

She is in Florida.

In Miami.

She has gone to find the congressman.

You call the Miami Police, and you tell them her location.

You are about to leave for the airport, but then you don't. In the best-case scenario, it will take you seven or eight hours to fly there, and you know someone who is much closer.

You call your mother. You're in a panic, but as soon as your mother answers the phone, you relax. When your mother is worrying about something, it means that you won't have to.

"Mom," you say. "I need you to go get Ruby. She's at the police station."

"Of course," your mother says.

You tell her which police station and the name of the police officer she should ask for. You begin to explain what happened, but your mother cuts you off. "We'll sort it out later," she says. "I should get going."

"Thank you," you say.

"You're welcome. What else am I doing today?" she says.

"You probably had things."

"Roz and I are going to the movies. That's about it," she says. "This will be better than the movies."

"What movie?" you ask. You want her to get to Ruby, but for some reason, you are reluctant to hang up.

"The one where the British woman has the bad American accent. Something to do with Jews. Roz picked it. There's a Q&A. Maybe we can still make it? Does Ruby like that kind of thing?"

"She does," you say.

"Will you fly down to meet us? It would be good to see you. Grandma asks about you."

"Give Grandma my love. I think about her all the time."

"So come down. Come see us," your mother says.

"I will," you say. "But I can't leave town right now."

"No? Not even to come get Ruby?"

"Would it be possible for you to fly up here with her?" You pause. "The thing is, I'm running for mayor. The election's next week, and the last debate's tonight."

"Mayor?" your mother says. Her voice sounds soft and warm and relieved and filled with awe and pride. Her voice sounds like a firefly looks on a summer night. "Aviva Grossman! A thing like that!"

"I probably won't win," you say. "They found out about me. It was only a matter of time."

"Did you explain to them?" your mother says. "Did you tell it from your side?"

"There's no defending me," you say. "I made those choices. I did those things."

"What did you do? It was sex. He was ancient. You were a girl. It was a bunch of *narishkeit*," your mother says. "Everyone in Florida behaved like little babies."

"Even so."

"Don't worry about Ruby," your mother says. "You have to stay. You have to fight."

AT THE DEBATE, your opponent leans into the ancient scandal and your double identity. You let him, and you don't even hold it against him. For the most part, he has behaved admirably. You know the thing about his wife, and you think about using it, but you decide against it. It's cheap, and she is beside the point. Honestly, who cares what the wife did? Who even wants to be mayor if you have to ruin some woman's life to do it?

You see her in the audience when the debate is over. She looks at you and she mouths, "Thank you."

Mrs. Morgan comes up to you.

"How did we do?" you ask.

"It'll be close," she says.

"Are you sorry you bet on me?" you ask. "I did warn you."

"Never! I bet on people, and I particularly bet on smart women. This was your starter election—get your scandal out of the way. Now they know what happened, and they're used to you. If we lose this one, we'll run again. We'll run for something bigger."

"You're crazy," you say.

"Maybe I am. But I've got a bigger checkbook than anyone in this town. And the biggest checkbook wins."

"That isn't always true," you say.

"Fine, but the biggest checkbook can always go the most rounds."

WHEN YOUR MOTHER arrives in Allison Springs with your daughter, you crush them into you. You want to melt their flesh into your flesh. You want to bond your bones to their bones.

You make Ruby go to school. She has missed enough school. "We'll discuss this later," you say.

Ruby doesn't protest.

After you drop Ruby off, you show your mother around town. "Such a pretty town," she says. "It looks like a movie set."

You show her your business, what you have built. "So impressive," she says. "All these people work for you?"

You show your mother to your guest room. "This is lovely, Aviva," she says. "Frette linen, like a hotel."

"What's wrong with you?" you ask. "Don't you have any complaints?"

Your mother shrugs. "What do I have to complain about?"

"I don't want to pick a fight," you say, "but you used to have a lot of complaints about me."

"I don't think so," she says. "I don't remember things that way at all."

"My hair. My clothes. My cleanliness. My—"

"Aviva, you're my daughter. I had to tell you things," she says. "If I didn't tell you things, how would you know them?"

"I go by Jane now," you say.

"My God," she says, "could you have picked a more gentile name?"

"There are plenty of Jewish Janes," you say.

"Maybe I mean boring. Such a boring name. Jane Young. There's your complaint," your mother says.

You leave your mother and you go to your daughter's room to say good night. "Mom, I'm sorry," Ruby says.

"You're home now," you say.

"No," she says. "He wouldn't see me. He can't be my dad if he didn't want to see me."

"I'm sorry that happened to you, but he's right. He isn't your dad," you say. "I never even had sex with him. I never—"

"No," Ruby interrupts. "I was thinking when I was on the plane back. Maybe it doesn't matter who he is. You're my mom and you're my best friend."

"I know I've made a lot of mistakes," you say, "but I've done my best."

"I'm sorry for something else, too," she says. "I was the one who told the newspaper."

"I know," you say. "It doesn't matter."

"But it does matter. You might not win now."

"I might not," you admit. "But the truth is, I might not have won anyway. When you decide to run for office, the only thing you know for certain is that you might not win."

"It's my fault," Ruby says. She covers her head with her quilt.

"It's not, Ruby." You dig her out from under the blankets. "Mrs. Morgan owns the newspaper. She could have run the story or she could have killed it. I told her to run it."

"Why would you do that?" Ruby asks.

"Because it's better this way," you say. "It would have come out eventually. I'm not ashamed of what happened, not anymore. And I'm not ashamed of what I did to improve my situation. And if people want to judge me and not vote for me, that is their choice."

On Election Day, Mrs. Morgan arranges for you to have the classic polling place photo.

You put on a red suit. You spend no time making this decision. You don't even consider wearing anything else. The fit is perfect and you know it will photograph well. You're older now, and you know what looks good on you. Ruby puts on a blue dress, and your mother wears gray pants, a white blouse, and an Hermès scarf. "Red, white, and blue," your mother observes.

You walk to the polling place, which is at the fire station, a few blocks from your office. You wonder what happens if there's a fire on Election Day.

Mrs. Morgan wanted you to get a car, but you decided to walk. The weather is cold but sunny and bright. You walk down the street with your mother and your daughter. A few people try to avoid your gaze, but for the most part, people wave at you and wish you luck. You're surprised by these displays of warmth, but you shouldn't be. You've planned their weddings. You've witnessed their most intimate days. You've discreetly handed packets of tissues to sobbing fathers, and you've held babies born six months after the wedding, and you've driven racist mothers-in-law to the airport, and you've forgiven bounced checks when you could, and you've looked the other way when a bachelor party got out of hand. The point is, they have secrets, too.

When you get to the polling place, a half-dozen photographers are waiting for you. The media beyond Allison Springs has picked up on the story. It's a juicy one. Sex scandal. Fallen woman. A girl who slept with a politician goes into politics herself. There *are* second acts in American political life.

"Aviva," one of the photographers calls. "Look over here."

"Jane," calls another. "Over here!"

You turn to one and smile, and then you turn to the other and you smile even more broadly. You smile with teeth.

"Who do you think's going to win?" a reporter asks.

"It'll be tight," you say. "My opponent's run a solid campaign."

You leave Ruby with your mother and you go inside to vote.

You usually vote by mail and it seems quaint and oddly intimate to be filling out your ballot in public. Even after you draw the curtain closed, you still feel exposed. The curtain makes you feel more exposed. You're a Catholic at confession. You're a teenage girl trying on prom dresses at the mall. You're a pregnant mother in an open-backed hospital gown, waiting to give birth. You're the Nurse in a high school production of *Romeo and Juliet*, standing in the wings. You're an intern who slept with her boss and everyone found out.

Speaking of which, you dreamt of Aviva Grossman last night. In your dream, she was running for mayor of Miami. You went to her for advice. "Can I ask you something?" you said. "How did you ever survive that scandal?"

She said, "I refused to be shamed."

"How did you do that?" you asked.

"When they came at me, I kept coming," she said.

You pull back your shoulders. You button your suit jacket. You smooth your hair.

You find your name on the ballot and you choose.

AUTHOR'S NOTE

There is no Allison Springs, Maine, but I can attest to the reality of Boca Raton, Florida: I grew up there.

Bubbe meise means a grandmother's fable or an old wives' tale in Yiddish.

Jane's favorite line is from the novel *One Hundred Years of Solitude* by Gabriel García Márquez. Roughly, it translates, "Humans are not born forever on the day their mothers have them; life necessitates giving birth to themselves over and over again."